Seventeen l ͻ

Take It to the Limit

to Lori
good luck
by Sally

i

Published as an e-book January 2012 by Take It to The Limit

E-book ISBN 978-1-617506-72-7

Paperback edition ISBN 978-1-617506-73-4

17 Degrees, 3 Minutes North

The latitude of the border that separates Juarez, Mexico from El Paso, Texas

Contents

Seventeen Degrees North   i

Take It to the Limit   i

Contents   iv

Part 1 Jack Sloan   1

Chapter 1 The Assassin   2

Chapter 2 Jack   5

Chapter 3 Lights Out   7

Chapter 4 Darlene   10

Chapter 5 Will Cowdry   13

Chapter 6 Durango   18

Chapter 7 John Thunder   24

Part 2 Carlos Santiago   28

Chapter 8 Juarez   29

Chapter 9 Mrs. Pendleton   35

Chapter 10 Come Up and See Me Sometime   38

Chapter 11 Che. 214466-A   41

Chapter 12 Ambush—Part 1   47

Chapter 13 Ambush—Part 2   49

Chapter 14 The Assassin   53

Chapter 15 The Briefing   55

Part 3 Southbound and Down   58

Chapter 16 I Shot the Sheriff   59

Chapter 17 Loaded Up and Truckin'   65

Chapter 18 Flagstaff	68
Chapter 19 Monroe	71
Chapter 20 The Assassin	75
Chapter 21 Cave Creek	79
Chapter 22 The Assassin	83
Chapter 23 Jack and Darlene	86
Chapter 24 Manuel Hoppe	91
Chapter 25 John Thunder	95
Chapter 26 Juarez	98
Chapter 27 El Jefe	103
Chapter 28 Frank	107
Chapter 29 Manuel Hoppe	112
Chapter 30 Home	117
Part 4 Rosa Lara	121
Chapter 31 Rosa	122
Chapter 32 Darlene	126
Chapter 33 Juarez	129
Chapter 34 Firefight	132
Chapter 35 Manuel Hoppe	134
Chapter 36 Frank and Carlos	136
Part 5 Mrs. Pendleton	140
Chapter 37 Virgin Gorda	141
Chapter 38 Miami Beach	144
Chapter 39 Cruisin'	148
Chapter 40 Making Port	153
Part 6 Jack and Darlene	157

Chapter 41 Break Time   158

Chapter 42 Rosa   163

Chapter 43 Connections   167

Chapter 44 Manuel Hoppe   171

Chapter 45 Rosa   174

Chapter 46 Explanations   180

Chapter 47 The Long Walk   183

Chapter 48 Unfinished Business   186

Chapter 49 Carlos   189

Chapter 50 Valdez is Coming   191

Chapter 51 Jack and Darlene   194

Chapter 52 Manuel Hoppe   196

Part 7 And So the Story Ends, We're Told   199

Chapter 53 Answers   200

Chapter 54 The Arroyo   205

Epilogue   209

Part 1

Jack Sloan

Pancho was a bandit boy, horse as fast as polished steel,
Wore his gun outside his belt, for all the honest world to feel.
Pancho met his fate you know, on a desert in New Mexico,
No one heard his dying words,
Ah, but that's the way it goes.*
*Pancho and Lefty by Townes Van Zandt (1972)

Chapter 1

The Assassin

"Make the first shot count and get out," were his employer's instructions. For insurance, he loaded the rifle's magazine to capacity with twenty rounds. One shot or not, no way the target survives. He guaranteed his work and hated to make refunds.

He ran his fingers down the top of the SIG SG 550-1 Sniper rifle. A thing of beauty, it had set him back fifteen grand, fifty percent more than retail, but U.S. law banned its sale to anybody except cops or military. He checked the settings on the Kahles ZFM 10X range-finding scope attached to the top of the weapon. Four hundred yards—a difficult but not impossible shot for a marksman with his skill. He locked the collapsible bipod barrel support into place, eased it onto the flat rock in front of him, and adjusted the rifle stock to his shoulder. The bullets, .223 seventy-five grain Hornady TAP rounds, would speed to the target at twenty-eight hundred feet per second. Impact would be brutal.

The decision to make the kill here had surprised him. He knew the territory, but not the precise topography. The direction the target would come from had dictated his shooting platform.

The hazy day made the landscape jump. Heat rose off the mesa fronting the Jemez Mountains and reminded him of Baghdad. He'd told the army psychiatrist about his father, but the jerk said it didn't excuse his wasting civilians and booted him on "a mental." He missed Special Ops, but he'd earn more today than he could in twenty years in the service.

He used the scope to scan the horizon. The mark came into view a mile or more off. Damn the sun, it had popped from behind a cloud and cut into his field of fire. The shadow might throw him off, and thunderheads moving in from the west could ball things up. Flexibility, he reminded himself. In this business, a shooter's most vital attribute. His skin felt cool and contained. No perspiration and no nerves, even after he took the precaution of donning the rain slicker poncho that he'd pulled from his backpack.

He checked out the landscape and spotted a suitable vantage point about thirty degrees to the right. A towering rock formation would deflect the sun and the rain, if and when it came. He cradled the rifle in his arms and duck-walked to the site.

He felt no wind, but through the scope he saw tumbleweeds skittering down the valley a few hundred yards away. A faint breeze struck his cheek. He knew the seasonal monsoons reared up without warning in this part of New Mexico. The small caliber rounds and the muzzle velocity of his rifle would mitigate much of a storm's effect, but he might need to make a windage adjustment. Thunder shook the sky and he realized he could take his shots without fear of detection if he timed them with the lightning bolts. He counted to himself after the next one. "One thousand one, one thousand two, one thousand ..." There, that's it. Strike, wait three seconds, kaboom.

The new ambush site suited him. He found a solid platform for the rifle's tripod, and the field of fire looked good. No, not good, excellent. His target drew to within a half mile, and he commenced to sight in the weapon. The Kahles scope accounted for bullet drop, once he dialed in the range and estimated wind affect. It made his job easy.

The storm struck with a fury. The sun disappeared and the sky went black. He pulled the extended poncho over his head. It covered the rifle scope so that only the front lens protruded. The cowling around the glass protected it from the rain.

Patience. Deep, slow breaths, and don't get excited. He'd done this dozens of times, but the rush still came. He ached to hear the explosion and feel the recoil and watch through the scope when the target's head exploded.

Lightning. *One thousand one, one thousand two* .... Closer now, the count quicker. He watched while the range lessened. Drops of scattered rain grew into large wet spots on his fatigues. Five hundred yards. Closing faster than expected. A bullet nestled in the chamber, and the gun's firing pin sat poised to strike. The wind howled and tried to lift him from the ground, but the outcropping protected him from the brunt of the storm.

Four-ten, four-five, four-one. He squeezed the double-action trigger and the gun came alive in his hands. He watched in fascination when the target's head turned to gravy and the bright crimson spray, magnified through his scope, mushroomed into a cloud. The target flew backwards, propelled by the violent rearward thrust of the bullet that destroyed his skull.

He packed the rifle and scope into a compact carrying case, picked up his spent ordinance, and scanned the ground for anything that might remain to mark his presence. Tracks, but electrician's tape concealed the tread, and his boots would burn in a wood stove before nightfall. Satisfied, he bent his head into the storm and began to walk in the direction of the blacktop two miles distant, where a car waited for him.

He thought of the driver and felt an erection push against his pants. He would lie inside of her and whisper the details of the kill into her ear. He fantasized about her response, and his steps quickened.

Chapter 2

Jack

Sapphire pulled against the reins and shied right. My six-year-old mare didn't like the steep incline, or the wind whipping up from the Jemez Mountains. Dark thunderheads roiled over the peaks, and I knew we were in for a blow. So did the horse.

Still a couple of miles to the barn. We picked our way down the ridge toward the wide *arroyo* below. Rivulets would morph into churning rapids when the runoff from the storm hit. The day felt warm, even at this altitude, and my shirt stuck to my back. I smelled rain and saw it sweep hard across the mesa that jutted between the mountains and our property. Sharp thunderclaps followed each brilliant lightning bolt that fractured the sky.

A bright flash a couple of hundred yards off made Sapphire buck hard and almost throw me. I decided to dismount and lead her. I untied the blanket from the back of the saddle and wrapped it over her ears and secured it under her jaw. It covered most of her eyes, but she could still see. She followed without resistance when I pulled on the reins. We walked toward the tame creek a short distance away.

Clouds wiped out the sun, and rain pounded us. It drummed on the saddle, and frequent thunder shook the ground. Sapphire jerked, and I adjusted the blanket. Her ears went back, but she quieted, and let me lead her. A mini-torrent swirled at the top of my boots, and Sapphire lifted each hoof like she was walking on sheep shit.

I glanced at the large canvas bag that I'd tied on her rump where I normally stored the blanket and poncho. It looked like a mail sack, but without the markings or logo. I wanted to kick myself when I thought about how I'd found it on the ridge and decided to take it. Who hid it there, and why didn't I leave it for the next passerby?

Our normal riding route took us through a switchback to get from the top to the bottom of Pojoaque Ridge. When we descended on today's ride, I'd noticed boot prints crossing the trail and leading directly down.

Out of curiosity, I urged Sapphire to tackle the slope. She had stumbled and dislodged a stone. The small rockslide revealed the rear third of a bag sticking from the dirt, and I dug out the rest.

A small suitcase lock protected the zipper, but I took out my Kabar knife and easily pried it open. The cash stuffed inside caused me to wince. This wasn't your mama's laundry.

Whoever stashed it would come back. Had I made a terrible mistake by bringing the problem home? I could unpack it right now and let it drift with the current down to the Rio Grande, but one of the neighbors might see it and get curious. Easy to backtrack and find the trail I left on today's ride, rain or no rain.

I couldn't turn it in to the police. My name might still spark a live wire in the FBI's database. And even though the cops hadn't come looking for me, and I suspected the firestorm surrounding the Sacramento fiasco had died down, I didn't want to rekindle it. Maybe I could talk to my friend with the Sheriff's Department. He knew how to keep his mouth shut, and he might come up with a few bright ideas. Brief flashes of what it felt like to be pursued by the law gave me butterflies. No way could I go back to living like that, and no way did I want to endanger my wife and home.

I crossed the *arroyo*, remounted, and approached the narrow road that led through a small valley to my house. The rain lashed my face, but in the distance I made out two dark smudges hurtling toward me—my half-German Shepherd dogs, Jem and Atticus—like messengers from Zeus. Jem pulled away from his slower sidekick. Behind them, a bedraggled figure in a sou'wester and high boots trudged along the trail. Jem came to a large puddle about twenty feet in front of me, leapt it in one bound, and skidded to a halt in front of Sapphire. She put her nose down and nuzzled him. Atticus, the imperturbable one, trotted up and gave Sapphire a big lick on the face.

My wife, Darlene, straggled in last, wiping water from her face. Strands of red hair stuck out from her rain hat.

"We went for a walk. The storm hit, but the boys must have heard you and Sapphire because they took off like rockets."

I smiled at her and turned my head toward a faint buzzing noise when a hard object smashed into the middle of my forehead. I felt myself thrown backwards off the horse, flashing lights playing on the inside of my eyelids, then nothing.

Chapter 3

Lights Out

Do the dead dream?

The blasts from two shotguns echoed through the pitch-black night. I heard the buzz of pellets over my head when I hit the ground, and a warm trickle flowed from my scalp across my right cheek. Muzzle flashes showed the direction of the shots.

I lifted my head and wriggled my chest into the earth, then propped my Glock with both hands, aiming for the pinpoints of light, and squeezed off a full clip. Grunts told me they struck home. I reloaded and stood.

I ran in the general direction of the shooters. Two large shapes loomed in my path. I stopped, aimed, and put five into the taller one on the right, but it didn't faze him. He grinned and kept coming. The rest of the clip went into his head, but by now, he was two feet in front of me with no signs of damage. One clip left. I jammed it home and emptied it into the zombies who had begun to wrap their arms around me.

Someone shouted my name, and I looked down. I lay on a slab and could see the yellow toe tag secured by a wire. "Sloan, Jack, Male, Caucasian." Then I felt hands on my face and the person was no longer shouting.

"Jack, Jack. Wake up."

A soft voice.

"Where am I?"

"The hospital. Thank god, you're awake. We were so worried."

Darlene stood next to me, her face and voice raw. I looked up and saw a fluorescent light and an IV filled with an opaque fluid. The trail of tubes led to my right arm where a needle rested in a vein.

"Why?"

"You and Sapphire had just crossed the river when a branch blew off a tree and hit you."

"When?" My throat felt parched, my voice squeaky.

"Two days ago. You've been out ever since. The doctor says you have a concussion."

"The bag. A mail pouch. Where is it?"

"In the barn with your saddle and other gear. Who cares?"

"Sapphire?"

"In her stall with oats and water. I knew you'd be pissed if I didn't take care of her first. I drove myself to the hospital."

"Who's taking care of the other animals?"

"Ray Green, the guy down the road."

I nodded, but it hurt.

"When can I go home?" I said.

"You just woke up after being unconscious for forty-eight hours, and you want to leave? Are you crazy?"

I saw a flash of anger illuminate her exhausted-looking face.

"I have to get home. Call the doctor, and ask him. Please?"

She threw her hands in the air, stomped from the room, and turned right. I reckoned she was headed for the nurses' station. I hoped so. I needed to take care of what I'd found, and to do that, I had to get home.

Two days later, I sat at my project table surrounded by guns. I still had a headache and the abrasions on my forehead itched. Darlene came in from the office she used for working on her romance novels.

"Jack, what in the hell are you doing?"

I'd received the requisite sympathy for the past couple days, but Darlene was pissed. She'd wanted me to stay another day in the hospital. I knew her well enough to let her fume and not start an argument.

"They need cleaning," I said. "Look at this barrel." I held the spotless unit up for her to see, knowing she wouldn't bother to look.

"You cleaned them last week, Cowboy."

I pretended not to hear the worry in her voice. The 'cowboy' reference was an inside joke and meant to be light-hearted, but I sensed the tension that roiled beneath the surface.

"You need to start practice-shooting again," I said.

I saw the tiny twitch of her head. She hadn't handled her gun since the night she used it to defend herself. She didn't answer, only turned and headed toward the stairs leading to the downstairs pool area. I remained at the rough work table and concentrated on my task. *Nice going, Jack, maybe you can come up with another way to irritate her.*

8

I thought about the hospital dream. It wasn't the first time. Darlene and I had both seen a therapist after the attack on our *rancho* three years ago. He said it was PTSD, a common reaction to what we'd gone through. Mine showed itself in regular nightmares where I fired my weapon with no effect. No matter what I did, I couldn't stop the people who shot at us. After a year, the images faded, and I felt normal—at least my version of it. Darlene claimed the same results, but I know that Abraham, the man she'd killed, still haunted her.

The ghosts never left me, but I didn't talk about it, and neither did she. Maybe a mistake. I'm living testament to the burden of guilt that settles on a moral person who's committed an immoral act. Taking a life, no matter the circumstance, transcends a person's boundaries and changes one forever. So it must be with Darlene.

Chapter 4

Darlene

Darlene walked in front as we headed toward the barn and the inevitable encounter with my folly. I'd put it off despite her curiosity. Her mood had improved since yesterday, but I still felt a chill wind blowing from that direction.

I watched, and it struck me again how fortunate it was that we'd found each other. She tolerated my excesses, and those were legendary—at least among people who knew me. I'd stopped drinking for a while, but now felt safe in taking an occasional sip. A psychiatrist friend told me that booze and anxiety have a way of finding each other. The tranquil life I led today let me do a lot of things I couldn't have done a few years ago. More reasons to forget the treasure I'd unearthed.

I talked to Sapphire while I wiped and brushed her down, then fed her oats and filled her watering trough. I dawdled and stalled until I thought it had become obvious to Darlene. Sooner or later, I had to deal with the problem.

I reluctantly picked up the satchel to carry it to the house. Darlene and the dogs followed. I dropped it on the mud room floor, and Atticus, the bigger of the two, took the handle in his teeth and started to drag it to one of his favorite burying grounds. Jem, the speedy one, snatched it and pulled the other way. It must have weighed more than either dog, but that sort of thing didn't deter those two when they sensed adventure.

"Come on, you guys, bring it here." My first laugh in a few days.

For once, they obeyed. Both sat, tongues hanging out, looking like they expected a treat for being so good.

"Let's get to it, Jack. I've been awfully patient." Darlene rubbed Atticus behind the ears and motioned with her head. She started to stride toward the back of the house.

"*Tranquillo, Corazón.* Give me a minute." I wanted to collect my thoughts.

10

A moment later, I put my arm around her, and we walked to the kitchen table. I massaged the spot between her shoulders.

"Sapphire stumbled and started a small rock slide. I found this stuffed into a crevice that opened up." I unsnapped the catch on the canvas bag and hefted it. Fifty pounds?

"Come on, Jack. Show me."

"Check it out." I turned it over, and the contents spewed across the table.

"My God." Darlene didn't often gasp, but she half-stood in her seat. "How much is there?"

"These are packs of ten grand each." I picked up several wrapped bundles and let them fall through my hands to the pile on the table.

Darlene stretched over and touched it. "I've never seen so much money."

"You start on your side, and we'll see what's here."

I made piles of ten packets, one hundred thousand dollars each. Darlene did the same.

"I count eleven stacks—one million, one hundred thousand." I glanced at her side.

"Fourteen over here. That's two and a half million dollars. It's a fortune." She opened her blue eyes wide and held her hands to her head.

"And a world of trouble," I said.

"Why? Finders-keepers."

"The sack is new." I picked it up and showed it to her. "No more than a day or two outdoors when I found it. It was stashed there for a reason, and whoever did it will come back. We need to find out who and why."

"We don't have to find out anything. Call Will and turn it over to the cops."

Will Cowdry worked for the Santa Fe County Sheriff's Department, and we counted him among our close friends.

"I'll talk to him off the record, but I can't turn it in. For all we know, I'm still in law enforcement's 'most wanted' database. If I hand it over, and my name comes up, I could go to jail. I wish to God I hadn't picked this up."

"Why haven't you ever asked Will to run your name? Find out once and for all."

"Because if I'm listed, a flag could pop and make them wonder why he's looking at me. It's not worth the risk."

"Sorry, Sweetie. I know." She reached across the table and stroked my hand. "But it's an awful lot of money." She flicked her eyes at the stacks on the table.

She smiled and the small lines on her cheekbones crinkled. Except for those, her complexion reminded me of porcelain-skinned Englishwomen you see in bodice-ripper movies.

Normal curiosity had compelled me to pick up and examine the satchel. I have many vices, but keeping another person's money never entered the equation. It reminded me of the old lawyer joke—an elderly woman who drops off a three-hundred-dollar cash retainer at her attorney's each week, puts three thousand dollars into the envelope by mistake. The lawyer is later faced with an ethical dilemma—should he tell his partners?

Two and a half million dollars abandoned in the wilds of New Mexico intrigued me. It meant trouble, and the person who put it there wasn't going to walk away and forget it. If he or she came peaceably, I'd hand it over—its origin wasn't my concern. Let the cops or whomever deal with it, only keep Darlene and me on the sidelines.

Chapter 5

Will Cowdry

I broke down my weapon of choice—a Glock 21. The .45 caliber Winchester parabellum bullets loaded in its fifteen-round clip would stop anything within range, and I never knew it to misfire. The same piece I'd used on the thugs with shotguns. In my dreams, the bullets were ineffective, but I'd seen what they could do for real, and it gave me pause.

Darlene's gun sat on the table. A Baby Glock, model 27. The ten-shot clip made it lighter than mine, but the stopping power was legendary, and I knew cops who swore by it. A Glock lightweight .357 magnum Pocket Rocket with an ankle holster and two shotguns completed my arsenal.

The first, a sawed-off, pistol-grip Remington twenty-gauge, could be concealed under a raincoat. The second, a Mossberg Special Purpose, boasted a nine-round shot capacity. Double-ought twelve-gauge ammo could take apart a vehicle at twenty feet. It didn't sound like much, but it represented a formidable collection in the hands of a person who knew how to use them, and I fit the category.

The boxes of shells stacked next to the weaponry offered further comfort. The main switch to the property security system hung on the wall about fifteen feet from where I worked. The marketers called it the most sophisticated protection a homeowner could purchase. We stopped turning it on a while back, after the shock of what had gone down succumbed to the erosions of time and memory. In much the same way we endure the loss of someone close, our minds help us rationalize other devastating traumas.

I considered myself one of the good guys, but I'd gotten in so much trouble during my short sojourn on earth that I could smell it coming, and ever since I picked up that satchel, its stench burned my nostrils. I pored over the Internet, but found no mention of a big heist or missing money. That meant it was connected in ways I didn't want to know about. I couldn't quite bring myself to burn the cash in the fireplace. I

13

knew too many people who would sell their grandmothers for that kind of dough, and aside from my desire for action, I wanted to do the right thing. Maybe Will would have answers.

Later that evening, we poured ourselves a couple of Absoluts on ice and sat in front of a muted television. CNN played the day's news, but neither of us was interested in the rest of the world. Darlene stood.

"Where are you headed?"

"I need a smoke, and I promised myself I wouldn't do it in the house. I'll go to the porch."

"I'll go with you." I snatched an ashtray off the kitchen counter.

Stars hung in the sky, brighter in the Land of Enchantment than most places. The altitude and thinner ozone layer give them a special brilliance.

"Seeing all that money was a turn-on, but after what you said and everything else that's gone down, I'm worried." She lit her Marlboro Light and fidgeted with the matches. "I know you, and you're not going to let it go without trying to trace it, are you?"

A breeze rustled in the cottonwoods and blew her hair across her face. She wiped it back and gave me one of her looks.

"I'll find out what I can from Will and the Internet, but I promise to give it up." I raised my right hand. "I swear."

"Do it, Jack. We have a good life here. Don't fuck it up." She crushed a half-smoked Marlboro in the ashtray.

I reached out to touch her arm, but she'd already moved inside.

The next day, I stopped by the Sheriff's Department off Route 14. I went inside and asked the receptionist if Deputy Cowdry was available. Before she could answer, Will burst through the inner door.

"Jack! Where you been keepin' yourself, you old Irishman?" He hugged me until he squeezed my breath out.

We both stood close to the same height, but at two thirty-five I had him by forty pounds, and I used the extra weight to untangle myself.

"Good to see you too, Will," I managed.

Will reminded me of Clint Eastwood in the spaghetti Westerns. I'd once told him what I thought, and he responded by saying I looked like Rooster Cogburn, only seedier. Will wore his gun belt slung low on his hip, and non-issue cowboy boots added to the picture. It didn't stop with appearances. Normally taciturn, Darlene and I found him honest and forthright, and unafraid to speak his mind. A man you could count on in a pinch or a gunfight.

He dragged me by the arm through the door and into his office.

"Have a seat, Pardner. You want coffee? Water?"

I said water would be good.

While he was gone, I studied the spartan office. Plain desk, small bookcase, 'Wanted' posters, and a couple of framed landscape photos tacked to the wall, plus piles of paper in every corner. The Sherriff's Department didn't overspend on décor.

After we covered old friends and old times, I asked him if he knew anything about a large sum of missing money which caused him to break his stoic demeanor to the extent he raised his eyebrows. He said he didn't know much, but the Feds were investigating a big-time kidnapping case. He showed me a bulletin that cautioned law officers to keep an eye out for two and a half million ransom dollars they couldn't account for. My stomach tightened, but I kept my face expressionless.

"I figure you'll tell me why you want to know about a pile of missing money when you're ready," he said. "But if there's something bothering you, best spill it now and let me help—if I can."

"I'd rather not say, Will. Don't worry. If what I'm thinking comes to anything, I'll bring it to you. Let's leave it there, if you don't mind.

"You're a real piece of work, Jack. Good thing I trust you like I do." He shrugged and smiled. "But don't do anything you'll regret."

"Any ideas?" I said.

"I'll call a cop I know in Juarez. See if he's heard anything. Carlos Santiago—a good guy."

"Thanks, Will. I'll check in later."

A reflection in the glass of the Taos ski area photo hanging behind his desk caught my attention. When I turned, Elias Hernandez, Will's boss, was entering his office across the hall. Maybe he'd been listening.

When Will phoned later in the day, he wanted to talk about the conversation that took place after my visit. I asked him to meet me that evening at Sheila's, the downtown tequila bar that Darlene, Tommy Crowfoot, and I owned. Consuela, our live-in housekeeper, cooked there three nights a week, and Will loved her grub. We sat at a corner table out of other patrons' earshot. Tommy worked a busy bar and couldn't join us.

15

"Elias came into my office, Jack. He asked about your business with the Sheriff's Department." Will cocked his elbows on the table and interlaced his fingers.

"What did you tell him?"

"'Passin' time, Elias'—but I know he didn't buy it. Hernandez is a major asshole, and he don't like you," Will said.

"Anything else?" My curiosity itched.

"He said he knew somethin' went down before with me and you that I never told him about, and I better not be usin' departmental resources to help you. He said my ass would be in a big sling if that were the case. I told him I knew who I worked for."

"I don't want to get you in trouble with your boss." I said.

"The guy's a cretin, Jack. I watched him try to tug his gun belt up over that sagging gut for the hundredth time this week. He makes me sick. I asked him why he had such a hard-on for you."

"And?"

"He said he didn't like you, or your snooty bitch wife. He believes you and Darlene think you're better'n him."

"He has that right."

"Hah." Will slapped the table, almost spilling his ice tea. "That's when he tol' me he knew somethin' was up three years ago and we never let him in on it."

I heard a note of genuine concern creep into Will's voice.

"He said he's gonna keep an eye on you and me and see what's cookin'. I tol' him, 'You do that, Elias, and if you find anything, let me know.'"

Now, I laughed. "How'd he take to that, Will?"

"Said I was gettin' smart-ass with him. Said I think I'm untouchable because my old man's a Commissioner." Will pushed back his chair and stood, stuck out his stomach, and did his Elias impersonation: "You're an employee of the county, and your job description says you take orders from the duly-elected Sheriff. Understand?" Will wiped his finger across the bottom of his nose.

"You think he was coked-up?"

"Coke or meth, but I'm not goin' there. I played the good ol' boy. I tol' him, 'You're the boss, and you know damn well I don't use my dad to get favors'—and that's the truth, Jack. What I wanted to say was, 'Maybe you need another hit of coke, you moron,' but I held my tongue."

The waitress brought our food. Fajitas for Will and my usual, Consuela's chimichangas—the best in the world. She refilled our ice teas and smiled shyly at me.

"We don't see you much anymore, Mr. Sloan," she said.

"I need to come by more often. Easy to forget what a fine place it is. Sorry, but I forgot your name?"

"Lucinda. I'm Tommy's oldest daughter."

Christ, what an idiot I am. My partner Tommy's girl, and I didn't remember her. It reinforced my thought that Darlene and I needed to get out of the house and pay attention to our old friends. It was hard to explain our hermit-like existence. We had wiped out the rest of the world and settled into a cocoon. I wouldn't call it fear—I chalked it up to caution. Killers stalking you change your perspective, and even though they were gone, the impact of those days remained.

"Of course, Lucinda. You're so pretty, and you've grown so much. Good to see you." She left the table, and I turned back to Will.

"Smooth, Jack." He smiled at me.

I shrugged and held out my hands, palms up.

"What's the upshot with Hernandez?" I said.

"Watch your butt. Elias might be a dork and a tweaker, but he ain't stupid. He'll try to jam you up." Will's expression turned serious.

"Any idea how?"

"There's lots of ways, Jack. Don't forget, he's the Sheriff. Even if you and I know what a jerk he is, he was elected by a majority of the people, and they'll take his word over yours. Lay low and don't stick your nose into this money thing. That's my advice."

Chapter 6

Durango

Less than a half hour after I came back from Will's, the phone in my home office rang. Caller ID told me it came from south of the border.

"Señor Sloan?"

"Carlos Santiago?"

"*Si*. Will Cowdry asked me to call. He said we might be able to help each other, and that it concerned the recent kidnapping in Juarez—the one that made the papers."

"Possibly, Carlos, but I don't know for sure if there's any connection between what's going on here and that case. Are you working it?"

"Technically, it's not mine. I'm with AFI here in Mexico. The FBI is handling things, but I have a temporary assignment to assist them. Anything you can tell me might be helpful."

"You tell me about the kidnapping, and I'll decide if what I know fits. Does that make sense?"

"No, Señor, it does not. You have an obligation to assist law enforcement, and I have a duty to maintain confidentiality. You go first, then we decide."

I resisted the temptation to make a joke about a Mexican standoff.

"Nothing personal, Carlos, but I don't know you. We should meet face-to-face. What do you say to Phoenix in a couple of days? Half-way for both of us."

"Sooner would be better," he said.

"Let me check my schedule and talk to my wife. I'll get back to you later today."

I didn't have a schedule.

"I need to go to Phoenix," I said to Darlene, "but first, we're going somewhere else."

She followed me outside and saw me throw the canvas sack of money into the back of our SUV, along with a small arsenal of weaponry and a gym bag with my overnight gear.

"Where?"

"Durango, darling. I need to see John Thunder. Pack a bag and let Consuela know we're leaving."

Consuela, our cook and housekeeper, and her husband Franco lived in the small *casita* near the main house. They'd been with us for years, and lived through the bad times when all our lives were in danger. Franco pretty much ran the property and Consuela managed the home. The four of us felt comfortable together, like family, and we took pains to give each other living space. I couldn't imagine life without them.

"Thanks for the advance warning, Rambo. When were you going to let me in on the secret?"

"Sorry, Sweetheart. I've a lot on my mind, and, honest-to-God, I only decided a few minutes ago."

"And why are you taking that sack of money? Wouldn't it be better to leave it in the safe?"

"Cut me slack on this one. I'll feel better if I can lay my hands on it. If we leave it here, it becomes another's responsibility."

She gave me a 'whatever' look and shook her head.

"I'll let Consuela know. Give me fifteen minutes," she said.

Then she grinned and my heart twitched. She walked away in her jeans, soft, high suede boots, and checkered shirt. Her hair ran every which way but straight. What gave me the luck to have a woman like her? I sure as hell didn't deserve it.

A few minutes later, I walked over to where Darlene and Consuela stood.

"*¿Dónde está Franco?*"

"In the barn, Señor Jack." Consuela said.

I caught him before he climbed to the loft.

"Franco, did you see me come in last night?"

"*Sí.*"

"Did you see the satchel?"

"*Sí, Señor.*"

"*Por favor*, forget about it. If anyone asks, *no sabes nada. Comprende?*"

"*Qué satchel, Señor?*" Franco held up his hands and laughed.

I completely trusted seven people in the world—Darlene, Tommy my business partner, Will Cowdry, Consuela, Franco, my lawyer, Zeke Martinez, and John Thunder.

19

John Thunder: Pueblo Indian, shaman, intrepid, timeless soul, and the person who saved our asses three years ago. By all rational standards, he knew things he couldn't have known without prescience. When John spoke, I listened.

John answered his cell, and we arranged to meet that evening in Durango. With time to spare, we followed Route 84, the scenic route, toward Pagosa Springs. A few miles past Abiquiu, traffic slowed near the Ghost Ranch. People drive past the entrance before they see it, and U-turning tourists present a danger. Beyond, the open road stretched into a phantasmagoria of crimson buttes, mesas, gorges and boulders, peppered with cholla, piñon, juniper, and chamiso. No wonder Georgia O'Keefe chose this as the place to live and practice her wondrous art.

"The dream, Jack. I'm scared. It's that bag of money." Darlene fired up a Marlboro and cranked down her window an inch so the smoke would blow out and not on me.

I'd told her that my nightmare had visited me when I was in the hospital.

"I dunno. If it doesn't stop, I'll go see Dennis again. You think there's something wrong with me?" I pulled back on the steering wheel to guide us around a sharp curve.

Dennis was the psychiatrist we'd both seen after the events of three years ago.

"Aside from being the craziest person I've ever known, not much. You need adventure—like doing the Indy 500 through these fucking curves—now, slow down a little and talk to me."

I eased off on the gas pedal. She crushed her cigarette in the ashtray and closed her window.

"I know that all this crap has shaken you, and please believe I don't want trouble to come around again, especially the part that hurts you. I don't know what else to say." I felt helpless.

"You're an odd man, Jack Sloan. You reduce everyday tasks to a routine so you can get through them without thinking. Then you look for ways to do it differently. There are times when you can't see the obvious, even when it smacks you in the face. If I didn't know better, I might say you were verging on autistic."

"Wapner."

"Boy, ain't that the truth? You're Rainman if ever I met him. Look at you and numbers. My God, you remember telephone numbers from thirty years ago, and you do math in your head that would melt a calculator. Maybe that's what's wrong with you." She laughed and rubbed my leg.

"I think I focus on the day-to-day shit because if I look outside myself, I'll understand how nuts I am." I relaxed a notch and eased my grip on the steering wheel.

"That's the most insightful thing you've ever said, but I love you anyway. At least our life isn't dull, but please don't start with the dreams again. I'm not sure I could take it."

We closed on Durango, and the terrain changed from high desert into Colorado mountains. Ponderosa pine scented the air, and I heard a stream tumbling through the rocks. The western sky began to streak red and yellow. I thought of the sunsets at our *rancho* when black clouds hung over the Sangre de Cristos to the east, and sunlight blazed west behind the Jemez range. When twilight fell, the darkness would turn purple, then the entire mass would sink into the tree line while the moon rose behind Truchas, the highest Sangre peak visible from our place. A few times a year, we saw a coyote moon—one that rose like an enormous ball and hung with brilliant light until you thought the sun and moon had changed places.

Descending the long grade into the town snapped me from my reverie. The ancient hotel stood like a monument on the corner. John and I first met there years ago when an old friend owned it. The former proprietor's body now lay under a pile of sand and rocks in the desert south of Santa Fe. He betrayed everyone who loved him and paid the ultimate price. I felt sad when I remembered the music and laughter we shared inside the red brick building.

We checked in and carried our things to the room. I didn't know why I brought the Remington shotgun. The Glock felt good in its old spot under my left armpit, but the other looked like overkill. Nobody waited to ambush us in Durango.

I thought about what I'd read concerning veterans who returned from Iraq or Afghanistan after two or three tours of duty. They experienced severe difficulty adjusting to civilian life and many tried to reenlist. My theory was that they were addicted to extreme danger.

My four years in the Army had given me problems. Combat can be a love/hate thing. I never wanted to return, but I held a secret place deep inside that I occasionally visited. No more, at least not until yesterday. I didn't want to tell Darlene that old ghosts had joined the more recent ones.

I rehashed the conversation we'd had before we left. In retrospect, it sounded stupid.

"Do me a favor. Let's keep the twelve-gauge in the house. I put your Glock in the stand beside your bed."

"Jack, what the hell is going on? I don't need a gun. We have two enormous dogs and a security system. Besides, the people who wanted us dead are long gone. Why are you doing this?" Darlene looked distraught.

"Humor me," I said.

I didn't see any sense in frightening her by explaining my foreboding, and before we hit the road, she agreed to go along with the idea.

"Because this much cash makes me nervous," she said.

"Thanks Sweetie. It can't do any harm to be careful until we find a place to dump it."

I had hugged her, in part because she agreed with me, but mainly because I loved her.

"You're Jack Sloan." The old bartender recognized me. "And you're his girlfriend. I forget the name, but not the face."

"Darlene." I nodded in her direction. "Good memory."

"Hard to forget a big, tall cowboy like you and that scar on your face. Besides, you were Abraham's best friend, and Darlene here is the best-looking woman that ever walked into the place. Damn, I miss him. You ever hear what happened? I mean, here one day, gone the next."

"Not a word." I shrugged and gazed out the window. Out of the corner of my eye, I saw Darlene cringe.

"Jack Daniels on the rocks?" He looked like he expected a prize.

"Like I said, good memory." I obliged his vanity, and he grinned while he poured our drinks.

"Music tonight?" I asked. Four scruffy country boys were gathered on the small stage tuning instruments.

"Bluegrass. Like the old days, and these guys are good. You stickin' around for a while?"

"Hmm. Hard to say. We're waiting for John Thunder."

He nodded and turned to take care of an older touristy-looking couple who pulled up bar stools. I contemplated my drink and the bottles stacked behind the bar. I'd sat in enough joints over the years to have perfected my inventory scans. One way to pass the time. John would arrive within an hour.

"See anything you want?" Darlene tugged at my shirt. "Come on, snap out of it. If I can stand to be in Abraham's old joint, so can you." She leaned over and whispered, "Remember, I'm the one who killed him."

Chapter 7

John Thunder

I ordered more drinks and carried them to a small table in a corner where Darlene and I could talk with John in private. The place started to liven up, and the fiddler played a little jig each time a new customer walked in the door. I guessed the band worked for tips or a percentage of bar sales. Serious Bluegrass would kick off in about fifteen minutes. I'm an amateur musician and partial to the old country genre. Singers like Waylon Jennings, Bob Wills, Johnny Cash, and Willie. My Gibson guitar still ran on all cylinders, and I liked to sit in with locals at Sheila's.

I hadn't seen John for almost a year, but when he walked through the swinging doors, old times came with him. His coal-black hair now hung well past his shoulders. A headband kept it out of his eyes—eyes that could burn a hole through a person he didn't like or trust. He walked with the casual grace of a human being comfortable with his place on earth. A man at home in the mountains or a honky bar on main street Durango. I jumped from my chair and hugged him.

"Christ, it's good to see you, *Hermano*."

"And you, my friend, but don't call me Christ." He held out his arms to Darlene. "Give me a squeeze, you beautiful woman."

"I always thought she might be why you put up with me." I tapped him on the shoulder with my knuckles and smiled.

"Not the sole motive, but it sure helps."

He waved at the bartender who put his hand on the draught beer dispenser and raised his eyebrows. John nodded and sat down.

"Not that it matters—seeing you for any reason is a treat—but what's the urgency?" John said.

"Something came up. I need your advice."

"That's what shamans are for, Jack. That and curing disease."

"You still drive the GTO?"

"I'll never give up that beauty. She's parked in the alley." He looked up when the bartender brought over his beer.

24

"On the house, John." He winked at us.

"Thanks, Sam. I'll catch you later." John turned to me. "Now, what's this all about?"

I told him about the events of the past couple of days, keeping my voice low.

"Let me get this straight," he said when I finished. "You found a bag full of cash. You don't know who it belongs to, but it might be a kidnap payoff. Nobody's claimed it, and you don't know what to do with it. How about sending me half and burying the rest?"

"It's more complicated than that, and you know it. First of all, I don't steal, and I'd never have taken it under normal circumstances. Second, I can smell the trouble associated with this dough. I wouldn't pass it on to anyone. Third, if I turn it in to the cops, I might draw attention to myself. I suspect I'm still on the FBI's 'wanted' list. And fourth, I found it on private property."

"Where?" John took a sip of beer.

"Pueblo land. I shouldn't ride there, but it's the prettiest ridge in the neighborhood. Can you imagine the hell to pay if the Indians found out I took that much cash off the reserve?"

"I could help. Most of the Pueblo Council are old friends, but when it made the papers, they might go nuts."

"John, convince my lover here that he needs to get rid of it. You know him and he's going to have a tough time keeping his nose out," Darlene raised her voice above ours.

"So what do I do?" I directed this at John.

"Did you hear what I just said?" Darlene jabbed me in the ribs with her elbow.

John shrugged. "I heard you, Darlene. The money belongs to the insurance company or the kidnappers. Take your pick. In my book, they're all crooks."

"Only if it's the ransom money. What if it's not?" I said.

"I see what you mean." He selected a toothpick from the jar on the table and began to chew on it.

"Will showed me a few newspaper articles, and I searched on the Internet. The kidnapping went down in Juarez and El Paso, or near El Paso. More questions than answers. Where'd the swap take place? How come they wasted the dude? Why in the hell would ransom money be anywhere near Santa Fe?"

Darlene sat and tapped her package of cigarettes on the table.

"You guys are ignoring me. I'm going outside for a smoke." She stomped away toward the front door.

25

John pulled a small pipe and plastic bag from an outside vest pocket. He opened the bag, stuffed a small amount of the contents into the bowl, tamped it down, and lit up. The unmistakable smell of weed wafted through the bar.

"John, for Christ's sake, you can't smoke dope in public."

"I'm a shaman. This is for religious purposes." He bowed his head a few degrees and shot me a serious look. "I'm contemplating your problem."

We sat in silence until Darlene returned.

He looked up. "I'm with Darlene on this one, Jack. My advice is to go home and have her turn the money over to Will. Make sure the media are aware. It'll be a great story. After it breaks, take a vacation. Get out of town for a couple of weeks until the whole thing is forgotten. Whoever left the money will read about it and know it's in the hands of the police. Maybe there's a reward."

"How about the reaction from the Pueblo Council?"

"Say you found it on the side of the road. Who's going to know the difference?"

I nodded and checked out Darlene's reaction. She looked relieved.

"We'll do it when I get back from Phoenix. I'm going there day after tomorrow to see a Mexican ATF Agent who Will hooked me up with and who's looking for missing cash. I'll see what he has to say."

"You're a piece of work, Jack. Why get involved at all? If you go to see this guy, you're going to get sucked in, and then what? Just dump it, pronto." John tapped his finger on the table for emphasis.

"All I have to do is convince myself it's none of my business, that I can't solve the crime, and I don't give a shit about two and a half million simoleons. Other than that, it'll be easy."

John shot Darlene what I took for an exasperated look and shrugged.

"I've offered my opinion. I know you'll do what you want, but be careful. That's a lot of money, and people could get hurt," John said.

We sat and talked for the next two hours. The ragtag band proved worthy performers and spun out great music.

"I have to get moving, Jack. I promised someone I'd stop by tonight." John plopped his empty beer stein on the table and half-stood.

"Thanks for the advice." I took his hand.

"I'll call in a couple of days. We shouldn't wait this long between visits. Darlene, come north in a month, and we'll go out to the mountains and do a little mescaline or peyote and wrestle with our inner selves. It's good for the soul."

"We'll come soon, my friend." She stood and wrapped her arms around him.

I turned my head to pull out my chair so I could stand, and when I looked up, he'd vanished.

Same old John.

Part 2

Carlos Santiago

Chapter 8

Juarez

6:00 a.m., Ciudad Juarez, Chihuahua, Estados Unidos Mexicanos.

Carlos Santiago slept fitfully, rehashing last night's argument with Maria. *So I quit, then what? Plant a bean field next to the house? I work for the Federal Investigative Agency, the AFI, in Ciudad Juarez—the most violent city in the world. Seven bodies a day. I want to make a difference, Maria. I can make a difference. The FBI and DEA respected me enough to train me. The Americanos call me the best fugitive hunter in the system. It means something. It's my job, and I'm damned good at it.*

Not that he gave a *carajo* about *gringos*. He knew enough of them to understand that the U.S. government didn't mourn the innocent Mexican nationals gunned down in the drug cartels' crossfire. Politics and statistics drove them. *How many metric tons of marijuana or cocaine did we seize on this raid? What's the street value?*

The next morning he walked to the door and looked back at Maria. "We'll talk when I get home. I promise."

Maria had propped herself on one elbow and rubbed her eyes, then brushed away the long glossy hair that hung in her face. Carlos' heart did a little flip.

"You're not listening, Carlos. We can make it without you being a cop. You're the smartest guy I know, and hard work never scared me." Her voice sounded thick with sleep. "It's more than talk. It's not safe here anymore." She turned her back to him and pulled the comforter around her shoulders.

"Maria?"

No response.

Maybe I will quit. Tomorrow. I'll make up my mind then. We could move to the States. Leave the battleground. I could sign on with a police force in another town—a quiet place where a man doesn't have to worry about catching a bullet every day.

The U.S. government refused to acknowledge that to stem the drug trade, they needed to curb demand. Carlos made the argument for the thousandth time to the man who sat across from him in the dusty South Phoenix pub later that same evening.

"Frank, your guys need to wake up and smell the crack. We didn't create the situation—you did." Carlos rapped his knuckles on the table for emphasis.

Frank Hunter, nicknamed Big Game in the Bureau, stared over a shot of tequila at his friend and sucked on a lemon slice. He pursed his lips and squinted.

"And as long as your criminalistas can make a living running dope across the border…?" Frank let the question hang.

"Take away the crime and you take away the dime. Remember that old one? Every cent the U.S. and Mexico spend on the drug war jacks up cartel profits." Carlos pointed his finger at Frank.

"Slackin' off ain't going to happen, Carlos. Washington's response will be more National Guard, more ICE agents, and a longer fence. Every time an American gets whacked south of the border, Congress increases the appropriation. There's no politician alive who would support your view." He downed the shot and licked salt off the back of his hand.

Carlos and Frank had first met four years earlier, working on a cross-border drug deal and homicide. Frank shared his pragmatism, but not his penchant for the unorthodox. Maybe that's one of the reasons Carlos liked him so much. He knew he could count on him. Rock-solid in a crisis, Frank understood the cop business. Carlos never worried about his back when he walked with Frank.

Carlos shrugged, tapped a Marlboro Red from a cardboard box, scratched the red-topped match on the book cover held between his thumb and forefinger—a jailhouse light—and inhaled deeply. The bar stunk of booze and smoke, and one more coffin nail wouldn't make any difference. Besides, Maria wasn't around to scowl at his smoking.

A small ruckus broke out near the juke box near the front of the bar.

"Frank, what do you like about this place? I'm not comfortable here."

"Habit, I guess." Frank shrugged. "I used to have a confidential informant who hung out here. I got used to it."

The argument up front grew in volume. Carlos squirmed in his seat when he noticed the two combatants looking his way.

"What are those rednecks staring at?" Carlos said.

"Don't pay 'em no mind. They're ignorant." Frank picked up his tequila, downed it in a gulp and signaled the waitress.

'Hey, Greaser," the taller of the men yelled and started to walk toward their table. "Your bar's down the street a few blocks. Get the fuck out of here. This is a white man's place."

Carlos tensed. The guy weighed in at about two-fifty, looked drunk, and ham-hocks dangled from the end of his wrists. *If I hit him first, I can take him. If I miss, I'm dead.* Carlos had taken his share of beatings, and he wasn't afraid, but he didn't want his evening ruined.

Frank moved fast for an old dude. The astonished look on the would-be assailant's face said it all. The forty-five caliber pressed against his mouth punctuated Frank's intent.

"F.B.I., Fuck-face. You have five seconds to vacate the premises before you lose those pearly whites." The yahoo lay backwards across a table. Frank pushed his knee into the big man's groin and rubbed the gun barrel on his lips. A small trickle of blood ran down his chin.

Carlos noticed a wet stain spread across the guy's pants.

Frank backed off, and the bed-wetter jumped up and high-tailed it toward the front door.

"He's fucking crazy," the man screamed at the bartender on his way out. "Call the cops."

"Don't come back." The bartender threw a wet towel at the man's retreating back. "Sorry, Frank. This one's on the house." He carried a shot of tequila and a beer to the table and patted Frank on the shoulder.

The hubbub passed with little notice from other patrons, one of whom punched "San Antonio Rose" into the juke box, and a couple began to dance.

Frank turned back to Carlos like nothing had happened.

"What are you doin' here, anyway? You're a fugitive chaser, and you ain't carryin' extradition papers. So what's the story?" Frank put down his glass. "Can I bum a weed?" He took one without waiting for a response.

"Thanks, Frank. You probably saved me from an ass-kicking."

"I've seen you in action. I was taking care of the other guy. Didn't want him to get hurt."

They both laughed, and Carlos leaned in toward Frank.

"Keep this confidential." Carlos trusted Frank more than anyone, except maybe Maria, and that might be a toss-up. "It's the Pendleton case." He watched the deep furrows in Frank's brow merge into an exclamation mark.

"The guy they kidnapped and killed a couple of days ago? You'll never catch them. Christ, there are what—two snatches a day that we know about? Besides, when did you get moved to that department?"

"Special assignment. It's high-profile, and the pressure from the American Ambassador is intense. Like you said, Washington reacts when a *gringo* gets killed, especially a big shot. You know the story?"

Frank shook his head. He loosened his tie and opened his shirt, but still wore his suit coat. FBI tradition—and it hid the gun clipped to his belt. Fine perspiration coated his face. He used a napkin to wipe it off, giving special care to the boxer's nose that lay semi-flattened between his high cheek bones.

"Nothing unusual about the kidnapping except where it happened. Why Ciudad Juarez? Rich businessmen with connections in both governments don't vacation in tough border towns." Carlos worked his shoulders around the stiff neck he woke up with. He'd removed his jacket, but still felt the day's warmth. He seldom strapped up on this side of the border except for special occasions.

"Maybe a woman?"

Carlos knew that Frank's reputation did not include the sobriquet "ladies' man," and since Frank had turned fifty-two a month ago, Carlos doubted he harbored plans of becoming one, but he knew that years of dealing with hard cases gave his friend an innate sense of peoples' motives.

"Maybe," Carlos nodded, "but it got weird after they bagged him."

"How so?" Frank stubbed out his cigarette after a few drags, shook his head and coughed. "I remember why I quit."

"They contacted the family here, in Phoenix, who agreed to pay the ransom. Pendleton's company carried insurance, so they came up with the cash. Two and a half million, U.S. The family let us know about it, but demanded no interference until Pendleton arrived safely home in the States. Our orders came straight from the Governor of Chihuahua. Hands off."

"Makes sense. Not much you—or we—could have done, anyway. Pay the ransom and hope for the best," Frank said and spread his hands.

"The company hired an abduction specialist who coordinated the payoff and recovery. He asked for and received 'proof of life,' although we don't yet know what it consisted of. That's when the rules changed. The criminals demanded that the swap take place on U.S. soil and specified a drop in New Mexico. The company agreed."

"Why chance committing an illegal act in the States? The odds of them getting caught here run ten times the risk of Mexico." Frank paused and shook his head in apparent disbelief. "Stupid fucking crooks. That's why the FBI always gets its man."

"My boss said the same thing, and then we started to think. What if the kidnappers weren't Mexican nationals? What if they were Americanos, and it has nothing to do with drug cartels? Damn nice if we could pin this one on *gringo* gangsters and get the heat off us."

"Now I see why you're here. But so what? They killed the guy two days ago and left his body—minus half his head—in the New Mexican desert. If your government's problem is diplomatic heat, it dies with Pendleton. In a month, no one will remember."

"Not so, Buddy. After the next kidnapping, the media will dredge up this one. Unsolved doesn't work, plus, no reason it went down that way. The specialist talked to Pendleton on a cell phone a half hour before the exchange. They'd assembled the money the night before, and the deal terms were simple: the kidnappers pick up and count the ransom, then free Pendleton within thirty minutes. No reason to kill him—at least none that we know of."

Frank tapped his fingers on the table and stared at Carlos.

"Whaaaat, Frank?"

"Any suspects?"

"Not really," Carlos said. "I didn't get a lot of details beyond what I told you, but you could make inquiries for me. My guess is that the Feds know more, but want to keep this a Mexican crime—like we want to pin it on *gringos*."

"As usual, nobody gives a shit about the victim—this Pendleton guy. Am I right?"

Carlos heard weariness in Frank's voice.

"We care because it's bad for tourism. Otherwise, you're correct. My gut tells me we're looking at a scumbag, anyway."

"That's speculation. I don't know much about him, but from what I've read, he enjoyed a reputation as one of the world's leading financiers," Frank said.

"But one more time: why Ciudad Juarez? It's an anomaly, and nine times out of ten, that means deceit. I want to get inside your outfit's investigation, Frank. Will you talk to your boss?"

"I'll see what I can do. First, I have to get access. I haven't paid any attention to the case since it's not on my desk, but my supervisor cuts me lots of slack, so I think he'll go along. Meet me at the office tomorrow morning."

"I'll see you then. Got to run now. Our Counsel wants to brief me on the 'public image' to project." Carlos shook his head and smiled.

Carlos and Frank stood, and each put a hand on the other's shoulder. Their friendship was way too old for a handshake.

"Hasta mañana."

Carlos turned and went out into the broiling afternoon sun. He carried his suit coat hung on one finger and draped over his shoulder. Arizona felt cool compared to Chihuahua.

Chapter 9

Mrs. Pendleton

Frank Hunter managed to convince his boss to allow Carlos to sit in on the widow's interrogation.

"Better if I don't come with you," Frank told him. "Takes the pressure off Forbes. Maybe you'll learn more."

Carlos doubted it, but maybe Frank was right. He'd felt an irrational dislike for Agent Forbes from the moment they met, and his discomfort increased when the questioning began.

"I know this is difficult for you, Mrs. Pendleton, but we need to find out all we can about your husband's activities the day of the kidnapping," said Forbes.

Carlos wished he could've brought Maria to Phoenix with him, but she wouldn't leave the kids, even with her mother babysitting. Maybe if she saw him in action, she might better understand why he risked his life.

He surveyed the living room of the elaborate spread in Scottsdale. Pendleton's spouse had received next-of-kin notification two days earlier, and based on her demeanor, Carlos figured that the initial shock had worn off. He studied her and found her composed and elegant. He'd met enough recent widows in his time to recognize the ones who might keep their grief inside.

"I have no idea why he went to Juarez. We don't go to places like that," she said and glanced at Carlos.

He held his palms up and outward to let her know he wasn't offended. She'd caught him examining her: A beautiful woman with an almost overpowering sexuality. He figured she might be fifty, or even a little older, but she moved and looked like a twenty-five-year-old. Tall, with long, dark, reddish hair, eyes that could cut straight to your heart, and a lithe, seductive body. If Pendleton spent his time fucking around in Juarez, Carlos thought he must have been an idiot—or gay.

"Didn't." Forbes said. "You said 'don't.' Sorry to say, it's past tense now, Mrs. Pendleton."

Carlos gave the agent a sharp stare.

"Please drop the Mrs. Pendleton. Call me Elizabeth." She gave a faint smile, but Carlos detected anger in her eyes.

"Could he have conducted business there, Mrs. Pendleton?"

In addition to being an asshole, it looked like Forbes played by the book—no 'Elizabeth' from him.

"Ask his secretary. She keeps—sorry, *kept* his calendar. I didn't know the details of his business travels. He didn't talk about them, and I didn't question. I do know that many of the companies he promoted invested in Mexico."

"You were married one year?"

"Two, next month."

She used her fingertips to brush away a tear that slid down her cheek. *Real—or a good actress?* Carlos wanted to jump in and ask his own questions, but he kept his mouth buttoned, like he had promised Frank.

"You received the first call from the kidnappers about 10:15 the night of the crime, correct?"

Carlos had read the copy of the official report Frank gave him. His mind drifted off while the agent bore in on who said what and when. *Typical Bureau. They'll spend days sifting through the minutiae and ignore what makes this crime different. That's where we'll find the answers.*

"Excuse me, Elizabeth," Carlos interrupted, "I need to use the rest room."

Forbes scowled.

"Down that hallway, first door on the right." Her smile dazzled him.

Please call me later. We need to talk. Carlos added his cell phone number, folded the paper, and placed it under the soap dish. He flushed the toilet, ran water over his hands, dried them, and returned to the living room.

He walked up behind Forbes, looked into Elizabeth's eyes, and jerked his head toward the bathroom. A few minutes later, she excused herself.

Carlos watched her walk back to her chair. He'd bet money she modeled in an earlier life. She nodded to let him know she'd read his note. He wished they were done with this leaden interview so he could meet her in

36

private. Then Forbes asked a question that yanked him back to the present.

"Mrs. Pendleton, did your husband have enemies?"

"A man in his position always risks offending someone," she said. "He ran a successful global hedge fund, but foolproof investments don't exist. People occasionally lost money and didn't like it, but dangerous enemies? I don't think so."

"This is a delicate question, Mrs. Pendleton, but I'm obliged to ask it. How will you profit from your husband's death?"

Carlos noticed that Forbes studied her, looking for 'tells.'

"We signed a prenuptial agreement. The estate goes to his children from a previous marriage, his former wife, a sister in Boston, and many charities. I came to the union with my own wealth. Robert's assets were his, and mine belong to me. I should add that I loved him very much and we were happy." Elizabeth choked and held her hand to her throat.

"I'm sorry, Mrs. Pendleton. I meant no disrespect."

Carlos saw her shoulders sag and sensed an end to today's questions.

She sat up in her chair and sighed. "Sorry to be so abrupt, but if you'll excuse me, I'm exhausted. Please let me know if you want to continue at another time. I'm at your disposal."

Elizabeth rose and extended her hand to each man, her face drawn. She walked Carlos and Forbes to the front door.

"Thanks for letting me listen." Carlos turned to Forbes when they stood outside. "If you don't mind, I'll keep in touch with her."

"I'll let Frank Hunter know when I'm coming back, and he can relay it to you, Agent Santiago. I have more questions for Mrs. Pendleton—not that she answered any of the ones I asked her today."

"Think she's involved?" Carlos didn't expect an honest response, but he wanted to see if he could rile this guy.

"Until it's solved, everyone's a suspect."

"I need to get moving," Carlos said. He didn't want his cell phone to ring with Forbes there. He hesitated, then added, "Look for something different. I have a feeling about this one—I don't think it's going to fit the usual pattern."

"You do your work, Agent Santiago, and let me do mine."

Forbes face looked tight with bottled-up anger, so Carlos dropped it. What the fuck did he care if this asshole wasted his time?

"Thanks again, Agent Forbes. *Adios.*"

Chapter 10

Come Up and See Me Sometime

Elizabeth Pendleton called Carlos and asked him to drop by her house that evening. She promised fifteen minutes. They sat in the same seats they occupied earlier.

"May I call you Carlos, Señor Santiago?"

"Please do." Her pronunciation of 'Señor' and his name indicated she knew Spanish. Interesting that she hadn't mentioned that.

"Carlos, how can I help? And I'm curious why a Mexican policeman is investigating a crime in the States."

"I'm here in the interests of the cross-border cooperation needed to fight drug cartels that kidnap innocent people and wage war on our streets." Carlos knew it ringed preachy, and blushed.

"Sounds impressive and important." Elizabeth poured two coffees from the urn on the silver service tray. "Cream? Sugar?"

"One of each, please."

She leaned over to give him his cup, and Carlos smelled her perfume. Her hand grazed his and raised goose bumps on his arm. *Must be careful of this one.*

"That's the official version," he said. "In truth, your late husband's abduction and murder is a big problem for Mexico. High-profile kidnappings get too much press. That sounds cold, and it is. We have garbage collectors snatched off the street in Juarez for five-hundred-dollar ransoms, but those cases don't sell papers or television programs, and they don't hurt tourism."

Elizabeth nodded.

Carlos pulled a notebook from his inside jacket pocket. He saw Elizabeth glance at the Walther semi-automatic that hung in a shoulder holster under his left armpit. *Did I wear it to impress her?*

"I want to ask you a few questions. I surmise you've heard them all from the FBI, but our memories can play tricks. Perhaps you'll recall a detail that escaped you earlier." He pretended to consult the blank pages in his notebook.

Elizabeth frowned and drummed her fingers on the arm of her chair. She rose and began to pace. Carlos stood out of politeness. Her height surprised him. He stood almost six feet, but her eyes were level with his.

"I'll do anything to discover what happened to Robert. What do you want to know?"

"I don't understand Juarez," he said.

"You mean why he traveled there? Like I told the other fellow, I don't know for certain, but his clients included Mexican companies." She paused, turned, and faced him. "Something compelled Robert, but he wouldn't tell me. His hedge fund had sunk into serious trouble, what with the stock market slump and all, but he always seemed so confident. I discovered a few days ago that he had made several trips to Juarez over the last year."

"Pardon me for asking, but could he have had personal reasons?"

"Did he cheat on me?" She shrugged. "Anything's possible."

Her voice sounded practical and pragmatic. She looked hard at him, and Carlos felt something feral move his way.

She came nearer, and he smelled her scent again. His knees wobbled, and he almost reached out to touch her. Her hip brushed his hand when she moved past and walked to the bar. *Is she coming on to me?*

"Something stronger than coffee?" Elizabeth took a glass, added ice, and poured three fingers of malt scotch. She turned to face him and put the drink to her lips.

"I'm on duty." He saw the wetness on her mouth and almost choked on the words. He took a deep breath, moved back to his chair, and sat. He folded his hands on his lap. No sense advertising how he felt. "Did he keep a home office?"

"Upstairs. The FBI searched it, but maybe there's a detail in his papers that they missed." Elizabeth shrugged.

"Mind if I take a look?"

"Not at all, but remember, I said fifteen minutes. Two people from his company will be here to pick up files on Robert's current clients. The Bureau vetted the data and okayed their release."

"Give me five minutes with those records. I want to see who he dealt with."

"There they are, but please don't tell anyone. I believe it's confidential." She indicated a small stack of boxes in the foyer.

Carlos opened the top box. Five thick files sat inside. He copied the names and phone numbers neatly typed on the index tab of each. He did the same with the other two cartons.

He stood, put his notebook in his pocket and buttoned his jacket. They stood facing each other.

"You have kind eyes," she said and smiled when Carlos blushed.

"I'll get out of here before your company arrives. *Hasta luego, Señora*," he said hurriedly and took her hand. It felt warm and smooth. "How about I ring you tomorrow and arrange to go through the office? If you come up with anything in the meantime, call

me." *Have a little mercy,* is what he wanted to say. He tried to swallow the regret he felt at leaving. "I'll let myself out."

He walked to his car, stopped, and looked back at the house. *If I hooked up with her, Maria would never know…. But I would.* And he had promised himself when he married that those days were over. *Think about the case*, he chided himself. *Don't complicate it—at least not yet.*

Chapter 11

Che. 214466-A

"Pendleton went broke," Frank Hunter told Carlos, squinting through the sunlight. "Let's get out of this heat, and I'll tell you about it."

Carlos followed him into a different South Phoenix bar. He noticed Frank's limp and the way he walked with his right foot at an angle.

"Bad back?" His father had suffered from one before he died, and Carlos knew the signs.

"Some days it kills. Getting old sucks."

"I hope I'm around long enough to find out." Carlos laughed and clapped Frank on the shoulder. "Let's get a load off."

They slid into the booth.

Both ordered Tecates with a slice of lime. Carlos rubbed the cool can on his forehead.

"How in the hell can one of Wall Street's richest guys be broke?"

"The way I hear it, when the stock market started to crumble, Pendleton's company took major hits. He considered the setbacks temporary and chased the losses. Each time he reinvested, he lost more money. He promised big returns, so he used cash reserves to pay dividends that didn't exist. Nothing esoteric, chalk it up to arrogance and stupidity."

"Does his wife know?"

Frank cocked his head. "You be careful of that one. I've met her, and I know a dangerous woman when I see one—and I don't know the answer to your question. Maybe you should ask her."

"Maybe I will. What does his being broke have to do with his kidnapping? If it were common knowledge, nobody would want to snatch him."

"It didn't come out until after he died. The Justice Department and the SEC swarmed his company's offices with forensic people, but they don't talk to us. It's like each agency works for a different country."

"Same in Mexico. I get more from you than from the Juarez police."

"Did you read the papers this morning?" Frank said.

"No. What happened?"

"Enough to push your boy off the front page. The Phoenix cops found four bodies. Mexican nationals by the look of it. Hands tied behind their backs and shot in the head. Whoever did it sprinkled cocaine on the corpses."

"Where'd they find them?"

"Close by—the Segundo Barrio Precinct. Sounds like someone wanted to send a message."

"Jesus Christ. We'll get blamed for this one too. Too bad they weren't *gringos*."

"Your compassion gladdens my heart," Frank deadpanned.

"You know what I mean. Those poor saps they use to run dope across the border have no money and no hope, so they go to work for the cartels. Once in a while, their fingers get sticky, and they give themselves a bonus. What a lousy world."

Carlos scanned the bar. He didn't want a repeat of their last meeting. A few professional drunks occupied stools, but otherwise, it was quiet.

"You want to see the crime scene? Since it looks cross-border, the Bureau will get involved."

"No thanks. If I go, I might get assigned to it, and I have enough to do. But I need a favor."

"What?" Frank said.

"I want to meet with the negotiator. He's going to be a better source of information than Elizabeth—I mean Mrs. Pendleton. Can you arrange it?"

"I'll see, but it might be better if I talk to him. To the best of my knowledge, nobody from the Bureau has contacted him. Pendleton's company gave us basic information, but that's where the trail ends. I don't even know the guy's name. And what's with this 'Elizabeth' bullshit? Maria would have your balls if she caught you screwing around with that one."

"I'm not 'screwing around' with anybody. She told me to call her that. Don't worry, Frank, I know what I'm doing."

"Yeah, but women like her eat guys like us for a snack. Mind what I'm saying. When do you see her again?"

"Tomorrow. She told me I could have a look at Pendleton's home office."

"We've inspected that place with a microscope. What do you think you can find that we didn't?"

"Forget the details. I want a sense of the guy. This stinks, and I have a feeling Pendleton left a clue that will freshen the air. I copied down names from Pendleton's files—customers. I want to telephone them. Any objections?"

"Suit yourself."

Carlos fidgeted, shifting his feet, while he waited for her to answer the door. *What am I nervous about? It's not like I'm cheating on Maria.* The door opened, and he did his best to maintain an impassive composure, but Elizabeth didn't make it easy. She wore a simple cotton dress that showed a lot more than most housewives. He felt dampness in his palms and wiped his right hand on his trousers before extending it.

"Elizabeth. Thanks for having me over again."

"Carlos, nice to see you." She stepped back inside and smiled.

"Like I said on the phone, I'd like to see your late husband's office."

"Fine, don't stand there, come in. Would you like a drink?"

"Thanks, but no. This will be a short visit."

She led the way up the staircase. Carlos watched her hips through the thin material. A scent of wildflowers wafted behind her. He felt his cock stiffen and blushed inside.

"In here." She inserted a key in the lock and pushed open the door. "I'll leave you alone. Call if you want anything."

Elizabeth gave him a look he knew he could interpret any way he wanted and closed the door behind her. He stood alone, looking at a room already scavenged by cops and the Bureau. Papers lay strewn on the floor and desk, drawers stood half-open, and an air of general disarray permeated the space. He wouldn't find anything in the details. He already knew that. He didn't know what he was searching for—maybe nothing. He closed his eyes and inhaled, trying to smell the man—if his traces had survived the hunters.

Carlos' job was to track fugitives through deserts and cities, and he found his prey more often than not. His fame extended across the border, and he had earned the respect of law enforcement agencies in the States, which was why his government had pulled him off his usual beat to work the Pendleton case.

He opened his eyes and swept the room. The Feds would've collected the evidence—if any existed—categorized it, analyzed it, and issued bulletins based on facts and conclusions. Sometimes it worked, but Carlos knew in his gut that this one didn't fit. He wanted to figure out how and why.

He stared at Pendleton's desk. A large antique cherry with a glass top. Must have cost fifty grand. Where it sat didn't jive. He moved stuff from the floor and looked for marks. *There! Somebody had moved the desk. Why? And why was there only one track of scratches? Like one of the legs held a nail in the bottom.*

Carlos took off his suit coat jacket and hung it on the rack next to the door, loosened his tie, and rolled up his shirt sleeves. He removed everything from the desk top and placed it in neat stacks. When it stood clear, he put his fingers under the glass and carefully slid it until it hung half-way over the edge. He went to the other side, pushed down, and with his fingers underneath, moved it toward the floor. *Wouldn't do to break it.* He grabbed the top, tilted it back, and lowered it into a clear space. He slid his fingers out from under. It thumped, but didn't crack. He pushed it backwards to give himself working room.

He repeated the exercise with the desk. It must have weighed two hundred pounds. He lifted on one side and tilted it backwards. He had placed two armless chairs on the other side and let the desk come to rest on them. They creaked, but held.

Carlos moved around to the other side, braced his knees, lifted the desk edge, and kicked away the chairs. He lowered it toward the floor. At the last second, the weight caused him to let go, and it hit with a crash. He waited, but Elizabeth either didn't hear or didn't care.

Despite the air-conditioning, Carlos felt sweat run down his chest. He stopped to catch his breath, then walked around to the back of the desk where four large footpads lay exposed. His excitement rose. The rear pad gleamed with a metal plate held in place by four flathead screws. He took a small knife from his pocket and opened the screwdriver attachment. The fasteners were Phillips head, but modern and scored to accept a flat blade. He removed the plate with little difficulty. A small sealed envelope dropped to the floor. He picked it up and put it in his pocket and reattached the piece of metal to the pad. No way would he get the table upright again, but he doubted the Feds would return, and if they did, they'd have a mystery to solve.

He considered his own mystery. If what was in his pocket belonged to Pendleton, how in the hell could he have maneuvered it under the pad and why? He rolled down his sleeves, donned his jacket, and left the room.

"Find anything interesting?" Elizabeth stood at the bottom of the stairs.

"Not really. Tell me, Elizabeth, did you or your husband have any work done on the house lately?"

"No." She put her finger on her cheek. "But Robert ordered a new safe installed a couple of weeks ago. He didn't believe the old one was strong enough."

"I didn't see a safe."

"Oh, it's there, but there's nothing in it. First place I looked when the kidnappers called. I thought I might need cash."

"Did you find any?"

"Not a cent and no papers of value. The FBI took the rest of the stuff."

"Thanks for letting me look. I may need to see you again."

"Do you have to leave?" She stood close enough that he could feel her breath on his face.

She's coming on to me.

"I do," he managed. Carlos twisted the door knob and backed out. "I'll call before I come over."

"You know where to find me."

He almost lost all dignity by stumbling on the top step, but managed to recover and stride to the rental car parked on the curb. He thought he heard her laugh, but didn't turn around.

Carlos waited until that evening in his hotel room before he removed the envelope from his pocket. Latex gloves would keep his prints from the contents in case it became necessary to turn it over to the Feds. He lifted the flap and a small paper fell to the floor. He picked it up and stared at it. A tiny flutter tickled his stomach. *Would this answer his questions?*

"Che. 214466-A," printed in tiny, neat block letters. Not answers, more questions. *What did it mean?* A cryptogram, numbers for a bank account, a password, the key to a code? Part of his AFI training had included four intensive weeks of cryptanalysis. He discovered he had a knack for it and almost entered the Mexican intelligence service as a code breaker, but detested the thought of sitting cooped up in an office all day studying diplomatic traffic. Besides, the people in whom the government expressed any real interest were the Americans, and their ciphers were too tough to penetrate.

Exhausted, he undressed and hung his suit, tie, and shirt in the walk-in closet that was part of the lavish bathroom, along with the Walther, then fell on the mattress without turning down the covers. A bottle of scotch and a container of sleeping pills sat on the nightstand. He reached over, popped an Ambien, took a sip of scotch, and turned off the lamp. Sleep came a few minutes later, broken by troubled dreams of Elizabeth and a headless man.

The next morning he awoke at 7:15. *Better get moving.* It took him a few minutes to orient himself. *Phoenix. Doubletree Resort.* The note lay on a desk near the bed next to a window. He made coffee in the kitchenette, stumbled to the bathroom and turned the shower to 'hot.' There were two nozzles in the large enclosure, plus a steam bath feature. He liked that the government let him rent a suite. The streams of water cascaded over him and vapor began to hiss from a valve near the floor.

He thought about Maria and his children. He'd call them after he cleaned up.

Chapter 12

Ambush—Part 1

The hired assassin waited in the hallway outside Santiago's room. He was dressed in coveralls and carried a tool kit. He glanced at his watch and noted the time—7:00 a.m. Every few minutes, he pressed his ear to the wall. He'd had no problem getting the room number.

"Front desk? This is José in Maintenance."

"How can I help you, José?"

"A guest, a Mr. Santiago, called about his air conditioner, but didn't tell me the room number."

"Mr. Carlos Santiago, room four-fifteen, José. Have a nice day."

"Thanks. You, too."

He stood there for fifteen minutes, and when anyone walked by, he busied himself with the overhead vent. He knew he would hear the shower before too long.

The call had come the evening before.

"I need you in Phoenix tonight. Something's come up."

"It's a six-hour drive, and I don't want to go to Phoenix."

"You can make it before midnight if you hustle—and you have no choice."

"Why? What happened?"

"You know I can't talk. I'll call you at 11:30 tonight from a different phone. Stay at the same place as before." The line went dead.

He had survived thirty years in the military and his chosen profession because he was flexible and knew how to be ready on short notice. Any ad-hoc assignment concerned him, and the idea of driving six hours looked like a non-starter. He logged onto his laptop and found an available 9:10 p.m., non-stop, Albuquerque to Phoenix, that would arrive in plenty of time. He'd rent a car and go straight to the hotel to wait for a call.

He heard the shower start and the door shut. Now he felt the familiar butterflies. Planned or impromptu, a kill constituted a kill, and he meant to enjoy it. He opened his toolbox and selected from his professional lock picks. The knob turned and the door swung open a few inches. The security chain stretched across the gap. He took a more substantial implement from the box, slipped it into the opening, and cut the restraint. He glanced up and down the hallway. No traffic. He closed the door and placed his tools back in the box. He lifted the removable top rack and pulled the silenced .22 semi-automatic pistol from the bottom.

He saw the slip of paper on the desk and picked it up. It fit the description of what he came for, so he put it in his pocket. Why not leave and give Mr. Santiago another day of life? Right.

One of his rules was to never move in haste unless pressed beyond compromise. He walked with deliberate care toward the bathroom door, checked his weapon, and chambered a round. The entry stood half-open and cloudy steam poured out. He pushed with his toe. The swinging door clunked on the wall. He waved away the fog and made out the shower. Empty. *Fuck.* He didn't panic. The target must still be in the suite, maybe with a gun trained on him. He crouched and swung his weapon level, sweeping the area in his view as best he could see through the steam. *Nothing.*

He backed into the bedroom, keeping his weight on the balls of his feet. He picked up his tool case, never taking his eyes off the room's perimeter. When he reached the entry, he opened it with his left hand and burst into the hallway. He'd secured the piece of paper his client needed.

The greaser cop still lived, but he did too, and he intended to stay that way. There would be another opportunity, one he could plan for.

He stooped to open the tool case, pulled out the top rack, and replaced the gun. A couple came toward him from the far end of the hallway.

"*Buenos dias, Señora.*" He touched his cap.

He waited until they'd boarded the elevator, then took the stairs. No problem. He took deep breaths of the fresh morning air and strolled to his car. *Mañana.*

Chapter 13

Ambush—Part 2

The hot water refreshed him, but Carlos took care with his feet near the steam nozzles. He shampooed and rinsed his hair and had begun to scrub when the shower stall door that he'd left open a couple of inches slammed shut. *Air pressure. Someone must have entered the suite.* The pulse in his neck pounded. *The maid? Too early.*

He stepped from the stall, turned the hot water to its highest temperature, and grabbed a towel. The walk-in closet in the bathroom where he'd hung his clothes and gun the night before stood five feet to his left. He moved toward it, crammed himself inside, closed the door, and pulled the Walther from its holster. If whoever it was outside opened the closet, he'd have a surprise.

He heard soft footsteps cross the floor and the stall door bang open. Carlos tensed. He remembered that he'd forgotten to cock the Walther. *Stupid!* If he did so now, the noise might alert whoever stood outside. He put his left hand on the slide, ready to chamber and fire.

His legs started to cramp, and he shivered. The A/C was set at seventy degrees. He couldn't hear anything more, but damned if he would walk into an ambush. *I wish I could see my watch. How long since I heard anything?* He counted a thousand and one, a thousand and two, until he come to sixty and started again. When he judged five minutes had passed, he decided to make his move.

He chambered a round, held his breath, and hoped the unmistakable sound hadn't warned the intruder. Nothing happened. He gritted his teeth and nosed open the closet door with the pistol barrel. Carlos surveyed the room. The steam still blasted from the shower, so he couldn't see more than a foot ahead, but a trespasser lurking in the fog would have the same problem.

He took a few tentative steps. The bedroom looked empty. He backtracked and found the steam shower switch, shut it down, and reached inside the stall to turn off the spigots. The silence startled him. No noise came from the other room.

The broken security chain confirmed his suspicions. The note had vanished. *Che. 214466-A* popped into his head. He picked up a pen and scribbled it on the hotel notepad by the phone. *Now what?*

He propped the desk chair under the door knob. He shivered and grabbed a robe from the door hook. His legs and hands were shaking. He snapped on the Walther's safety, laid it on the bed, and plopped down beside it.

The note. Elizabeth. No one else knew he'd searched the office. He reached for his cell phone beside the bed and dialed Frank Hunter's number. Voice mail.

"Call me back. I need to meet you at nine in the hotel coffee shop. Let me know."

He clicked off and lay back down, drained. A minute to rest, then downstairs.

"You look like you didn't get much sleep, my friend," Big Game said to Carlos across the outdoor coffee shop table.

A fresh carafe of French Roast steamed between them, and Frank poured two cups.

"Maybe I'm going nuts, but I think someone tried to kill me this morning," Carlos said while he stirred in cream and sugar.

"Whadda you mean, kill you? For Christ's sake, Carlos, tell me."

Carlos relayed the story of the intruder and his escape, trying to keep it low-key. He looked down and saw his hand shaking like a maraca. Delayed shock.

"My God, Carlos, you have to take care of yourself. You ain't too popular with the bad guys. If the cartel boys heard you're on this side of the border, they might have tried for a little payback. You've played hell with them for the past couple years."

Carlos willed himself to relax. "I think this has to do with Pendleton." He took out the hotel note paper with the number he found in Pendleton's desk. His hand stopped vibrating. "What do you make of this?"

"Where'd you get it?"

"Pendleton's office. I think it's an offshore account number." He took a sip of coffee and reached for a cigarette.

"I can run it through our computer models and see what happens," Frank replied.

"Can you do it without turning it over to your office?"

"What's the diff? I thought we were talking joint operation." Frank picked up the Marlboro pack and played with the cellophane. He put a cigarette in his mouth, but didn't light it.

Carlos reminded himself of the real reason for his assignment to the case, and it had nothing to do with solving a crime. A simple goal—shift responsibility to the *gringos*, and make this a U.S. problem. His boss had called before he left the hotel room. The newspapers and TV talking heads in Mexico had jumped all over the kidnapping of the Americano big shot. The FBI wouldn't like it if he could put a wrap on the evidence and present the package to his office and the media. He shook his head.

"Sorry, Old Friend, but my cooperation has limits. I want yours, of course, but if I fuck this up, I'll be planting beans in the Yucatan. Run with me, and I won't forget it." Carlos took a deep drag and blew the smoke away from Hunter.

"You're not allowed to smoke in here," Frank said and looked around the room.

"When they bust me, I'll put it out." Carlos felt defiant, but removed his cup from its saucer and crushed out the weed, burning his fingertips in the process.

"Who knew you found the numbers?" Frank said.

"I'm not sure. If it's Elizabeth Pendleton, she would have known where her late husband planted it. It wasn't sitting out in the open. Maybe another interested party came looking. In any case, I didn't have a warrant, so it's not going to stand up in court, but it might help us figure out why he died."

"You're right. If I bring it in and it's tainted, my ass will be grass. If you follow through, no waves on this side of the border. Write it down for me, and I'll see what happens when I plug it into our computers."

"Thanks. I mean it. I have a feeling that we're looking at the key to the puzzle. While you're at it, can you find out more about the grieving widow? If she sent a killer to my hotel this morning, she's in it up to her eyeballs."

A pretty Hispanic waitress came to their table. "Have you decided yet, Gentlemen?"

"Rancher's special for me—with pork chops." Frank said.

"Scrambled with toast." Carlos ordered, though he wasn't hungry.

"And you gentlemen know this is a non-smoking area?" She gave them a big smile that showed perfect teeth.

When she walked away, both men watched her hips sway through the short pink skirt. Frank shook his head in appreciation.

"Mmmm-mmm."

"You got that right, *Amigo*." Carlos poured both of them another cup of java.

"Back to the lady in question. Why don't you stop by her house, bone her, and get her to confess?" Frank almost choked on his coffee from laughing.

"Bite me, *Hombre*. Get serious. A *maton* came for me this morning, and it wasn't a booty call."

"Okay, you're right, but I still like the image. I'll run the number and the lady this morning and call you if we get any hits."

"The way things sit, Elizabeth Pendleton has moved up to Number One on our suspect list. Maybe not for the murder, but she could be in on the financial scam, and the two things must be linked. Another reason I don't want your Bureau to know about the note is because they might swarm her and drive her deeper into cover. I have a better shot at finding the truth," Carlos said.

"Yeah, I agree. The Bureau can get a little overzealous. We're lookin' at the tip of an iceberg. We don't want to plow the ship into it."

"You want to go see the negotiator this morning? Assuming we can locate him," Carlos added.

Frank shook his head. "No can do. We're scheduled for an all-hands meet this morning to review where we stand. The DOJ forensic guys are briefing us on Pendleton's Ponzi scheme."

"Let me know what they say, will you?"

"Sure. When do you see the gorgeous Mrs. Pendleton again?"

"I'll call her later. I want to see her face when I ask about the upstairs office. Might give me a clue about her involvement in what happened at my hotel."

The waitress brought the food. Frank waited until she left before he continued.

"How about Pendleton's customers? Have you called them yet?"

"Same reaction from all of them. They don't want to talk. A couple mentioned their portfolio losses, but when they realized I wasn't calling about that, they clammed up."

Frank reached over and picked up the tab for breakfast. "This one's on the Bureau."

Chapter 14

The Assassin

He held the throwaway cell phone to his ear. "It's not there," he told her.

"What do you mean, 'not there'?"

"Not there, like in 'gone.' It's fucking gone."

"You said you left it in a safe place. Where'd you stash it? Go look again. Maybe you missed something or forgot."

"For Christ's sake. I grew up there. I put it in my old hiding place on the side of the ridge. Nobody knows about it."

"Did you see anything?"

"A small landslide and hoof prints. I followed them until they hit loose dirt, then they washed out. A horse must have stepped in the hole and broken loose a rock. Godammit."

"What are we gonna do?"

"What are *we* gonna do?" he mimicked her. "I'll find out who took my dough and rip his fucking heart out. That's what *we're* gonna do."

"Why'd you hide it in the first place? You could have been in Mexico by now with no worries."

"I wanted to find out how much heat there was. It's cross-border. The beaner cops would have their eyes open for cash crossing over. They'd take the dough and shoot me. But my inside guy says there's not even an alert out for the ransom. Who the fuck knows?"

"I'm scared. I don't want you to get caught."

"Me neither, Baby. I got to come to Phoenix tomorrow."

"Why so soon?"

"That's my business."

"Will I see you?"

"No. Lay by the pool, read a book. Don't worry your pretty little head about me. I've done what I do for a long time, and I know the ropes."

"So do I, Darlin'. And I don't have a 'pretty little head.' The last thing either of us wants is for you to get nabbed, so don't take any chances."

"I've never been arrested or even been a suspect. And who knows anything about us? There's nothing to connect me to anything."

"*I* know you."

He thought for a moment.

"You got me there, Sweetheart."

He went back to where he lost the trail and used his compass to sight in the direction of the hiding place. West by northwest. A straight line. If he followed a bearing of south by southeast, he might stumble across the thief. He could see a house in the distance at the bottom of a small rise. He raised the field glasses. Stable, chicken coop, and a coyote fence surrounding the entire property. Maybe his target. He chambered a round into a silenced .22 caliber Colt Woodsman, switched on the safety, and dropped it back into his shoulder holster.

He came to a small depression and knelt down, taking his binoculars out of the case that hung at his side. He adjusted them for the estimated distance to the house and began to sweep the property.

Two dogs romped in the yard. Big enough to be shepherds. He'd have to come back tomorrow. He loved dogs and could never bring himself to kill one. A powder he used in the past, mixed with hamburger, should put them in la-la land for the time he needed. He looked at the sun and guessed about an hour until darkness. He found a comfortable spot to relax where he could keep the glasses trained on the compound.

Two *gringos*, a man and a woman, and two beaners—another man and woman—lived on the property. A big house and a *casita*. The Mexicans must be hired help. At least two horses occupied the stables, and several goats roamed inside the coyote fence. There didn't appear to be a lock on the gate, so entry would be simple.

He needed to postpone his trip to Phoenix. Deckert could wait. The best time to pull this off would be mid-afternoon, siesta time. The big dude might be out riding, and the wetbacks and the *gringo* woman, napping.

If they turned out to be the ones who stole his money, they'd be in for a good long nap.

Chapter 15

The Briefing

Four agents and half a dozen staffers sat in the conference room of the DOJ Phoenix field office. A slim, fortyish brunette wearing dark-rimmed glasses stood in front of the group, scheduled to make a presentation on the current status of the Pendleton financial investigation.

Frank Hunter fidgeted and sipped his lukewarm coffee. This would be his last field assignment, and the closer he edged toward mandatory retirement, the edgier he became. Maybe he needed someone. Cynthia had walked out on him twenty years ago, no longer willing to live alone for extended periods and desperate for the child Frank expressed no desire to father. He looked at the woman standing a few feet in front of him. Pretty in an understated way. Bookish. No ring on her left hand. He missed her name when she introduced herself. Maybe he'd ask her to meet him later for a drink.

What if she doesn't drink? His ineptitude with the opposite sex had assumed legendary status among friends and coworkers. Women found him attractive, and he liked to tease and flirt, but the trouble came when they asked a serious question. He answered the best he could, then fled the scene before they could pose another. *What in the hell is wrong with me?* He made himself a mental promise to follow up on the drink idea before the day ended.

The lights dimmed and the banner for the presenter's PowerPoint demo flashed on the white wall.

"Pendleton Financial Enterprises," she said in a soft voice.

He strained to pick up her words. *Maybe it's a way to get everyone's attention.*

"Total cash under management at the end of their fiscal year, March 31, reported at seven billion dollars." A new slide played on the screen. "Average annual return to investors over the past twelve years of ten and one-half percent, far above the standard hedge fund, but not outlandish. I think everyone here knows what happened when agents seized the books last week." She looked around her audience. "Less than one hundred million dollars in assets were located." She seemed to derive satisfaction from this.

"To the best of our ability to sort it out at this early date, Pendleton stopped investing client money two years ago. It wasn't a typical Ponzi scheme. He ran a legitimate shop for several years, and paid the returns he advertised."

A different-colored slide came into view, and she continued.

"Two years ago, Pendleton began to use assets to pay dividends, depleting accounts and never replenishing them. When new money came in, he used it to cover losses. Clients received quarterly position statements that led them to believe their investments were safe. If one of them wanted to cash out, Pendleton used another person's money to pay them off. When the markets went into steep decline, his customers were delighted that their statements showed them making the same returns they always earned."

The woman shook her head, and Frank assumed she wanted them to recognize her deep disapproval and disgust.

"A large sum of money found its way offshore. We don't know how much, and have no idea yet where it is, but without a doubt, it topped five hundred million dollars. We suspect this represents Pendleton's payoff to himself. The business became untenable when investment money dried up and the markets fell even further. He must have known the day of reckoning loomed, and we think his kidnapping and murder all connect to his failing company."

She launched into the details of the forensic examination, and Frank slipped away to an alternate universe. The lights going back up to a smattering of applause startled him, and he sat up straight in his chair. He felt his ears redden and hoped he hadn't fallen asleep. He looked up and caught the woman's eye and saw a smile play across her lips. *Busted.*

People stood around her asking questions and receiving a handout copy of the presentation marked "Confidential." He edged his way to the front and tried to think of something he wanted to know.

"Can I help you, Rip?"

Rip Van Winkle. She'd noticed.

"Yes, ah, one question, but I may have overheard the answer when you spoke to the last gentleman."

"Oh, you mean his request for an analysis of portfolio positions?"

"Yes, that's it." He gave her his biggest smile.

"He didn't ask me that. He wanted to know if I could meet him for a drink later."

"What?" Frank felt flustered and searched around for a way out of the room.

"How about it, meet me later?"

Her eyes laughed, and Frank fell in love.

Part 3

Southbound and Down

Chapter 16

I Shot the Sheriff

I read the message Will Cowdry left in my computer mailbox during the night.

> *The negotiator's name is Manuel Hoppe. Suggested by the family and approved by the insurance company. Ex-Special Forces. Has handled several hostage situations out of Mexico over the past five years. Record looks clean. I couldn't get current contact information. He uses temporary numbers when he's working a case, then disappears until the next job. The insurance people give him high marks and say this is the first hostage they've ever lost when he's handled the swap.*
>
> *Pendleton also carried a five-million-dollar term life policy. His company is the beneficiary. Wife looks clean, doesn't financially benefit from his demise.*
>
> *I'll let you know when I find out more.*
>
> *P.S. Watch your butt. Hernandez is gunning for you and thinks you and I are conspiring!*
>
> *P.P.S. There's a Mexican cop out of Juarez working the case—same guy whose name I gave you. He's on TDY Phoenix. Carlos Santiago. Currently staying at the Doubletree Resort.*

The man I was supposed to meet in Phoenix tomorrow.

I called John Thunder and relayed the gist of Will's message.

"Manuel Hoppe? Not familiar. I'll see if I can find anything off the record. The 'tom-tom highway' reaches into Chihuahua. People know

59

stuff they don't talk about to *gringos*. However, it's a moot issue if you do what we talked about. Is that still your intention?"

"I didn't bury it, but it's safe. I want one more conversation with Will to make sure we do it right, and I'm going to Phoenix to meet with an AFI dude who's working the Mexican side of the case. I want to know the money's source before Darlene walks into Will's office and dumps it on his desk. You agree?"

"Yeah. Anyone else know about this?"

"Not yet, but I'll bring Tommy up to speed so he doesn't have to read about it in the papers."

"In the meantime, be careful. The money's a time-bomb. I don't like it."

I needed to take care that Hernandez didn't suspect anything. That ruled out a visit to Will's office—or even a phone call. Maybe he, Darlene, Tommy and I could get together at Sheila's later on tonight.

Tommy Crowfoot, my joint manager, partner, and closest friend—next to Darlene. A Ute Indian who'd done his time in the slammer and alcohol rehab, and one of the most solid people I ever knew. I would trust him with my life, and did exactly that three years ago.

"What's happening, Jack?" Tommy stood behind the bar working on what looked like an inventory list.

I slid onto a barstool. "Your fiftieth is in a couple of days, right? How about if you call Will and get him down here tonight? Darlene and I'll come in about seven, and the four of us can toast your becoming a senior citizen."

"You're a bad influence, *Amigo*. I haven't sucked down a drink since the last time you 'stopped by.'" Tommy raised his eyebrows and smiled.

"Me either. But a shot of tequila every six weeks helps your digestion, and I have great weed that John Thunder gave me."

"You're on." Tommy turned to the phone on the bar.

Fifty—hard to believe. He moved with an athlete's grace, and his broad shoulders and arm muscles made him look like a man you didn't want to fuck with. Ditto for the scars around his eyes. His hair, tied back in a ponytail, hung shorter than John Thunder's, and gray streaks ran its length

"Will says he'll be here." Tommy picked up his inventory notebook. "Sorry, Jack, but I need to finish this before the liquor salesman gets here." He nodded toward the storeroom.

"There's something I need to talk to you about, but it can wait until seven."

Tommy and I had worked together at Sheila's for several years, and I'd made him a part-owner, but about ten months ago, I turned the day-to-day management over to him. The business bored me, and I wanted to try other things, like farming and raising horses.

Sheila's turned into a cash cow, and both of us made a great living from its proceeds. Good music, great food, and the best margaritas in Santa Fe meant overflow weekend crowds. Tommy's and my reputations didn't hurt business either, and a few people came in to see if they could spot us.

The Legend of Sheila's started after we busted up a biker bunch in the alley behind the bar years ago. Tommy's Indian brothers spread the word to the Pueblos with liberal hyperbole. The young men who ventured off the rez to try their luck in the city idolized Tommy, and I enjoyed the reflected glory.

The drive from our *rancho* to Sheila's stretched fifteen miles, the majority of it four-lane freeway. Perhaps the most radar-monitored road in the universe, each of the three Indian Pueblos along the way boasted its own police department in addition to the Highway Patrol and the Sheriff. The speed limit signs read 65mph, but I knew from experience that 74 would make it through any radar trap. I set the cruise control.

Darlene fired up her pipe and the smell of Humboldt County weed rolled through the vehicle. I don't smoke while driving.

"I brought a bag for Tommy out of the ounce John gave me. Better than yours," I said.

She snorted to show her disbelief. Darlene was a connoisseur.

Tommy reserved a large corner booth. Consuela still cooked at the bar three nights a week, and brought out a plate of miniature chimichangas the moment we sat down. A pitcher of Silver Coin margaritas, condensation wetting the tablecloth, sat waiting along with a bowl of salt for those who liked to rim their glasses.

Will arrived a few minutes after us and picked up a Coca-Cola at the bar. He drank alcohol sparingly, and never on a duty night. Soft moans of delight over the appetizers were the only sounds in the room—unless you counted the incessant background music blaring from the jukebox in the front drinking area.

61

Tommy leaned forward. "Jack. What did you want to talk about?"

I looked around to make sure no one was in hearing distance, then told him the story of the two and a half million dollars.

His eyes widened, and he turned to Will. "Did you know about this?"

"I knew about missing ransom money, and I knew Jack's nose was into something, but I didn't connect the two." Will gave me a wry smile.

"I wanted to talk to John Thunder before I told anybody else," I explained. "Both you guys are familiar with the relationship between me and the FBI. John suggested that the best way to handle things would be to have Darlene turn the money over to Will, let the news media in on the story, and for us to take a vacation until the heat blows over."

"Sensible," said Tommy. "What's my involvement?"

"None of us are involved," I said. "I just didn't want you to be surprised when it all goes down. No doubt, reporters will make a connection and arrive en masse at Sheila's, so I thought it best you know all the details."

"Thanks, Pardner. When you going to do this?

"Darlene will bring the bag to Will late tomorrow afternoon." I glanced at her. "I intend to confirm a few things with a Mexican AFI agent in Phoenix tomorrow morning. Darlene will join me tomorrow night, and we'll take off for parts unknown."

Darlene nodded.

We spent the rest of the evening on our usual chatter about politics, the state of the world, and other, more arcane, subjects. I managed to slip Tommy the bag of weed from John Thunder without Will noticing. An officer of the law, he didn't condone our pot smoking. The clock showed 9:30 when we packed up to leave.

"See you tomorrow, Will." Darlene kissed him on the cheek, then hugged Tommy.

"We'll be back in a couple of weeks. Call my cell if you need me." I directed that at both of them.

When we pulled onto the freeway, I reset my autopilot and leaned back in the seat. I'd imbibed in one drink and knew I wasn't impaired. Four miles down the road, flashing red grill lights told me to pull over.

"Fucking-A. There's a cop car behind me."

"Were you speeding?" Darlene had lit up again. She tapped her pipe into the ashtray, crushed the embers with the stem, and rolled down her window, fanning the fumes with her other hand.

"No more than usual."

I dug in my pants pocket for my license, and Darlene reached into the glove compartment and extracted the registration and insurance card.

I opened my window and watched in the rearview mirror. The Sheriff Department cruiser's door opened and a familiar figure with a sagging belly pulled himself out and plodded toward the car. *Hernandez. Just what I need.*

"What's the problem, Elias?" I attempted a smile, but I think it came off more like a grimace.

"You're in trouble, Sloan. Speeding, your taillight's broken, and I suspect you're driving under the influence."

"So give me a ticket, but you're wrong about the light and the drinking."

"Really?"

He ambled to the back of my SUV, unclipped the nightstick from his belt, and whacked something. I heard glass break.

It's nothing. Keep cool, or this will turn bad.

He came back, and I kept my anger in check. "Like I said, officer, sorry about the taillight. Can I have my citation, please, and be on my way?"

"Please step out of the car."

I felt the muscles in my jaw tighten and my face flush. *Must control my temper.* I kept my eyes fixed on Hernandez' when I exited. His pupils were dilated. He must have snorted a few lines while he was waiting for us.

"Turn around and brace, hands on the car." He paused and sniffed the air. "I'm pretty sure I smell marijuana. Hope it's not in felony quantity."

I leaned on the car, but kept my weight on the balls of my feet. A bad feeling washed through me. I looked up and saw the dark outline of an early full moon. Serenity. The word floated through my mind. The nightstick's blow on the backs of my legs caught me off-guard, and I came close to collapsing from the pain.

"I said 'brace' on the car, Numb-nuts, or I'll pull you in for resisting arrest."

The snarl in his voice told me I needed to move, and do it fast. I half-stood, grabbed my legs, and began to moan.

"Mr. Tough Guy, huh? Quit giving me shit, or the next one will be to your skull."

"Please, Elias. No more. What do you want?"

I stayed in a crouch, partly from the pain, partly because at full height, I stood half a head taller than Hernandez, and I wanted a clear shot.

I waited until he raised the stick, then pushed to my feet, hitting him flush in the nose with the heel of my left hand. He started to crumple, and I landed a crushing right hook to his gut. Crimson spurted from what looked like a pile of mashed potatoes in the middle of his face, and he retched violently. He clawed at the service weapon dangling under his belly, but I snatched his index and middle fingers and bent them back until I heard a click. Hernandez screamed and fell to his knees. I reached down and removed his pistol from its holster.

"You're a dead man, Sloan," his voice slurred before he passed out.

I took his cell phone and stomped on it, went to the cruiser, ripped out the mike on his radio, opened the hood, and tore off several wires. I ejected the shells from Elias' gun onto the side of the road and tossed the weapon on the front seat before I walked back to my car.

"*Adios*, Elias, you prick. Don't come after me."

I jumped into the driver's seat and squealed onto the road. My legs hurt, but adrenaline helped anesthetize the pain.

"Move it, Jack. Head home and pack. I think it would be better if you disappeared for a while."

"What about Will and the money?"

"It can wait. We need to get you safe for now."

A cool customer, my Darlene.

Chapter 17

Loaded Up and Truckin'

"Where will you go?" Darlene gave me an anxious look and brushed the hair from her forehead.

"Phoenix. Maybe I can still meet the Mexican cop who's working the kidnapping." I hadn't thought it through, but it sounded good.

"Forget the kidnapping. It's the least of your worries now, Jack. That's one mean temper you have."

"He pushed too hard. Sorry, Baby, but that's who I am."

I pulled a plastic bag from our safe that contained my bolt-hole stuff. Passport, driver's license, five thousand in hundred dollar bills, Social Security card, new cell phone, Visa, and a registration doc for the Corvette we kept in the barn, all in the name of Monroe DeLong. I picked the moniker years ago. I assume alcohol influenced my choice, but I couldn't remember. I stuffed the escape kit into my always-packed overnight case. I kissed Darlene on the mouth and turned for the door.

"Keep the shotgun in the bedroom tonight. Fly to Phoenix tomorrow, and call me. Ring up Tommy and tell him what happened. I'll phone Will from my car."

"Why don't I stay here and deal with the money?"

"I have a bad feeling. I want to be around when you do it, and I don't see a big rush if it's not in the house." I couldn't explain, even to myself.

She nodded and looked doubtful. "Be careful, Sweetie. Don't do anything stupid."

"Have I ever?"

I went to the barn, dug the canvas bag from its hiding place, and locked it in the Corvette's trunk, along with my Glock and an overnighter.

The car started on the first crank, and the deep rumble went through my fingers and straight to my balls. Okay, so I did something bad, but getting on the road jazzed me. I hit the door opener and idled the car outside. Darlene stood by the end of the driveway. She leaned over and kissed me through the open window. I saw lights go on in the *casita*. Must have disturbed Franco and Consuela.

"Make sure to tell them not to talk to Hernandez or anybody else that comes calling."

"Don't worry. They know the score about you."

Within an hour I was southbound and down. A Johnny Cash CD blasted from the player. *I been everywhere, man.* I pulled into a rest area fifty miles from town and dialed Will on my cell phone.

"What in the heck did you do this time, Jack? There's an APB out for you. Says you assaulted a police officer."

"Hernandez stopped me on the way home and braced me. Clubbed me with his nightstick, and looked ready to break my skull, so I popped him one. If he wasn't flying on coke, I'll kiss your ass in the middle of the Plaza."

"Where are you now?"

"Better you don't know, then you won't be tempted to lie. I'm safe, but I'm worried about Darlene. Can you swing by and check on her later? Better call first, 'cause she's strapped and scared."

"No problem, Buddy. Listen, I don't know if I can make this assault go away. Hernandez was treated at St. Vincent's ER for a broken nose, dislocated fingers, and a bruised gut. You 'popped' him more than once."

"He deserved what he got. Take my word for it. You know my lawyer. Talk to Zeke tomorrow and see if he has any strings to pull. I don't think Hernandez would like his drug problem advertised, even less so in an election year."

"Can't Darlene call the attorney? Not that I mind, but it seems more logical. She bringin' the money in tomorrow like we talked about?"

"She's leaving town. The money? Way too complicated for a phone conversation. I'll get in touch after I'm sure of Darlene's safety. I have the satchel with me in the car. We can take care of it after this blows over."

"You always amaze me, Jack. Don't get your butt in a wringer again. We need you around for entertainment."

I put the top down and donned a leather jacket to keep warm, then spun out of the service area and back to the highway. Light traffic flowed and there were few oncoming headlights to drown out the beauty of the heavens. I read on the Internet that New Mexico enjoyed a reputation for being one of the ten best places on earth to view the stars. Whoever wrote that piece must have been staring at a night sky like this. The

66

Milky Way wrapped itself around the horizon, and Orion's Belt showed the way west. The new moon had risen higher, but the darkened ball I saw when Elias clubbed me no longer hung on the mountain peaks. My legs ached, and I chewed on a Vicodin for the pain. I didn't intend to drive six hours straight, but I wanted to cross the state line before I stopped to nap.

Chapter 18

Flagstaff

The pain in the back of my legs persisted, and I didn't want to take any more Vicodin while I drove, so instead of turning south to Phoenix, I stayed on I-40 toward Flagstaff. I planned to stop for two or three hours of shuteye, then call Darlene, and arrange to pick her up at the Phoenix airport. There were other calls to make.

The sign on the Hampton Inn east of Flagstaff advertised a vacancy. The night clerk dozed behind the counter, but sprang to attention when he heard the door. A nineteen-year-old working at night and going to school days. The corporate shirt didn't quite fit him, and his hair needed washing. I noticed the pile of textbooks next to his chair.

"One bed, one night." I stumbled on the words. My cheeks felt rubbery from the cool breeze that had washed over me and kept me awake for the past few hours. I worked my fingers and shoulders to get out the cramps.

"Welcome to Hampton Inn. Major credit card and ID please?"

I handed him Monroe DeLong's Visa and driver's license. I looked at them and, for a moment, thought, *Who the hell is this?* Then the reality of last night came crashing back.

"Are you all right, sir?"

"I'm tired, Kid."

"Please sign. If you stay past eleven tomorrow, you'll be charged for another night—unless you call the front desk for late checkout." He looked at his computer screen. "If you do want to stay later, I don't think there'll be a problem. Not a lot of visitors this time of year. The heat, you know."

"Is there an ice machine?" I figured I could fill the bottoms of a couple of those plastic laundry bags they leave in your closet and put them on the swelling.

"Same floor you're on. Five doors to the left of your room. You should have an ice bucket, but if not, call me."

"Thanks again, Kid." I dug in my pocket for a five and handed it to him.

"Gosh, sir, you don't have to do that." But he didn't try to hand it back.

I limped through the lobby and took the elevator to the third floor. The room smelled antiseptic clean, which beat the alternative, but I didn't bother to check the amenities. After preparing two ice packs, I tossed my things in the closet, took off my clothes, set the alarm for nine, and crashed. A shower could wait.

I called Darlene on my new mobile. "Did you book a flight yet?"

"Southwest 160. It arrives at 2:55. I'll meet you outside at the baggage claim level about 3:15 unless there's a delay. Are you okay?"

"Tired, but functional. My legs are bruised and hurt like hell. I'll get over it. What's happening there?"

"Two deputies I've never met came looking for you this morning. Will swung by in the middle of the night to check on me and told me to expect them. No problem, except he riled up the dogs, and I had a hard time getting back to sleep."

"I stopped in Flagstaff to rest so I'm a couple of hours from the airport. I'm gonna sleep and leave here about 12:30 to make sure I get there on time."

"Then what? Do you have a plan in mind?"

"Will's calling Zeke this morning, and I'll talk to him later. There might be a way to get Hernandez to drop charges. In the meantime, I want to use the time here to check into our other problem."

"Okay, Sweetie. I'll call you when I deplane so you don't have to circle."

"Love you. See you soon."

My next call went to Zeke Martinez, the best lawyer in Santa Fe.

"Will called and briefed me this morning. You're a real piece of work, Jack. I hear you busted up that asshole Hernandez."

I could picture Zeke pushing his reading glasses up on his nose while he doodled on a notebook. One of the smartest people I ever met, the one time I ever saw him in a neatly-pressed suit with a necktie that wasn't half untied was in court. In front of a judge, he could've stepped from GQ—in contrast to most of the hacks who plied their trade around the state capital. I once asked him why he stayed in the sticks when he could have run with the big dogs in D.C.

The best answer that I managed to squeeze from him was, "I like it here."

"I don't want to get arrested, Zeke. Can you handle it?"

"Kind of difficult to assault the County Sheriff and avoid incarceration. I'll talk to the prosecutor and see if he'll cut you slack since you claim Hernandez hit first."

"There's a guy they call Tubby who hangs at the Cowboy Saloon. He sells gram bags of coke, but I hear Hernandez buys in bigger quantities. He definitely looked coked-up when he stopped me. Talk to the Sheriff in private and mention Tubby's name. He might consider dropping charges."

"Whoo-wee, Jackson, that's sweet. I'm seeing the prosecutor this morning anyway, and I'll ask him about a deal. If he doesn't bite, I'll give Hernandez a call."

"Thanks, Zeke. I'm incognito for now. I'll check in tomorrow."

"Take care of yourself, my Boy. Life wouldn't be half as entertaining without you around."

"That's what everybody keeps telling me. I'm starting to feel like a Chia Pet."

I disconnected and headed for the bathroom. A long, hot shower sounded good. I anticipated a difficult day ahead.

Chapter 19

Monroe

Before I checked out, I called Carlos Santiago. I identified myself as Monroe DeLong, Will's friend. The Mexican cop sounded dubious about meeting, but when I mentioned the Pendleton kidnapping, his interest level increased a few notches.

"Another guy from up there called me a couple of days ago—Jack something or other? Said Will told him to call."

"I'm here, and if you want to talk, I'm available."

"Is it okay if I bring a friend? He's FBI," he said.

"You can if it's off the record. I don't want to make anything official yet."

"I'll find out and call you back."

Five minutes later my phone jarred me out of a daydream. My fantasy included a massage table and a beautiful therapist who worked the cramps from my thighs. She asked me to turn over so she could ring my bell. Too bad the clanging came from Verizon.

"He said 'Roger' about the off-the-record, but wanted to know why."

"It's personal. Maybe I'll tell you about it one of these days."

"One more thing, Mr. DeLong, Frank can't meet until later this evening. How about you and I get together first?"

"Let's do it. Tell me where you're staying, and I'll come to your hotel around 5:30. I'm driving an old Corvette—easy to recognize."

He gave me the address. "See you then," Santiago said. "Look forward to it."

When I picked up Darlene at the airport later in the day, I gave her a heads-up about meeting with Santiago and the FBI.

"Are you nuts, Jack?" She damn near jumped out of the 'vette. "You can't go near the Feds. I don't want you in prison. What about the plan

71

for me to hand the money over to Will? Why should we get involved in any of this crap—and why aren't you looking at me?"

"Santiago said it would be unofficial, and for an unknown reason, I trust him. Besides, who knows if I'm clean or dirty?" I paused and raised my head to look in her eyes. "And why stick our noses into the kidnapping thing? Call it insatiable curiosity, and maybe I can help."

I knew I didn't need to get involved, but I couldn't resist, and I might be able to put my fears of the FBI to bed for good.

"Where do we meet him?" she said, resignation in her voice.

"I'd prefer you to wait in our hotel room and let me check these guys out before they know who you are. You're my last refuge after Monroe DeLong."

"I don't like it, but okay—this time."

The bitten lower lip told me she didn't like it at all.

Santiago met me in front of the hotel. I wanted our first conversation in my car. I'd purchased a bug detector a couple of years ago from an online survivalist store. The little light on the box glowed green on all-clear, but switched to red if it found a listening device—not foolproof, but better than nothing.

"Hop in. We'll drive around." I had the top down and I pushed open the passenger door.

"Nice wheels." He ran his hand over the upholstery. "You know the town?"

"A little. I know enough to avoid traffic."

"Head North on Scottsdale, and we can tour the homes on Mummy Mountain."

I've never been a big Phoenix fan. Too hot in the summer, and too many people, but they know how to build expensive neighborhoods. The sun began its descent into the Western sky and scattered clouds cast moving shadows on the almost-prehistoric profile of the rocky outcropping they used to call Horseshoe Mountain. The homes looked like overkill, but many were architectural marvels.

We drove and made easy conversation. A few rare people you like when you meet them. Carlos Santiago fit the category. He looked and sounded intelligent, and it felt comfortable. I wanted to open up to this guy, but common sense told me to wait and listen.

"I don't know where to begin," I said.

"Let's start with Pendleton. You said you wanted to see me because of something you know."

"Something I *may* know. I'm not sure it's connected, but it's almost too strange not to be. But before we get into that, tell me about yourself. Where are you from, who do you work for, and why are you in Phoenix? Sound fair?"

Carlos spent the next fifteen minutes giving me a capsule biography. When he finished, I thought I'd made a good decision so I took the plunge.

"Okay, Carlos, as to why I'm reluctant to meet with the FBI, believe what you choose, but I'm no criminal, and I don't think the Feds are looking for me, but they might see it differently. I got involved in a fracas a few years ago and defended myself. Extenuating circumstances said it might be better to vamoose than explain what happened."

"That's a U.S. jurisdictional problem. Doesn't affect me." He said and shrugged.

"How about your running mate?"

"He sticks by his word. We're interested in the Pendleton kidnapping, not you—unless you're involved, of course. Now, tell me what you know."

I hesitated for a brief moment. Quick decisions based on gut feelings were my strength, and I sensed I could confide in Carlos without fear of repercussions.

"I found a large sum of money four days ago when my horse stumbled over a canvas bag stashed in the *barranco* behind my *rancho*. Later, I read about the shooting near Los Alamos, which is about a dozen miles from where I picked up the item. I talked to a lawman friend of mine, put two and two together, and came up with a connection."

"How much money?" Carlos said.

"Two and a half million in cash."

"That's it, the Pendleton ransom amount."

Carlos radiated excitement. He had slouched down in the 'vette passenger seat, his arm resting on the console. Now he sat up straight and slapped his hand on it and almost spilled my coffee.

"Any ideas about what it means?" I said.

Carlos held out his hands, palms wide. "The kidnappers hid it there after the exchange and murder and intended to come back for it?"

"What if the murder and payoff happened in different places?"

That stopped him for a moment.

"Where is it now? The money?"

"It's safe. I've no intention of keeping it, but I want answers before it gets turned over to the authorities. Uh, the problem I mentioned with the Feds…"

"Yes?"

"I'll introduce you to my wife. She's going to turn it in so my name doesn't get involved. My real name."

"Who's Monroe DeLong?" he wanted to know.

"A solid citizen with impeccable paperwork and records. Once we know each other better, I'll give you the rest."

"Whatever makes you comfortable. What did you mean about 'different places'?"

"I found the money a little after two in the afternoon. The newspaper said Pendleton's murder happened between four and four-thirty on the same day."

This brought Carlos straight up in his seat.

"Whaaaat? How could that be? The money was handed over to one of the kidnappers, and the delivery man saw Pendleton get shot."

"Maybe I confused the time, but I don't think so. It's worth checking out."

"Could you drop me back at the hotel now? I need to see Frank Hunter, my FBI partner, and arrange for you to meet him."

"How about dinner tonight? You, me, my wife Darlene, and Hunter? I know a few good places here."

"Sounds fine, Monroe. Let's say seven, and you call with a location."

I looked around and saw I'd driven back toward the hotel. Traffic jammed the road, and I wanted to get to my room and take a shower. I decided to drop Carlos off in front and circle around. I didn't want to tell him we were staying at the same place—inbred paranoia.

"*Hasta luego, Señor. Mucho gusto.*" Carlos closed the 'vette door.

"*Lo mismo, Amigo.*"

I liked to try my Spanish whenever I could.

I watched him walk to the hotel entrance. Darlene would like him. He seemed to possess John Thunder's common sense—which reminded me, I should call John and update him on my travels. Same with Tommy. I could take care of it when I arrived back at our room.

Chapter 20

The Assassin

The hot afternoon sun cooked his arms. The bush hat settled low across his eyes as he marched cross-country to his target. No need to follow the trail from the hiding place. This route would save at least a mile.

The familiar terrain rekindled hated memories of a childhood spent hiding from his father and his leather strop, and later on, the Pueblo police. He had come to know the *barrancos* that crisscrossed the area like his own backyard and could lose himself in them at will. *The seventh circle of hell.* After his last visit, he had vowed never to return, but the opportunity offered by this remote area to pull off the biggest job of his life had beckoned too strongly. Now, he cursed the miasma of bad luck that hung over this place.

His head jerked when he came to a tree he recognized. An old cottonwood with a crooked, low-hanging branch. A few days after he turned fourteen, the Pueblo cops had arrested him and pretended they were going to hang him. They put a rope around his neck and threw it over the branch and laughed when he pissed his pants. Years later, he'd made a return trip to the little town and cut the ringleader's throat while he slept. *Not my class reunion.* He laughed to himself.

He slowed when the *rancho* came into view. Quiet. No barking dogs, no people in sight.

He shucked the small haversack from his back, opened it, and reached inside to feel the coolness of the iced hamburger. He'd laced it with Ambien before he left his room at the resort—not enough to kill, but sufficient for a good night's sleep. He donned a pair of thin gloves, eased open the unlocked gate, and whistled softly. Within a few seconds, he heard the dogs pound in his direction, making lots of noise, but that didn't matter. Anybody at home would see him soon enough. He placed two portions of meat on newspaper from his haversack and offered them when the German shepherds stuck their noses through the opening.

They gobbled it down, and he sat back to relax while the drug did its work.

He dozed and awoke when he heard snoring on the other side of the fence. He poked his head inside, and saw the dogs, fast asleep. He smiled and removed a glove to ruff their necks when he passed. The yard looked empty, but he heard the sound of a tractor behind the barn. Guinea hens and chickens raised a ruckus when he strode by their coop. He smelled new-mown grass and gasoline. It reminded him of his childhood when he worked on a farm.

"Shhhh, Little Chickies," he said and waved at them, putting the glove back on.

A small orchard stood between him and the barn, and bees buzzed through the fruit. A smallish man on a tractor seat a hundred yards away stared at him with a puzzled look. He raised his hand in greeting and smiled.

The man got down from the tractor and walked toward him and looked around, probably wondering where the dogs were.

"Can I help you, Señor?"

"I'm looking for a brown canvas satchel that I lost on the *barranco*. Have you seen it?"

The farmer blinked and looked away.

He knew this was his man.

"*No, Señor. No comprende.* Satchel?"

"You fucking greaser. Where's my money?"

He grabbed the man by the shirt and shook him violently. A shout from the *casita* caused him to look up. A woman ran toward them.

"Let him go!" she screamed.

"Go back inside, Señora. This is man's business." He nodded toward the house.

"Consuela. *Esta bien.*"

The woman stared for a moment and ran back inside the *casita*. She emerged a few seconds later toting a big shotgun.

"Tell her to stop and drop, or I'll kill her." He showed the pistol in its holster.

"Consuela," the man shouted. "Put down the gun and go back. Do it."

She hesitated, a frightened look on her face, but bent down to place the shotgun on the ground, then walked backwards towards the door.

"Tell her not to call anyone, or I'll kill you."

"Don't call anyone. Don't call the police, or he'll kill me," he shouted in Spanish.

"Good fellow. Now, tell me about the bag you found."

"I didn't find anything. Please, Señor, let us go. We know nothing."

"What's your name? That's Consuela up there in the *casita*. Your wife?"

"*Si*. I'm Franco. We work here. This isn't our property."

"Who are the owners?"

"They're gone. Out of town. Not back for two weeks. Now can we go? *Por favor, Señor*."

"I didn't ask where, I asked who."

"Navarro. Their name is Navarro."

"Did Mr. Navarro find a bag? Now, if you lie to me, I'm going to take you to your *casita* and shoot your wife in the right elbow. If that doesn't loosen your tongue, I'll take out the left. Move it."

He shoved Franco by the shoulder in the direction of the little house. He stopped and picked up the discarded twelve-gauge on the way.

"Nice weapon," he said and hefted it for weight. "Maybe I'll use it to blow out her stomach."

Franco dropped to his knees and grabbed the man around the thighs.

"Please, Señor, don't hurt my Consuela. I'll tell you anything."

The man felt Franco's arms tighten and his body push against his legs. He lifted the shotgun in his right hand and crashed it down on Franco's skull. The pressure increased and he felt himself start to fall backwards.

Tough little spic bastard. He dropped the shotgun and put out his hand to catch his fall. *Too bad I have to kill you.*

He lay on his back, Franco on top, clawing for the Colt. He watched Franco's efforts, a bemused expression on his face. He reached down, took a knife from the sheath on his boot, and sliced off one of Franco's fingers. The screams brought Consuela outside.

"I called the police, you *gringo* shit. They'll be here any minute. You let him go."

The situation became tedious. He rose to one knee and drew the Woodsman from its holster, tripped the safety, and took casual aim at the woman. The long rifle hollow point caught her forehead and she flew backwards into the door frame.

"Noooooooooo!" Franco's scream shattered the quiet after the explosion.

The man stood and used the pistol butt to rap Franco on the side of his head. Franco fell in a heap, blood congealing around a two-inch cut in his temple.

The man walked to the *casita* and dragged Consuela inside. He pushed and rolled Franco's inert body close to the porch, recovered the twelve-gauge, and sat back in a lounger to wait for the police Consuela had called. He checked the load in the shotgun. Sweet. A nine shot magazine crammed with double-ought shells. Should be fun. He pulled the bush hat lower over his eyes and dozed.

Chapter 21

Cave Creek

We picked up Frank at his hotel after Carlos joined us downstairs at ours.

"I made reservations at Cave Creek," I informed him.

"Great food," Frank said, "if you like steaks."

I rented a limo since the four of us couldn't fit into my 'vette. I couldn't help but look at the two of them—Frank and Carlos—side-by-side and wonder at the differences.

Frank exuded frumpiness. Tall, gawky, a suit that didn't quite fit, crushed necktie, the remnants of a broken nose, a small stain on the front of his white shirt. Carlos could have been a movie star. Handsome, great smile, tall, lean, and dark. Short hair like most cops, but combed straight back so it showed pizzazz.

"Know where it is, *Amigo?*" I asked the driver.

"*Claro qué si.*"

We became acquainted on the ride to the restaurant. Frank seemed laid-back and friendly compared to most Feds I knew. I could tell Darlene liked Carlos from the git-go.

They seated us near an outdoor fire pit—close, but not too close. The distinctive smell of juniper permeated the air, and the dark outlines of distant mountains illuminated by a slice of rising moon created an ethereal atmosphere. I almost wished Darlene and I had come alone.

"I haven't told Frank anything, Monroe. Could you tell him what you told me?" Carlos leaned back in his chair.

I spent the next twenty minutes telling Hunter the same story I'd relayed to Carlos. His facial muscles tensed when I told him about the timing.

"It can't be, Monroe. We received an accurate account from the negotiator, and the time of the drop and killing is reasonably exact." He shook his head like he wanted to clear the cobwebs.

"Like I said to Carlos, maybe I'm wrong, but I doubt it. I think you need to revisit the details."

"I took the dogs for a walk," Darlene said. "We left the house about two in the afternoon, and ran into Jack, er, Monroe, a few minutes later." She sounded sure of herself, despite the stumble.

Both Hunter and Carlos smiled at her slip. A voice in my head told me they already had me pegged.

We ordered dry Sapphire martinis, straight up. I told them how I named my horse after my favorite gin.

Far too beautiful an evening to rush things, we sat and talked for an hour before we placed our order. A clue that others occupied the restaurant came from clinking ice and murmured conversation. When the food came, it more than met the expectations raised by Frank's prediction—even after a second drink.

I leaned on both elbows and eyed my newfound friends.

"What's next? Darlene's going to turn in the money, but first, I need some assurances."

"What kind of assurances?" Frank said.

"It will stop there. No investigation into her or me. No repercussions."

"Are you afraid of what we'd find?"

"Yes, but like I told Carlos earlier, I'm not a criminal, so you don't have to worry on that score."

"Let me pose the obvious question—you have the ransom money, or so we think. Why shouldn't we arrest you for participating in the kidnapping?" His cop voice.

"If I were the kidnapper and had escaped with two and a half million bucks, why would I be sitting here talking to you and Carlos?"

"I needed to ask. No offense intended."

"So, one more time, what's next?"

Carlos sat up straight, a gleam in his eyes. "We all agree there's something fishy about everything surrounding the kidnapping, the payoff, and Pendleton's murder."

The three of us nodded.

"If this is the ransom money, and I can't see it otherwise, we use it to flush out the killer or killers and the motive. Mrs. Pendleton moved to the top of my suspect list yesterday, so we'll start with her."

Carlos told Darlene and me about his brush with the intruder and the mysterious coded message he discovered in Pendleton's desk leg. "I'll call Mrs. Pendleton now and ask if the four of us can visit her tomorrow. It should be interesting."

80

Carlos stepped away from the table and took his cell from his pocket. We watched while he engaged in animated conversation for the next few minutes. I decided to put a question to Frank.

"Darlene and my best friend think she should turn the money in tomorrow and we should butt out of this. Any reason why not?"

He appeared to consider for a moment before responding.

"If you turn it in, and it hits the papers, we lose leverage on the kidnappers. On the other hand, if you hang on to it and assist us in the investigation, we might be able to solve any problems you have with the Feds." He gave me an inquisitive look.

"Hate to sound like Marathon Man, but is it safe?"

"I should think so. Nothing connects you with the money, and if we keep a tight lid on things, nothing will. I wouldn't worry."

Carlos returned from his call before I could answer.

"Late tomorrow. Four p.m. I asked her a few questions, and I think she lied about the meaning of the note I found."

"Would you care for coffee or a nightcap?" The waiter stood next to Darlene.

"I'll have both," she said. "How about you boys? Can you handle another one?"

I didn't bother to tell them that she could put all of us under the table if she concentrated.

We sipped great coffee and good cognac, then ordered another round of the latter.

"I don't know about you guys, but I have a busy day tomorrow. I'm the only one here with a legitimate job—I don't count Carlos'—and I need my shuteye." Frank included us all in his smile. "Monroe, you and I will finish this conversation later. In the meantime, can I count on your discretion?"

Carlos didn't blink, and I nodded.

We dropped Frank off at his hotel and headed for ours. I told the driver to leave Carlos at the front door. Darlene and I sat in the back while she lit up a Marlboro.

"Fascinating night, yes? And nice people, Carlos and Frank."

"Exceptional. You trust them?" Darlene said.

"I don't think we have a choice."

"Let's sleep on it. We don't have to decide tonight."

"I have a better idea." I leaned over and nuzzled her neck. "Let's not go to sleep quite yet."

The best laid plans. We went to our room, and I undressed to walk to the shower.

I heard Darlene jump from the bed, then she placed her hands on my shoulders.

"My god, Jack."

"What?"

"Your legs. They're purple and blue from your butt to your knees. Doesn't it hurt like hell?"

She massaged my neck, and for the first time in a while, I thought about Hernandez and the whack he'd given me.

"I guess it does, but I forgot about it for the evening."

"We need to get you to a hospital, *pronto*," Darlene said.

"Get ice from the machine and wrap it in towels. It's nothing fatal."

"What if it were me? Would you toss it off like that?"

"No, but it's not you, and I don't have the time or inclination to sit around an emergency waiting room. I'm sure it would make it worse. Do the ice. It'll clear up in a few days."

Instead of making love, Darlene played nurse, and I fell asleep on my stomach, which meant my back would ache in the morning.

Chapter 22

The Assassin

He heard the siren from a mile away. He threw water on Franco and moved him half-off and half-on the small portico outside the *casita*. Franco moaned and tried to lift his head, but fell back after each effort. The pool of blood underneath his hand began to stiffen. The intruder went inside the partially-opened door and sat on a kitchen chair with a clear view of the porch, the shotgun across his lap, a frying pan dangling in his right hand. He knew the cops would see Franco and come to assist.

The police car roared through the open front gate and skidded to a halt in the driveway. Two Pueblo constables leaped from the vehicle and raced toward Franco. The killer laughed when he saw Franco try to wave them away, his hand making feeble flaps, his voice an unintelligible croak. The cops crouched over him and appeared unable to decipher his warnings.

He dropped the pan and they looked up and peered into the open doorway. Their hands moved toward their gun belts. He let them start to draw their Glocks before he blew the first one to hell. The other stood stupefied, his weapon halfway between holster and firing position, not knowing what to do. A second later, he turned to bolt, but a load of double-ought caught him between the shoulder blades and he went airborne, skidding to a halt, face in the dust, blood gushing from the wound and coloring the ground.

The man walked to each of the deputies, unholstered the Woodsman, and put a round in the back of their heads. He turned and saw the horrified look on Franco's face.

"Not yet, *Amigo*. We have things to discuss."

He pulled Franco into the living room after moving Consuela out of sight. A man with nothing to live for would be more difficult to crack.

He found rope in the pantry and used it to tie Franco's hands and feet. He lifted a table lamp and ripped off the cord. Using his pocketknife, he skinned the wires bare. He grunted when he moved Franco near the light socket and smiled when he noticed the fear in his eyes. He undid Franco's belt and slipped down his trousers and underwear. The flaccid penis lay there like an overcooked tuber.

He found the circuit breaker box in the pantry and opened the door to check it out. After returning to the living room, he wrapped the bare wires around the penis and pulled his chair next to the electrical outlet.

"Now, my friend, you're going to tell me where the money is. Do that and I'll let you go so you can call an ambulance for the Señora—and I won't plug this in."

"She's alive?" Franco croaked through cracked lips.

"Wounded, but bleeding. She needs help."

"The money, Señor. I don't know. Señor Jack left and took it with him."

"Señor Jack? What's his last name?"

"Navarro, Señor. I told you."

The man inserted the plug into the outlet. Franco's screams drowned out the sound of the circuit popping. A burnt hair odor permeated the room, and Franco's pubic region smoldered. The man removed the plug and went to the pantry to reset the breaker.

"Let's start again. Where's the money? I don't have much time." He leaned forward in the chair. He heard the police radio crackling outside. The dispatcher must be worried about her charges. They'd soon send another car.

"I swear to you I don't know. Please stop. I don't care about money. I want my Consuela. I'd tell you if I knew. Give me water, *por favor*." It came out in a garbled rush.

The man considered for a moment. "I believe you, Franco. You're a tough *hombre*. Too bad you have to die."

He inserted the plug one more time for the fun of it. The wailing sound of an approaching police vehicle woke him from his murderous haze. Franco's lucky day.

"*Adios, Amigo*." He turned and sprinted out the door.

He trotted to the main house and used the shotgun to blow away the deadbolt lock. The alarm sounded, but he didn't care, he knew what he wanted. Easy to locate the office. He opened the unlocked filing cabinet and saw the neat rows of income tax returns. He opened the most recent folder and removed the 1040 copy. He suspected he would find all he needed to know about Mr. Navarro in here. He turned to leave when he noticed the photograph. A man and woman smiling with their arms around each other.

He picked up his backpack in the barnyard, stuffed the file and the picture inside, and ran to the still-idling police car, tossing the bundle in the back seat. He dropped the vehicle in gear, hung a U-ey, and headed for the back gate. The dogs were still comatose, and he used care not to hit them. He passed through, stopped the car, pulled the dogs outside, and closed the gate. It would take the next pack of cops a few vital minutes to figure out which direction he'd gone. Back in the auto, he stomped on the accelerator and sped toward the *arroyo* he'd crossed earlier.

The six-inch deep water proved no obstacle to the tough police cruiser, but a large rock that punctured the oil pan did. The engine ran for another ten minutes before it began to smoke and wheeze. It froze up, and the vehicle skidded to a halt. He abandoned it and set out on foot after strapping the haversack on his back. He patted his armpit to make sure the Colt snuggled in its holster. No problem jogging the mile to where he parked the Hummer.

Chapter 23

Jack and Darlene

Darlene looked worried. "I called home early this morning, but no one answered."

"It's a nice day. I reckon they're both outside. Did you check the answering machine?"

"I couldn't remember how to do it from here. I ended up leaving a message."

"Try later. I'll call Will and ask him to drop by and check things out."

I unplugged my cell from its charger and glanced at the display. Six missed calls. I must have set the ringer to mute by accident. Big fingers on a small electronic object make funny things happen. I flipped the top and dialed voice mail. The messages came from Will and told me to call him ASAP. He answered on the first ring and didn't sound good.

"Jack. Come home. There's been an incident."

"What do you mean, an 'incident?' What happened?"

"Jesus Christ, Jack, I don't know where to begin." His voice faltered. "A home invasion at your place."

Indistinct words followed.

"What? Our home? Talk louder, Will. When? Is everyone okay? Is stuff missing? Are the dogs okay?" Anything else would be unimaginable.

"The dogs are fine. It's Franco and Consuela."

"Are they injured? For Christ's sake, Will, spill it."

"They're both in the hospital. Two Pueblo cops are dead."

The phone fell from my hands onto the bed.

"Jack, you look sick," Darlene said. "What is it?"

"Jack, Jack, you still there?" Will's voice echoed from the handset.

I picked up the phone and gripped it like it had betrayed me. A red haze dropped over my eyes.

"How bad are they? Why?"

"We don't know why. We found the police cruiser in the *arroyo*. No prints, no clues. He or she drove it that far, then walked. We think we discovered where the assailant parked his or her vehicle, and by the tire tracks, it looks like a Hummer. Beyond that, I don't know. You have to get back here *pronto*."

"What's Franco and Consuela's condition? You said they're in the hospital."

"Consuela's still critical. She was shot in the head. The bullet passed through her scalp and fractured her skull. They don't think there's any brain damage. Franco lost a finger and has a severe concussion. Also, it looks like he was tortured."

I hung up and sat there in shock. *Shit!*

I felt Darlene tug hard at my shoulder.

"It's my fault …," I said

"What about Franco and Consuela? They're hurt?"

"Consuela's in the ICU. Franco's hurt bad. I hauled that stupid-ass canvas bag home, and now two cops are dead and our friends are wounded." I held my face in my hands.

I remembered the animals after I hung up. I called Will back.

"Do me a favor."

"Anything."

"Stop by Ray Green's place. He lives three houses east. I board his horse. Ask him to stop by for the next few days and take care of the animals. I'll come out when I can."

"Consider it done."

"Thanks, *Amigo*."

The next few hours went by in a surreal blur. I called Carlos and told him. He would call Frank and let Mrs. Pendleton know we weren't dropping by today. Darlene wept and raged, but didn't blame me.

"No one could have known, Jack. It's not your fault." She wrapped her arms around my neck, giving and seeking comfort.

But it was, and neither she, nor anyone else, could convince me otherwise.

Could I go back now, given the trouble I was in? I called Zeke Martinez to find out if he'd made any progress with getting the charges against me dropped. He said Elias showed marked signs of stubbornness, but he could feel him cracking. Zeke knew about the cop murders and sounded heartsick. It looked like we had no choice but to drive home and take our chances with the constabulary.

87

The cowboys and Indians game I had been playing since I found the money loomed like pure vanity. Who cared about Pendleton or the cash or the kidnappers when two of my closest friends were in the hospital, gravely injured, and two policemen lay dead? I couldn't imagine walking to the barn and not seeing Franco's smiling face or hearing Consuela call everyone to dinner. How long before they would rejoin us?

We drove in silence, each of us wrapped in our own memories. I kept my speed within ten miles of the limit, not wanting to risk a stop and a test of the Monroe DeLong credentials. Later, Darlene, who had been leaning her head on my shoulder, drifted off. She came to when we neared Santa Fe.

"Godammit, Jack, what are we going to do about this?"

I heard an edge to her voice that told me she wasn't kidding.

"We'll find the person who did it, and take care of business."

"I want to put my foot on the fucker's chest and a bullet in his eye."

"That's two of us. Be calm. We need the law's help, and I have to fix it so I can resurface."

I checked into the El Dorado near the Plaza using the Monroe DeLong alias, and Darlene took a separate room under her own name. I wouldn't be able to show my face around town until Hernandez backed off, but Darlene could cover what we needed to do.

I had fucked up a lot of things in my life, but never anything like this. The feeling that hit me when I found the money remained. Franco and Consuela, the cops, and the stash. I knew in my heart they were part of the same package.

A knock on the door of my suite. I checked the peephole. Will. He walked in, then hugged me.

"Jack, I'm so sorry. A man shouldn't have to worry about the sanctity of his home."

"Do you know what happened? Who did it?"

"Sit down, and I'll tell you what little I know."

He had picked up a call on his radio about trouble at our place. Our *rancho* didn't fall within his southern jurisdictional patrol, but he red-lined the tachometer and reached our property in twenty minutes. Normally, the North County Sheriff's Office would have handled the original 911 call, but Pueblo Police had heard it and responded.

Will arrived first on the murder scene. The deputies lay sprawled, one on the porch, the other farther away, like he'd been gunned down running toward the car. Will unlocked the riot gun from its rack on the front floorboard of his cruiser and eased open the car door. He crouched behind it and shucked a live round into the chamber. No noise came from the house.

Will reached inside the vehicle and thumbed the two-way radio, telling the dispatcher there were officers down.

"Send four busses and backup." He gave her the address.

How long do I wait? What if Franco and Consuela need help? What if I'm in the perp's gunsight right now?

"Hello in the house. Throw out your weapons and come out with your hands in the air." His shout echoed back at him.

He cradled the shotgun in his elbows and began to crawl toward the porch. It felt like boot camp all over again, except there were no live rounds screaming over his head. He worked his way past the first deputy and the reek of blood and shit almost overwhelmed him. When he came to the porch, he sprang up and braced against the side of the door jamb.

"Franco. Consuela." Silence. Not even a clock ticking.

Will peeked around the corner. Franco lay sprawled on the floor.

What the fuck. I have to get to him.

He held the shotgun at his waist and moved into the living room, sweeping the perimeter. He heard flies buzzing and a bird sing outside the window. He spotted Franco. Congealed blood had pooled around his hand and head. He gagged when he saw the wires wrapped around his penis. Franco's chest rose and fell in regular rhythm, so Will knew he wasn't dead.

He stepped over Franco and tiptoed to the bedroom. Consuela lay curled on the floor at the foot of the bed. He propped the shotgun against the wall and bent down to feel her pulse. Faint, but regular. Thank God, they were both alive.

Will sounded like a man in a trance, and I shook his arm.

"Why, Will? Why would anyone try to kill those gentle souls?" I wanted to shout or scream, but couldn't. "And the Pueblo cops. What were their names? Did we know them?"

He snapped back to the moment.

"All I can figure, Jack, is that the killer came looking for the money you found. He shot Consuela and tortured Franco. You might have known the policemen. Luis Alvarez and Tony Gallegos."

I shook my head. "Godammit, why didn't I do what you said and have Darlene turn it in? Why did I lose my fucking temper and assault Hernandez? Why? This is my fault. All of it." I started to pace back and forth, running my fingers through my hair.

"You didn't tell some psycho to steal the money or invade your home, shoot Consuela, torture Franco, or kill those cops. You couldn't have imagined this."

"I should have seen it coming. I knew that money meant trouble the moment I laid eyes on it. Me and my macho crap." I kicked at a footstool, but only managed to graze it.

I went to the mini-bar and pulled out a small bottle of Patron. I needed a drink. I didn't bother with a glass, twisted open the top, and swallowed it in one gulp.

"Easy, Jack. That won't help, and you know it."

"It'll help me get through tonight, Will."

At the policemen's funeral, I discovered the meaning of 'extended family.' At least two hundred people showed up to pay their respects to the dead officers. I huddled in a back room with a window, afraid that Hernandez might have the poor taste to show up and try to arrest me, but he didn't. Good thing because I came strapped and would have faced serious charges after I burned him then used the window to escape. Later that day I called Zeke.

"Offer Hernandez ten grand in cash to withdraw the charges."

"That's bribery, Jack. It could land you in the slammer."

"Couch it in terms of a civil settlement offered to head off a lawsuit."

"I'll see what I can do."

He called me the next morning to tell me Hernandez had agreed. I drove over to Zeke's office and gave him one of the bundles from the satchel. I didn't want to show up at my bank and withdraw that much cash. I could make it up later.

"Make sure I'm clean. I want to take care of business."

"You look like hell, Jack. Have you slept?"

"I feel like hell. I don't know if I can get past this one, Zeke. It's tearing me up and Darlene too. I've never seen her so enraged. We need to talk about it, but neither of us wants to discuss anything but revenge."

"Maybe you need to talk to a professional. A priest or a shrink."

"I don't do priests or preachers. I'll call John Thunder."

"Take care of yourself. Call me this afternoon."

"Thanks for everything, Zeke." I didn't know what else to say.

Chapter 24

Manuel Hoppe

The insurance company's claims division occupied the fourteenth floor of a sleek glass building in downtown Phoenix. Built when the Southwest broke the real estate growth sound barrier during the first few years of the twenty-first century, it offended Manuel Hoppe's aesthetic instincts.

He stood at the desk of the assistant to the Assistant Vice President of Claims.

"Please let Wayne know I'm here." He gazed over her head at a distant object.

"Right away, Mr. Hoppe." She pressed her intercom and spoke in a hushed tone.

"Please, Mr. Hoppe. Go right in. I believe you know the way to his office?"

"Thank you." He turned to the familiar hallway on his right. The office door stood open.

"Manuel. Thanks for coming in on Saturday." Wayne Deckert rose from behind his desk and extended his hand.

"Not a problem, Wayne. I know we need to talk." Deckert's hand felt clammy, and Hoppe experienced the familiar revulsion engendered by physical contact with another of his sex.

He did his best to relax in the visitor's chair. He looked across the desk at his employer and suppressed the sneer that tried to curl his lip. Deckert's Scottsdale suntan and over-stuffed face made him feel ill. He reminded Hoppe of the guy who used to command the Starship, Enterprise.

"If you don't mind, Manuel, perhaps we could get right to it. I'm getting pressured from the brass, and you know how that goes." Deckert made a good old boy face and shook his head. "In addition to the ransom insurance, we wrote a five million dollar term life policy on Pendleton. Unless there's an irregularity, I can't delay payment more than thirty days."

"And you're hoping to find a detail out of line?" Hoppe put a sardonic inflection into the question.

"Of course not. But we do need to investigate the circumstances of Pendleton's death. They were anything but normal, although his policy did not preclude payment in the event of either homicide or suicide."

"You've read my report, but take out your pen and paper, and I'll give it to you again. Maybe I overlooked critical information." He kept the edge in his voice.

"Now, now, Manuel. No one questions your professionalism. I'm sure the original report is complete, but you and I are on the same page. Let's do it one more time."

Deckert pushed aside a large actuarial tome to clear space, placed a legal tablet in front of him, primly selected a pen from the cluster on his desk, and looked up in expectation. "Please. Start at the point when you assembled the cash."

Hoppe leaned back and closed his eyes. He maneuvered his fingers into a pyramid around his nose and took a deep breath. When he opened them he could see Deckert's feet under the desk, tapping like Bojangles. *You're stressed out, aren't you, you fat little faggot?* He smiled inside and began his narrative.

"The bank responded beautifully. Four hours after the insurance company made the decision to pay, the bank delivered two and a half million dollars to the safe room on the eleventh floor. I counted it and packed it into a brown canvas bag. I negotiated a simple arrangement with the kidnappers, even though it was bizarre, with respect to location."

"That's putting it charitably. Why would Mexican kidnappers want to do their business near Los Alamos, New Mexico, several hundred miles from their base?"

"If you want to hire me to solve that question, I'm available."

"Ha. First things first, Manuel—but in all seriousness, we may want to do that."

The laugh sounded nervous to Hoppe, and he filed it in his memory bank.

"I flew to Albuquerque, rented a vehicle, and traveled an hour and a half to the *rendezvous*. Based on their instructions, I drove to an abandoned National Forest Service tower and waited. Fifteen minutes after I arrived, my cell phone rang. The caller directed me to look southwest until I saw a yellow flag. I did, and saw Pendleton. He waved the flag to signal me. A jeep with covered license plates pulled up to the station, and a Mexican came up to me, held out his hand, and I passed him the satchel."

"Could you describe him?"

"I already did. A Mexican. He wasn't my concern."

Deckert made a sour face and ran his hand in a circle to signal Hoppe to continue.

"I watched Pendleton through field glasses. I estimated it would take him a minimum of twenty minutes to traverse the distance between us. They warned me to stay in the Ranger station and not approach him. He closed to a few hundred yards, and I heard a shot. I was watching through the binoculars when his head flew in several directions."

"I wouldn't want your job, Manuel."

"I hit the ground. Pendleton looked dead, and I thought the shooter might still be out there. I called here on my cell, but no one answered. I called the local Sheriff, and they came inside half an hour."

"Sounds like a setup. Any thoughts about why?"

"They're criminals. Maybe they did it for kicks or target practice. Maybe he saw their faces. I'm not paid to apprehend the kidnappers, only to rescue the hostage, and in this case, I failed miserably."

"It wasn't your fault, Manuel. You risked your life to go up there and meet with those animals. We don't hold you responsible."

"I appreciate that, Wayne, but I can't shake the feeling I did something wrong. Seeing him die while being passed to my care hit home." Hoppe sat up in his chair and hung his head, resting his elbows on his knees. "I'm taking time off to get it back together." He felt the shakiness in his voice.

"Sure. We understand. Do you want me to contact you when we need your services again?"

"Please. A few weeks, and I should be fine. If you still want to work with a negotiator who lost a client, I appreciate it."

"There's one more thing, Manuel." Deckert twisted in his chair and rubbed his hands together.

Now we're getting to it. Squirm, you little bastard.

"I'm sure you've read about Pendleton's financial predicament. Lot of money missing from his hedge fund. This part hasn't made the news yet, but, between you and me, we're talking more than five hundred million dollars." He raised his eyebrows.

"Yeah. So what?" Hoppe kept the surprise he felt out of his response.

"Pendleton went to Juarez for reasons unknown, was abducted, murdered, and big money's missing. We think it indicates a possible criminal conspiracy. If we could prove it, we could avoid paying off on the policy. It would be worth a lot to us."

"Who's the beneficiary?" Hoppe stalled. He needed time to think.

"His company. They paid the premiums—same with the kidnap insurance."

"So the widow gets *nada?*"

"Correct. I don't think he even left money in his checking account, but she's flush on her own. She had more money than he when they married. Oh, and one other thing—a cop stopped by here the other day asking about you."

"Me? Why me? What did he want?"

"Not you, exactly, but he wanted to meet the person who negotiated the ransom for Pendleton. I told him we classified the information as confidential, and he needed to obtain a warrant. It didn't make a lot of sense. None of this does."

"When nothing makes sense, everything's wrong."

Chapter 25

John Thunder

I spoke at the memorial service for Luis Alvarez and Tony Gallegos, or so I'm told. I don't remember anything I said. I felt gratitude that none of the relatives or friends knew I blamed myself for their deaths. Will theorized to anyone that would listen that maybe a random home invasion took their lives, but I didn't buy it. John Thunder's face in the crowd was the only good thing about the day

We stood beside the priest and the immediate family to shake hands with the mourners. John Thunder came near the end of the queue.

"I'll stop by your house tonight if you want."

"We haven't seen it yet. I don't want to yet, and neither does Darlene. Meet me in the bar at the El Dorado."

"Seven, Jack. See you then." He squeezed my shoulder, then made it a full embrace. "God, I'm so sorry. Those guys were good cops, and what's to say about Franco and Consuela? But you can't blame yourself."

Darlene and I started to talk again about practical matters.

"I went to the hospital and talked to the doctors. I told them whatever Franco and Consuela needed, they should get. The people in the Administrative Office were great. Turns out that the medical insurance we pay for every month covers almost everything. There'll be a co-pay, and I asked them to bill us. We can't visit either of the patients yet, but maybe tomorrow."

"We'll see John tonight, Darling." I caressed her brow and hair.

"Good. I don't know about you, Jack, but I need someone to tell me what to do. I feel like I'm wandering in the desert with no place to hide. I mean, an evil person violated our home and killed two people. There must be an answer."

"One of the costs of agnosticism. It helps me understand why people need God."

"Ain't it the truth? How about going down to the bar now? I could use a margarita—or two."

"Our church, I guess." I took a joint from my jacket pocket. "How about a toke before we hit the road?" I lit it up, took a drag, and passed it to her.

"This helps." She sucked with enthusiasm on the needle-thin paper and inhaled the sinsemilla, John Thunder's finest.

I looked at her. Neither of us had worn anything resembling dress clothes for so long, I forgot how beautiful she could be in them. The silk skirt hung a couple of inches below her knees and showed great legs. The matching blouse draped her bosom like a Greek statue. I looked in the full-length mirror and startled myself when I saw the dude in the sport coat and loosened necktie. The first laugh in a few days. It must have been the grass.

We had poured down three Silver Coin margaritas each by the time John arrived. That, plus a couple of trips to the bathroom for a quick hit of dope, and we were pretty hammered. When he came through the door, I couldn't help but smile at how incongruous he looked in his mountain clothes. Nobody dressed up in Santa Fe except tourists, but those were the denizens of this particular bar tonight.

"Jack, Darlene."

We moved to a table in the corner, and Darlene excused herself to go outside for a smoke before we dug into the hard stuff. In her absence, I let John in on what we knew. When she returned, she brushed back hair that had fallen over her forehead and looked at us expectantly.

"First question is the most obvious—how do you know it wasn't a robbery or simple home invasion? Maybe if you and Darlene had been there, we'd have buried you today along with the two cops."

"We haven't done an inventory yet. Will told us everything looked in place."

"So you think it's connected to what you found?"

"That's what makes it my fault."

"And why haven't you returned home to check things out for yourself?"

"I'm angry. There are times when I want to burn it to the ground."

Darlene nodded. "I feel the same, John."

He bent his head to his chest and gave out a long sigh, like he had made a decision.

"Let me tell you a story I've never told anyone. I'm a Capote Ute. I became a shaman after my Sundance when I turned nineteen. Any young man can perform and seek medicine power by participating in the Sundance if summoned through a dream, and I had a strong calling."

John paused to look at us.

"The ceremony starts with a four-day fast, no food or water, and is held inside the Sundance Lodge. It may not sound difficult, but that long without any form of sustenance wears on the body and mind. The only way to survive is with the support of your family who are camped on the outskirts of the dance territory. They sing and chant and offer up to the Great Spirit so that the dancer may realize his full potential."

"After four days, I saw a vision. My people, who lived in poverty, ignorance, and disease, grew strong again and rose up to stand chest to chest with the white man. I could see pride in their eyes and smiles on the children's faces. I told this to the Sundance Chief, but he looked at me like a crazy man, so I ran to the tipi where my family waited. When I arrived, they sat outside, their heads hanging, the women wailing."

"What happened?" I asked my mother.

She shifted her eyes to the tipi entrance. I lifted the flap and saw my grandfather wrapped in a burial blanket. Grandfather had become my guide and mentor. We loved each other, and when I saw him dead, my world collapsed. I began to moan and weep until my father came inside the tipi."

"Get up," father spoke in Ute. "You are a man, and your grandfather told us you possess strong medicine. He has gone to the Great Spirit, and your duty is to do what you promised. If you lament, it is for yourself, not him."

"Father, he was too old to come and sit for me. If he had stayed home, he might be alive."

"You don't know that. He did what he wanted and lived his desires. Do not dishonor him by forsaking your strength. Use it to fulfill what your vision promised."

John came back to the present and sagged in his chair. "I've done my best to give my people spiritual strength, and I've seen them prosper, not because of me, but because of my grandfather and others like him."

He looked me straight in the eye. "I've never advised anyone to seek revenge, but I make an exception for this crime. Find the person who injured your friends and killed two lawmen, and serve up justice." He once again bowed his head. "And go home tonight and honor the dead. Make peace with yourself. You didn't choose their path, and you cannot change what is."

Chapter 26

Juarez

I needed answers, and Hunter and Carlos could provide them—if they were willing. Darlene stayed in Santa Fe, and I took an early flight to El Paso. I asked them to meet me in Juarez. El Paso and Juarez—an old Mexican once told me they were the same city with two different souls.

Darlene promised me she'd carry her gun at all times and not stay in the house alone at night. The Pueblo cops stationed guards 24/7 at our front gate, but, according to Will, they'd be pulled off in a couple of days. I berated myself for leaving. Would she be in danger? My actions and decisions of late had not produced great outcomes—but what sane person could have anticipated what would happen? I wanted to start searching for whoever invaded my property, hurt Franco and Consuela, and shot the cops, and The FBI seemed like a logical place to start.

"Monroe, I can't tell you how sorry it made me to hear the news. Something like that in your home, and those poor policemen ..." Frank Hunter patted me on the shoulder. For a Fed, he was an okay guy.

"Thanks. Darlene and I are dealing with it. Now I need to get back to business."

"I think this is the part where I'm supposed to remind you that you're a civilian, and to leave this to the professionals. But if I were in your shoes, I'd dismiss the advice and follow my instincts. I suspect you'll do that anyway."

I ignored the implied question.

"I need your help, Frank—and Carlos'. Will he be here soon?"

We had crossed the border to Juarez. I hadn't visited in several years, but nothing seemed to have changed. Frank had hesitated for a fraction before agreeing to meet on this side. From my experience, G-men like to stay in a jurisdiction where they have power, a lesson I learned when they pursued me. Carlos was home, visiting his family, and this place suited him, so here we were. I gave Frank credit for keeping an open mind. His badge also made the trip through customs a lot easier.

The air conditioning in the bar cranked away the afternoon heat and the dust that tried to seep in from outside. It amazed me that the joint appeared to be evenly populated between tourists and locals. I thought that *gringos* avoided Juarez due to the kidnapping danger and the drug wars, which were real, and the frenzy the Border States media created with their unending investigative reports and exhortations to the government, which were part fact, part fiction. But here they sat in cheap straw *sombreros* and Bermuda shorts, sandals dangling from their toes while they sipped on local tequila. The Juarez denizens who occupied the regulars' section appeared friendly and unmenacing, except for two gangly dudes in dirty white pants and shirts with kerchiefs tied around their heads. They glared at Frank and me like we carried the bird flu virus.

I remembered the city I once knew. Normal, cheerful people and old nuggets of beauty like the Catredal Plaza at night, or the Kiosko that sat in a peaceful garden in the middle of the city. The Misión de Nuestra Señora de Guadalupe in El Centro, beautiful outside and in, smelling of old wood, flowers, and sacraments. A few great eating places. My old favorite tourist trap, Frida's, located on Triunfo de la Republica. I didn't know if it or its sister restaurants were still there. Juarez offered a variety of food. I'd chowed down on Chinese that ranked right up there with Hong Kong eating. Of course, the best places were the small bars like this one. Tucked away in an alley and reeking of Old Mexico and its past.

Carlos arrived and waved at the two men who had given me pause. Their expressions changed from Jack the Ripper to Jack in the Box. I saw them through a haze, and it struck me that everyone in the bar smoked. Once the smell flooded my nose, I couldn't avoid the other odor of spilled *cervezas*. Part of the charm.

"I asked them to keep an eye on you," Carlos said. "They work for me part-time. If we need local help, we can count on them. Both have lost relatives in the war." He focused on me. "You coping, Monroe? Sad to hear about your troubles."

Another round of condolences. Maybe if I stopped hearing how sorry people were, I could put Franco and Consuela and the dead cops out of my mind for a few minutes. *Knock it off,* I chided myself. *They want you to know they care.* I could be a real asshole when I tried.

"How are your friends doing? Any progress reports from the doctors?"

"Fine, Carlos. Thanks." I shrugged.

"So, where do we stand?" I looked at each of them in turn.

Frank nodded toward Carlos. "You tell him."

"Right now, we're at a dead end." He used his fingers to enumerate. "Mrs. Pendleton left the country on vacation, and I'm not sure we could have pried anything else out of her, anyway. The numbers I found in the desk haven't led us anywhere, although Frank's people are still working on them. The hostage negotiator, Hoppe, stopped by the insurance company last Saturday and confirmed his report, but the executive Frank talked to wouldn't tell him squat unless he showed him a warrant. The SEC and FBI are analyzing Pendleton's finances and securities transactions, but that'll take weeks before we have final answers. And we have no proof that the mayhem at your place is part of our situation."

"I'm convinced of the connection," I said. "The only way I'm going to find out who did it is to get to the bottom of the two and a half million dollars I found in the *barranco*. So what's next?" Judging by their response, things didn't sound promising. "How could Mrs. Pendleton leave U.S. soil? Isn't she a suspect?"

"We haven't charged her or even cited her as a person of interest. It's a free country. Funny thing is, we can't figure out where she went or how. We ran a cursory check on airlines, and she didn't fly. Maybe she traveled south using private transportation." Frank shook his head.

Carlos signaled the waiter for three more beers and lit up a cigarette. Frank and I both reached for the pack at the same time.

"Six years for me." I felt sheepish when I drew in the smoke.

"A dozen here." Frank looked like I felt.

I coughed hard and put it out, but it tasted good. First time I ever missed them.

"How about my question—what's next?"

"We have an idea." Frank hesitated. "Well, not 'we' exactly. It's Carlos' play, but I approve. Tell him about it." He motioned to Carlos.

"There's a local drug boss." Carlos gazed at his fingers instead of at me, which made me nervous. "Not the top guy in the cartel, but he runs Juarez and reports to the kingpin. He's agreed to talk, but not law enforcement. He must have his own agenda, otherwise, he wouldn't bother."

I looked around our table and found the one person who fit that description.

"You're shitting me. You want me to meet with one of your *bandidos*?"

"The Pendleton trail is cold, and your killer's enjoyed a week to run. Unless we get a new lead, we're out of business."

Darlene wouldn't like it. Hell, I didn't like it, but these guys were cops who knew their business. I either trusted their judgment or I didn't. Time to choose.

"Let's say I agree. How and when?"

One of the patrons dropped pesos in the juke box and loud mariachi music bounced off the walls of the room.

"We can do it tonight if you're game."

My palms started to sweat. I once read that courage doesn't mean absence of fear, it means doing a thing that scares you witless. The sudden rush took me back to my days in the service when being afraid came with the territory. But back then, I ran with a team, and we took care of each other. One dies, all die. This would be a solo run.

"We leave you here. Tito, one of my guys," he nodded towards the pair in the corner, "will let the other side know you're ready. They'll come for you an hour after Frank and I split. You do what they say. No monkey business. *Comprendes?*"

"*Comprendo*, Carlos, but I need more details. What should I ask?"

"Nothing. Let him talk. The boss must want us to know something."

"Do I wear a wire?"

"If you want your head cut off."

"Standard punishment for rats," Frank interjected.

The song on the juke box ended, and another one blared across the room. I looked around for a *vaquero* to strangle.

"Tito put the money in the machine, Jack. The noise blocks anybody from electronically eavesdropping." Carlos gestured toward one of our protectors and smiled.

"Christ, are they that sophisticated?"

"More advanced than you can imagine. Weapons, computers—you name it, they have it. Makes the war on drugs difficult," Frank said.

I saw Carlos become restless. I hadn't answered him directly, and he needed to know.

"So, you'll do it?" He raised his eyebrows.

"I have choice?" My stomach fluttered, and for an instant, I imagined I sat with Darlene in the courtyard of a fine hotel in Puerto Vallarta, drinking good tequila and listening to the small band that strolled from table to table while dusk settled around us. I could even smell the ocean.

Carlos stood and nodded at Tito, anxious to get going.

"*Buena suerte, Amigo.*" He squeezed my shoulder.

"You forgot one thing, Carlos."

"What's that?"

"What happens later? How do I get back to El Paso?"

Carlos laughed. "An important detail. Whoever drives you will drop you at your hotel. These guys have no problem crossing the border."

"Remember what I said, Monroe, and play it cool. You'll be fine. They've no reason to harm you." Frank rose in his heat-wrinkled suit and shook my hand.

His hand felt dry. All in a day's work for him. *I wonder if he carries his gun over here.* It didn't matter. He'd wear that jacket in the middle of the jungle.

I watched them walk out the door and glanced over at Tito. Inside my head I heard my clock ticking. I asked the waiter for another Tecate and took the half-crushed Marlboro from the ashtray. Carlos had left matches on the table. I lit it and enjoyed the sensation. *All I need now is a blindfold.*

An hour later, Tito motioned to me. I followed him outside, surprised that smoky streetlights and the smell of burnt firewood and garbage had replaced daylight. A black Suburban with tinted windows sat in front of the joint. The back door opened and I got in. Before I could get a look at the occupants, a hood dropped over my head, and it was cinched loosely around my neck.

"Sorry for the precautions, Señor. It won't take long to get there."

I fought the rising panic in my chest when claustrophobia kicked in. *I can breathe, I can breathe.* It became a mantra. At least my hands weren't shackled. I asked my unknown friend to crack a window, and he obliged. The breeze helped convince me I wasn't suffocating.

Chapter 27

El Jefe

The day's heat fled with sundown, but it hung on inside my head bag. Sweat trickled down my eye sockets, along my nose, and dangled there, poised to drip onto my shirt, but Godammit, it wouldn't. I felt an insatiable urge to wipe it off, but I kept still.

That's when the rage began to build. For the past week, I had wallowed in remorse, guilt, and self-pity. Now, anger overwhelmed my senses. Whoever tried to kill Consuela and Franco would pay. I meant to find him or her and take care of business—the law be damned.

I lose track of time and it jars me when the Suburban slows and halts. Muffled conversation before I hear a gate slide open. We travel another hundred yards and repeat the drill. Double-gated. A shorter distance. We grind to a halt, still on asphalt. Doors slam, and mine open. Someone takes me by the elbow and leads me from the car to a gravel walkway. My guide speaks in Spanish, and the ensuing buzz tells me we're going through a security door. I stumble once or twice, but the man next to me is solicitous and steadies me. A rush of cool air through an open portal, and I'm guided inside. I smell gardenias, expensive cigars, fireplaces, and leather. A chair scrapes on stone, and I feel pressure on the back of my legs.

"*Por favor, Señor.* Sit down and relax." A polite, cultured voice with a trace of an accent.

"May I remove the hood?" My hands rest on the chair arms, ready to move.

"Of course. A necessary precaution. So many newspapers have printed pictures of me that it won't matter if you recognize me. The route here, however …" A barked laugh. "That's a different story. Would you like a drink?"

"No, but I need to use your bathroom. I drank beer at the cantina."

My eyes adjust, and I can see him. I recognize the face, but search for a name. Handsome and smooth. Compelling dark eyes. I want to dislike him, but he has that indefinable quality that makes people seek his approval. I find myself drawn to him. I want to resist and chide myself for my reaction. The anger has left a metallic taste in my mouth, and more than using the facilities, I want to rinse it.

"Of course." He chuckles and motions to the man standing behind and to my right. "Please escort El Señor to *los baños*."

The décor in the toilet speaks of wealth and taste. The small Impressionist painting on the wall looks original, and I try to decipher the artist's signature, but it's old and indistinct. A bathroom's a good place to assess a person's prominence.

My guard brings me back to the salon, where I take my place across from my host. I immediately recall his name, Villenueva. A high government official and well-known philanthropist. *Hard to believe he works for the cartel.*

"I see you're confused, Señor. You're wondering if I'm a cartel Jefe or a police official. Mexico is more complicated than your fine country— distinctions between good and evil more difficult. Let me assure you, however, that we're on the same side."

"It doesn't matter to me whose side you're on, Señor. My business is elsewhere."

"*De acuerdo, Señor* DeLong. In that case, what I have to tell you may be of little use to you personally, but of enormous value to your *amigos*."

"Have you heard what happened at my *rancho*? To my friends?" I found I didn't want to say their names aloud to him.

"Yes. I promise that if any information comes to me or my people that would be of assistance to you, I'll convey it to my contact."

I took a deep breath and let it go.

"Please, Mr. DeLong. I have information crucial to the Pendleton matter and to my *compadres* on this side of the border."

"I'm listening." I tried to keep my voice neutral.

"Neither the cartel nor any Mexican organization or person took him. The setup was designed to confuse the trail and motive."

It sounded like the truth.

"How do you know?" I needed to validate the information. It changed the equation.

"My contacts extend into every enterprise that operates in our little corner of the world. I have received assurances about these things."

"Did it happen in Juarez?"

"Yes. Pendleton kept a mistress here, and whoever snatched him knew about her, his habits, and his itineraries. According to the woman, Pendleton came to her apartment three weeks ago at his usual time. He left four hours later. When she went to close her drapes, she heard noises outside. She looked out the window and saw two men dragging Pendleton to one of those RV's you Americans adore so much."

"Did she call the police?"

"Of course not. She's an intelligent woman ... although, at my request, she later gave a statement."

I rubbed my fingers over my eyes, then drew them down across my cheeks. My skin felt rough and unshaven.

Excitement mounted in my chest and blotted out exhaustion. Perhaps my mysterious friend didn't know anything about Consuela and Franco, but his information strengthened my belief that the same person may have butchered Pendleton and the Pueblo cops.

"That's all, Mr. DeLong. Any questions?"

"If I trace this back to the assault on my home, would you let me talk to Pendleton's mistress?"

"One of my men will ask her." He shrugged. "I have no objection."

"Is there more information that might be useful to the AFI? A license plate number or the mistress' identity?"

"We doubt she participated in the abduction. In Juarez, a beautiful woman must use caution and not offend the wrong person. These are dangerous times, more so if you carry a high profile. At the moment, her desire is to fade away and blend in. If she were part of a plot, she would have fled weeks ago. Is there anything else?"

"Why me? Why not make direct contact with your friends at the AFI?"

"Eyes and ears are everywhere in Juarez. A dozen people know you are sitting here right now, and you would not enjoy meeting any of them. I couldn't risk exposing my relationship with our mutual acquaintance." He stood, and his height surprised me. We stood eye-to-eye. "It took courage for you to travel here, and for that, I thank you."

"Thank you, Señor. May I call upon you in the future?"

"No promises, but you know how to reach me."

He shook my hand, and I felt the hood slide over my eyes.

"*Adios, Señor*. I trust you will keep details of our meeting to yourself, except for that which you need to pass on to our mutual friends. It would be to your benefit to do so."

"You have my word." My voice sounded muffled, even to me.

The ride back proved uneventful. At the hotel, I checked my voicemail and saw a message from Frank. When I listened, I discovered he and

Carlos were on their way to Phoenix. Could I please meet them there tomorrow morning? *They couldn't have worried much about me.* I called and booked a 7:35 a.m. flight. My mind swirled with possible scenarios, and I wanted to talk to Frank and Carlos about what I'd learned. The clock on the bed stand registered well after midnight, so it would have to keep until tomorrow. My skin crawled with a burning need for action. The next few hours would pass like days.

Chapter 28

Frank

Frank Hunter struggled to unwrap himself from the bed sheets without disturbing Amanda. He looked at her and felt an affection he hadn't known for years. She might not be a classic beauty, but she took away his breath. *Oh, to hell with it.* He leaned over and kissed her on the cheek.

"Have to run. I'm meeting with Carlos and another guy in half an hour."

She half-opened sleepy eyes and nodded.

"Uh-huh. Call me later." She waved a tired hand at his retreating back.

After that first smitten night, they'd spent the maximum time together their jobs allowed. Amanda knew about Monroe Delong's trip to Juarez and told Frank she wanted details. He promised to provide them, even though Department regs forbade discussing open investigations. Frank liked talking to her, but the transgression nagged at the back of his mind.

Carlos had awakened him earlier and told him about big news that they needed to discuss in private. Well aware that his ass would be grass if the Bureau discovered his role in arranging an unauthorized contact with a cartel chieftain, Frank took precautions when he left Amanda's place.

He checked every parked car on the street and looked in windows across the way. The sun had not yet shown its full force, and the glare was minimal. He turned off his cell phone—a few blackout minutes wouldn't matter—and felt under the bumpers and fenders for GPS trackers. Call it paranoia, but he couldn't shake the feeling of being played. Satisfied, but not positive, he climbed behind the wheel, flipped a one-eighty, and sped away. The view in his rearview mirror looked clean.

A glance at the dashboard clock told him he could take an extra five minutes. For the hell of it, he went through standard tail-shaking procedure. Again, he didn't detect anyone following. *Getting old if I'm worried about my pension.* He grinned in the mirror and gunned the

Crown Vic up to seventy-five. He parked two blocks from the coffee shop and walked the rest of the way.

I watched Frank through the glass door. He approached, looked right and left, and entered. He smiled when he saw us in the corner booth.

"Hey, *Amigos. Buenos dias.*"

"Frank, you look like a man in love. What aren't you telling us?" Carlos returned his greeting.

Frank's ears reddened. He held up his hands, palms outward, and shook them back and forth. *Don't ask questions.*

I had told Carlos the highlights of my excursion and saw the fire it ignited.

Last night, when my adrenaline had stopped pumping, I popped half an Ambien and enjoyed a few hours' sleep—the first REM time in over a week. Going to see El Jefe had been therapeutic. A story I could get my mind around, and perhaps a track I could follow to the killer. Now, I saw hope in Carlos' eyes and wanted to see the same in Frank's.

"Tell him what you told me, Monroe." Carlos nudged my elbow.

Frank poured a coffee and held it over my cup.

"Thanks, but I've swilled three already. Better eat before I jump through the ceiling."

Frank looked at me and raised his eyebrows.

"First, I want to thank both you assholes for abandoning me in Juarez last night." The inflection in my voice said I wasn't joking.

"My fault, Monroe," said Frank. "I needed to get back, and we couldn't risk calling on your cell. Might make the boss-man suspicious."

"It must have been damned important."

"Bureau business." Frank blushed.

I figured it for bullshit, but I let it pass.

I repeated the story, playing down my role. I wanted Carlos and him to focus on the new twist, tear it apart, decipher what it meant, and help me to an answer.

"You got big balls, Monroe. Nice work."

I saw new respect in his eyes.

"What does it mean?" I don't know what I expected. Maybe for Frank to apply his knowledge and acumen and come up with an instant solution.

"I'm scheduled to talk to El Jefe after lunch," Carlos said. "With luck, he'll give us information on the mistress."

He and Frank had decided to use my code name for Carlos' cartel contact.

"Anything on our other mysterious woman?"

"Elizabeth Pendleton must know the ropes. Maybe she crossed the border to Mexico and went from there. We're ninety-nine percent certain that she didn't fly out of any U.S. airport. Homeland Security may not be geniuses, but they keep pretty accurate tabs on citizens traveling on a passport, and the new computer systems give us rapid access." Frank said.

"Doesn't it make you suspicious? Innocent people don't disappear. I bet a dollar to a *burrito* that it has to do with the money her husband pilfered," I said.

Frank spent the next twenty minutes relating Amanda's briefing.

"You could have told us before. Sounds like motive to me." Carlos looked agitated.

"It's preliminary, and I honest-to-God forgot. Everything's based on guesswork, and Amanda says it's going to be hard to prove unless we find the deposit accounts."

"Have you run a full background on Mrs. Pendleton?" I chimed in.

Frank's face reddened.

"That's another thing I forgot."

"For Christ's sake, Frank. You're acting like a lovesick schoolboy. You don't tell us about the forensic exam, now this?"

Other people sat at a nearby table, and Carlos kept his voice to a subdued roar. "Tell me."

I looked at one of those God-awful velvet matador paintings hanging on the wall. No way did I want to get involved in this pissing match.

"The name on their marriage license application was Oliveras, but there's no SS number or tax returns for an Elizabeth Oliveras that match the age or current and former addresses. That's not unusual. Maybe she was married when she met Pendleton. There's a ton of possibilities. Another thing—we couldn't find a passport issued for either Elizabeth Pendleton or Oliveras, but we know she and her late husband traveled abroad." Frank blurted it out.

"How about their tax returns?" Carlos said.

"Married for almost two years, but he listed himself on a request for extension last year as 'married, filing separately.' Nada for this year, and he missed the October 15 deadline. He paid what he estimated he owed, so no IRS flags. If I were forced to guess, I'd say he predicted the future and made plans."

"How about her returns? If they filed separately, she must have used either Pendleton or Oliveras," I said.

"We'll keep checking. That part doesn't add up."

Carlos jabbed a finger at Frank. "They were in it together. Find her, and we wrap up the whole *enchilada*."

"What do you care? We already know from El Jefe that no one can prove a crime occurred on Mexican soil. That's why you came here. When we get authorization to release the information, you're off the hook." Frank looked dejected.

"And they won't release it until we solve it from this side of the border. It's a chicken and egg thing."

Frank hunched over his coffee and shook his head. "I'm fucking this up, ain't I?"

"Don't be an ass. You're distracted. I'm sorry I lost my patience. If it weren't for you, I might be cooling my heels in a FBI bureaucrat's waiting room right now. You're my friend and ally, and I haven't forgotten either of those facts." Carlos punched him lightly in the arm.

"So what's next?" Frank's spirits rose visibly.

Carlos glanced at me, then turned in Frank's direction.

"I'll set up a meet for Monroe and the mistress. You track down a warrant on the hostage negotiator's report. And we both need to chill. Mrs. Pendleton can wait until we find out what went down in Juarez."

"Wait a minute. What makes you think I'll go back to Juarez to see anybody? And don't talk about me like I'm not sitting here." I was angry.

"What do I tell a judge to get a warrant—a Mexican drug lord told us such and such? I need to think about how we play this." Frank chewed on his bottom lip, ignoring my outburst.

Carlos tapped the table. "Don't forget, Amigos, El Jefe has to remain our secret. It would be dangerous for all of us if it slips out, and I'll lose my best resource."

"Hey, listen to me." I slapped the table, and both flicked their eyes my way. "You'll set up a meeting for me and the mistress? First I've heard of it."

"Tell me about your meeting with El Jefe. What did he look like? Where did he live?" Frank switched subjects, avoiding eye contact.

"I gave him my word. Hell, if you can't get that kind of information from Carlos, what makes you think I'll give it up?" I was momentarily distracted, but becoming frustrated.

"Fair enough. Call it curiosity. I thought it was worth a try." He slumped back in the soft booth cushions and shot Carlos a wry look.

"You need to talk to the mistress." Carlos nodded at me.

"Thanks for asking. Exactly how do we do that? He didn't tell me her name or how to contact her. He said she wants to stay out of it. I asked him if I could see her provided I found a connection between Pendleton and the murders at my home. He said to contact him through you."

"If I can set it up, will you go?" Carlos said.

I hesitated a fraction before answering. "I don't like it, and I sure don't like you two assuming I'll do whatever you decide for me, but I'm in for the duration."

My mind jumped to what I could tell Darlene. She wouldn't like me going to Mexico to meet with Pendleton's beautiful former mistress. "I need to talk this over with Darlene and establish a schedule. Right now, we're scatter-shooting. The information from the cartel boss looks promising, but I need coherence. How about you two?" I checked out Frank who was gazing out the window.

"Don't forget what I said about us being at a dead end," Carlos said. "We're still there, except for the glimmer of light you've provided, Monroe. I'll work on setting you up with the mistress, and one of us needs to get on Mrs. Pendleton's trail." He jerked his head Frank's way.

Frank snapped back from wherever his mind had drifted.

"She must have left a track when she vamoosed. We'll find it. And there's the code Carlos discovered. We have so many computer models for that sort of thing that one of them is bound to come up with a suggestion. Once we get it, either Carlos or I can investigate its origin. Where's Darlene now?"

"She's staying in Santa Fe. A neighbor's been caring for our animals, and the house …. We have things we need to do. I think I should give her a hand. Call me and let me know about the mistress. I can be in Juarez in three hours."

"We'll go together—like last time," Frank said. "A lot easier for you to cross the border if you're with me, and since we're not yet revealing the suspected U.S. origin of the Pendleton crime, I have reason to go."

The meeting over, I rose to leave.

"Take care. I'll see you both day after tomorrow—if things go the way we want. But don't fuck with me like this again. *Comprende?*"

They looked startled, but both nodded.

Once more into the breach.

Chapter 29

Manuel Hoppe

Darlene ran her finger across the dining room table and studied the mark it left in the dust. The unforgiving dryness of the high desert doesn't offer mercy for a week's neglect. She sprayed the table and started to wipe it with a paper towel. She had wanted to come home before Jack returned.

Police tape still wrapped the *casita*, and when she looked out the window, she could see Franco's bloodstains on the porch. The cops had cleared the scene, and she'd contacted a cleaning service. They promised to come *mañana* and clean where she couldn't. In the meantime, busy hands offered salvation. That and the animals.

The dogs had gone wild when she pulled up in the rental car earlier that day, jumping on her, licking, and barking insanely. She'd hugged them and gone inside to greet the cats. They seemed indifferent compared to Atticus and Jem, but they were cats, and that said it all.

Ray Green stopped by to relay scanty animal news, and she devoured every tidbit. Solace comes in many shapes.

"I'm so happy you're coming home," Darlene said.

I heard her voice crack.

"Must be rough. Alone there. I thought you would wait for me."

"I found something, Jack, and it makes me nervous."

"What?"

"Whoever tried to kill Franco and Consuela searched our office. They left the tax return file open, and last year's is missing."

"Jesus Christ. He knows our names. Are the cops still on the gate? Are you carrying your gun?"

"Yes to both, and I'm not sleeping here tonight. I'll stay in town with Lilly."

"Good idea. I'll visit the Pueblo after I get back and see if I can hire security guards from the casino to work part-time. Half a dozen of them could cover our place night and day. Tough young dudes."

"Why do we need them? Aren't you staying home for a while?"

"A day. There's something I need to do. I'll tell you about it when I get there."

She groaned and I wished I could be the bearer of better news.

"I can't let this rest, Sweetheart, and Frank and Carlos need my help."

"When do you get in?"

"Tomorrow morning. I'll rent a car at the airport and drive up. Easier than you coming to meet me. The 'vette'll be safe in the hotel garage here."

"Thanks. I couldn't face the hundred miles." She hesitated. "I almost forgot—Will called, and you're clear at the courthouse, so you can put Monroe DeLong back into mothballs."

"Zeke came through. Good. I'd rather be Jack than Monroe."

"I was kind of looking forward to sleeping with a different man."

The first laugh from her in several days.

"I'll wear a mask. You won't know the difference. By the way, have you been to visit Franco and Consuela again?"

"Of course. I've gone every day. They ask about you. Consuela's still suffering from a bad headache, and Franco is coming around, but the doc says it'll be another week before they come home."

"Yeah, I feel guilty about not being there for them, but I'll make it up later. You know how I hate those places anyway."

I'd only been hospitalized twice in my life—the knock on my head from the tree branch and at an army field installation many years ago. I'd caught a spent round in my left shoulder. I tired of hearing how lucky I was that it hadn't hit a few inches to my right and damaged my spinal cord.

Everything was so complicated. I wanted to think a simple answer existed, but I knew it didn't. That night I dreamed of Juarez, drug lords, beautiful women, and blood. Ambien, vodka, and Nyquil—the perfect cocktail if you hungered for sleep.

Manuel Hoppe had already driven by the property three times. The cop on the gate didn't concern him. He'd purchased a 1982 red Chevy pickup from a local, a guy only too happy to take five hundred cash, no questions asked. No rust—after all, the car grew up in New Mexico—but dusty and beaten. The straw *sombrero* looked like every other farmer's in the county. He thanked whatever gods he worshipped that the AC still worked.

He focused on his primary objective—recovering his money. Death and mayhem might have to take a back seat to practical matters, although it pained him to forego these pleasures.

The rental car parked on the hill leading to the house told him that someone had arrived earlier in the day, but who? Maybe Jack and Darlene? He loved that he could put names to the faces in the picture he had taken from their house. If they were home, the ransom money was with them. They'd be on high alert and dangerous. Better play this smart. Case the *rancho* today and return tonight. If the cop still guarded the entrance, he'd take him out.

His fourth drive-by came at six-thirty. He saw Darlene pull out of the gate, wave at the sentry, and take off down the road. He followed at a discreet distance. Fifteen miles later she pulled into a driveway of a home not far from the Santa Fe Plaza. She carried a small overnight bag when she walked to the door.

Hubby must still be out of town. No sense in breaking in tonight. He might get one shot, and why waste it if the money's not there? Besides, getting Jack to talk while he put cigarettes out on Darlene's stomach would be much more fun and productive. Best to wait until they were both in his sights.

His other problem—Mrs. Pendleton. She had pointed out that she knew his identity, which made her expendable. Trouble is, he didn't know where she was, though he had a good idea. Lots of loose ends. He didn't like it, but it gave him things to think about.

He thought he needed to fight the urges. Cool. He'd been efficient and deadly for so long he almost believed that person was him. But inside, he wanted other things. He sat in his truck, a block away from the house Darlene had entered. The window down, he chain-smoked and tried to make his eyes bore through the walls. He wanted to see her naked.

After three attempts, Darlene reached Jack on his cell.

"I'm at Lilly's, and I'm edgy, Jack. I think someone's watching me."

"I don't want to frighten you, but it's possible. Stay inside. Call Will and ask him to swing by Lilly's place tonight. Don't go home tomorrow. Call Ray Green and ask him for one more favor. I'll be there soon."

"God, I hope so. There's another thing…"

114

Darlene looked down at her left hand and realized she'd marked her palm with her nails.

"The picture of you and me that sat on your desk is gone. I didn't notice it at first, but knew the room seemed out of balance. You know the one I mean?"

"Yeah. Christ. So he knows our names *and* what we look like. It has to be connected to Pendleton. Break-in artists wouldn't care about a photo."

"Can't we get rid of the money?" She spoke in a low voice so Lilly couldn't overhear.

"We could, but it's our link to whoever took a shot at Franco and Consuela and killed the cops. Frank and Carlos think we need it for bait. Once it goes on the news that we've recovered it, our boy will high-tail it out of Dodge."

"We need to find a solution to the animals until this is over. I think it's dangerous for Ray to go to the house to care for them. I hate to do it, but we might have to kennel them for the duration. We can put enough food out for the chickens and guineas to last a week, but the dogs and cats need constant attention."

Darlene knitted her brow while she considered options.

"Work on that from Lilly's until I get in tomorrow. We'll pack them off to that high-end kennel and close the house." Jack said.

"I can do that. Please hurry home, Baby. This is the toughest spot we've ever landed in, and I need you." She took another peek through the side of the window curtain.

Hoppe dozed off, but an inner alarm woke him when the Sheriff's car pulled around the corner and onto his block. He laid his head on the passenger seat and pulled the Woodsman from his shoulder holster. He extended his arm so it wouldn't be impaired if he needed to fire.

The flashlight beam swept through the window and illuminated the cab, but he felt certain the cop couldn't see him, laying down as he was. If he did, too bad for him. He heard the car stop and honk twice, then start up and pull away. Decision time.

The pickup truck sat on a slight grade. He pushed in the clutch and allowed it to roll fifty feet down the road. When he opened the driver's side door, the interior light flashed, but he doubted if anyone noticed. He might not get this good an opportunity again, so while he wanted to kill them when they could look in each other's eyes, this might be almost as satisfying.

The Woodsman dangled in his hand, cocked and ready to fire. He took small steps to avoid stumbling in the darkness. No streetlights on this side of town. Not quaint enough for the neighborhood elitists.

The living room looked dark, but a left rear window gleamed with light. He opened the metal gate and winced at the squeak. He sidled around the corner, back brushing the stucco walls. Not more than ten feet to the window. He half-raised his pistol.

The flashlight beam missed his eyes, or it would have blinded him. The report of a heavy-caliber handgun rang next to his ear, and stucco chips flew, cutting his cheek and sending warm blood coursing down his face. He emptied the Woodsman's clip in the direction of the shot, then turned and ran. He leaped the fence like a sprinter and pounded down the road to his truck. No more bullets came his way, and he didn't hang around to find out what damage his fusillade may have caused.

The old pickup groaned when he popped the clutch and gunned the gas, but it screeched from its parking spot. He slowed down and turned on the headlights a block later. His haversack lay on the seat within hand's reach. He pulled a pint bottle of tequila from the outside pocket and took a long swig. A close call. His hand shook, not in fear, but in anticipation of his next encounter with Darlene. Killing her was going to be a pleasure beyond his dreams.

Chapter 30

Home

The drive home from the Albuquerque airport seemed to take forever. I'd made it dozens of times, but this felt different. When Santa Fe came into view, I released a long breath. Twenty more miles. I took the bypass that circumvented downtown and headed north on the 599. I punched my speed dial and heard Darlene pick up.

"On my way home, sweetheart. Stay put at Lilly's. I'll check a few things out at the house, pick up clean clothes, and meet you there in two hours."

"Jack, we're in trouble. I moved to a hotel."

I knew from her voice that this was serious.

"Lay low. Nothing will happen downtown in daylight. Did you make arrangements for the pets?"

"Listen to me, Jack. Something happened at Lilly's last night. I didn't call you because there wasn't anything you could do."

"What? Are you okay?"

"I'm alive, but a prowler took a few shots at me. It scared me—scared me bad."

I heard the tremble behind the words, but I also recognized resolve.

"Who? Did you see him?

"No. It was dark. A truck was parked outside Lilly's house that I'd seen earlier in the day near our gate. It made me suspicious, so I took my gun and used the back door. I waited by the corner, and this guy came creeping around the wall with a pistol in his hand. I took a shot, but hit the edge of the stucco. There was blood, so I must have done a little damage."

"My God, Franco and Consuela's attacker. Did you call the police?"

"They came right away. Neighbors reported the gunshots. They didn't find anything, but they insisted that Lilly and I move here."

"I should never have left you alone. What do you want me to do?"

"I'm worried about the animals. I don't want to go back to the house without you, and they're by themselves. Can you take them to the kennel?"

"Of course—add an hour to my time. I'll have to do the paperwork."

"Where are we staying tonight?"

"Wherever you are now. Don't move."

"I'm paying for Lilly's room. She's been fantastic about this."

"Don't worry about anything except staying safe. I'll put out enough food for your birds and make sure the house is locked down. Anything you need me to pick up?"

"I didn't unpack my carry-on. I can get by with whatever's in it."

"10-4. One of the many things I love about you—you're a minimalist."

"What are you going to do with the bag?"

It took me a second.

"The money? In the trunk. I'll stop by Wells Fargo and get a safety deposit box."

"Are you totally nuts? You're carrying two and a half million dollars around in your Corvette?"

"Seemed like a bad idea to leave it around the house. *Tranquillo*, Baby. I'll put it in the bank today."

"Good. I don't want to be anywhere around that thing. Have your gun with you?"

"I checked my suitcase when I flew. No problems. It's locked and loaded."

"Later."

I heard her kiss the phone.

A cop car sat parked next to the mailbox with a guy I knew dozing in the front seat. I pulled up alongside and rolled down my window. His opened at almost the same time.

"Hector, I'm locking the place down for a few days. Check with your sergeant. We won't need a guard for now." I'd decided hiring security people from the casino wouldn't work. Two dead cops were enough.

"Hey, Jack. How you doin'? I heard about the shootout last night. Darlene okay?"

"Scared, otherwise unharmed."

"She's a tough one. I'll let the Sarge know you want him to pull us off."

"Thanks. Made me feel better knowing you were here."

"No problem. I hope we catch the fucker that did this. The cops who bought it were both friends of mine—Franco, too." He scowled and made a fist.

"Yeah. It's hard on all of us. Anyway, thanks again." I pressed the window switch, waved, and turned into the driveway. About halfway down, I hit the remote for the gate and watched it slide to the right. I was glad I'd remembered to pull the opener from the 'vette. My chest constricted when I saw our place wrapped in police tape. I shouldn't have let Darlene come back here last night. When I jumped from the car, the dogs rushed me and knocked me back with their enthusiasm. They'd be heartbroken to go to the kennel.

I sped through my chores, putting out a week's worth of pellets and half a dozen heads of cabbage for the 'ladies'—Darlene's name for our chickens and hens. The eggs would have to accumulate. I put the two kitties into cat carriers and left them on the porch. Protest meowing filled the air.

Back inside, I grabbed clean clothes. The twenty-gauge lay beside the bed. I stuffed it and a box of shells into Darlene's extra overnight bag. Extra firepower wouldn't hurt. I used a small duffel from the top of the closet for a liquor cabinet. Bottles of Patron, Absolute, Johnny Black, lime juice, agave syrup, and Cointreau. Might be a long stay at the hotel. What else? I checked the freezer and pulled out a carton of Marlboro Lights for Darlene. Satisfied, I rattled the doors, noting the temporary repair job where the intruder had broken in—I wondered who fixed it. Windows closed, recirculating fan on, alarm set. I locked up and carried my load to the rental car.

Jem and Atticus sat by the back door, noses in the air like they knew something was about to happen. I put the bags in the trunk, the cats on the front seat, and opened the back door for my boys. They jumped in without hesitation and waited for me to roll down their windows. They loved to ride with the wind blowing in their faces.

I talked to the animals on the way to the kennel. It wasn't like transporting them to a gulag. The animal habitat cost what you might pay for a first-class human hotel, and offered individual exercise and care. Still, they'd miss their freedom, a sensation I understood too well.

Atticus and Jem sniffed the air within a couple of miles of the place. They looked at me with those big brown eyes that said, "How could you, Dad?" I left them in the car while I completed the paperwork, then took all four to their new home—for a week at most. It wasn't easy to leave them, but I kept telling myself they were better off here. Safer, at any rate.

I talked to Ray Green about the horses. He agreed to stop by every day for grooming and feeding and to check on the goats. Exercise would have to wait until I returned, although Ray said he might be able to take them for a run in a couple of days. Sapphire and her pal romped in a good-sized pasture, and a lip of the river cut under the south-side fence so they always enjoyed plenty of fresh water. I didn't worry about them.

I stopped at the bank and signed forms for a large safe deposit box. *Should I swallow the key?* I laughed to myself. I felt like I had accomplished a great deal by taking care of the animals and stashing the money—none of which would've been necessary if I hadn't stumbled across that satchel ten days ago. No time for regrets. *What's done is done—but now it's time for payback.*

Part 4

Rosa Lara

Chapter 31

Rosa

In her sixteenth year, Rosa Lara murdered her mother. She buried the body behind the shack where they lived in Chalco, east of Mexico City. Rosa knew nobody would miss a notorious drunk, crack addict, and whore who had lived in and out of jail from the time Rosa could remember.

For a couple of years after the killing, Rosa felt happy. She lived alone in the shanty. Without her mother around, she could give it a good cleaning and erase the stale smell of the vile woman who gave birth to her. She went to school and waitressed nights in a run-down café, earning enough to feed herself and pay the utilities. When mail came for her mother, Rosa dumped it into the trash, and, in so doing, missed the delinquent tax notices the State sent. When *la policia* came to evict her two days after her high school graduation, she felt more bemused than alarmed. Rosa packed her meager belongings, went on the road, and hitchhiked to Juarez.

"What's your name?" she had asked the Indian-looking boy behind the counter at the KFC located near the Hotel Lucerna in Ciudad Juarez.

"Steadman." A shy smile pulled at the corners of his mouth. Dark and handsome, his long, thick, braided hair hung well over his collar. His looks bespoke a way with the ladies. "What's yours?"

"Call me Rosa." She felt like the butterflies in her stomach swirled around her head. "What's with the name?"

"I'm Meskito Indian." He stood straighter. "My family escaped from Honduras many years ago. I'm named after a great hero."

Rosa discovered instant madness with Steadman and started living with him a week later. After three months, Rosa turned up pregnant and Steadman once again escaped.

"Pregnant? Are you nuts?" She stared at the nurse in the clinic where she went to check out why her periods no longer visited her. Rosa wasn't stupid, but you could call her careless. It took her five months to realize she'd missed her cycle and to notice the excess tummy weight. "How about an abortion? How much does that cost?" She grabbed the nurse's arm.

"*Pobre ángel.* You might be third trimester. I wouldn't recommend it unless there were complications, and you look healthy to me. You could cross the border to El Paso, but it would be expensive."

She gave birth a month before her nineteenth birthday in the charity ward of Hospital Angeles. She couldn't remember everything she shouted out during labor, but knew it referenced her dead mother. She lucked out. Neither the doctor nor nurse in attendance at the birth appeared to give a shit about the burdens on their patients' minds. No one ever mentioned her confession.

Preternatural beauty proved a blessing and a curse. She sensed that it opened doors for her and made it easy to get a job, but it also made her lazy. She came to rely on her looks and fabulous body to see her through life, and what better or easier way than to dance in a strip bar. When she looked in the mirror, she saw thick, copper-colored hair, and a suntan that almost covered the freckles across her nose and forehead, a memento from her father.

She performed the lap-dance routine in the best Juarez strip joints and found it repulsive. Much easier to find a rich *gringo*. It would make her a whore, and she hated the thought of it, but she needed to support her baby. When Pendleton walked into the club one warm winter's evening, Rosa knew she'd met her man.

Pendleton treated her like a lady. She moved to a good address with a swimming pool and furnished it from stores across the border. He visited every two weeks. She grew fond of him and their lovemaking, and never thought to betray him. For over a year, they enjoyed what she considered a perfect relationship. A few weeks before his kidnapping, an encounter had occurred, one that would prove pivotal in her life.

"Señorita Lara."

The preemptory command caused her to stop in the middle of the street. She turned and came face-to-face with a swarthy, though well-dressed man.

"You don't remember me, do you?" he said.

Rosa shook her head.

"A customer of yours when you danced at the club."

She felt a sinking feeling in her stomach.

"My boss wants to talk to you. Don't be afraid. No harm will come to you or your child."

The mention of her son carried an implicit threat she couldn't ignore.

Within the hour, the man Monroe DeLong had nicknamed 'El Jefe' sat across from her. She pressed her hands on her thighs so he wouldn't notice their trembling. His face looked familiar. She'd seen it in newspapers and government television ads against the drug cartels. She took the same trip Monroe DeLong took, hooded to conceal the location of this house. She didn't want the man to know she recognized him.

"Señorita Lara. Thank you for agreeing to see me. Believe me, I have no ill will toward you. I want your help. And, please, I am sure you recognize my face, but I feel safe with you possessing that knowledge." He inhaled an American cigarette, careful to blow the smoke away from her. "Can my butler bring you a cool drink? Perhaps a lemonade?"

"*No, gracias, Señor.*" Her voice sounded firm.

"Very well, let's get on with it. Please do not lie to me or evade. I know everything about you. Do you understand?" He lifted his hand and the servant placed a glass of lemonade next to him.

"*Sí, Señor.*"

"Mr. Pendleton is a man of great wealth. Business associates have informed me of his inquiries about certain transactions he would like to carry out."

"I know nothing of this, Señor."

"Of course, but no matter. You can do him and me a great service."

"And what would that be, Señor?"

"I have what he wants. He has what I want. You become our intermediary. I will compensate you well, and you have nothing to fear."

"Please explain." Rosa's confidence in her survival grew.

"He has money to sell. I will buy it from him and place the proceeds in a safe place. Trust me, this is a thing he wants very much." He sipped on his drink.

Rosa thought for a moment. She knew he referred to money laundering. Why would her lover want to move money? Perhaps things were about to change in her life. A little insurance wouldn't hurt. After all, fidelity to Pendleton meant one thing, but her first loyalty lay with her son. She recalled the conversation with Pendleton when he had told her he wanted her to leave Juarez with him. She dismissed it as married-man talk, but perhaps he meant it.

"*Si*. I will do this. Tell me how." She felt her fortunes wane and wax with each turn of the conversation.

"The next time Señor Pendleton comes to see you—I think that will be the day after tomorrow—tell him of our conversation. Explain to him my position in Juarez. After he has agreed to hear my proposal, contact Enrique, the man who brought you here today. You and Enrique will arrange for Pendleton to visit me."

"And, if he refuses?"

"Make sure he doesn't. He cares for you and wouldn't want anything bad to happen to you or your son. If necessary, you may say this to him. Am I clear?"

"*Si, Señor*." Her hands started to shake again. This situation loomed as something her beauty could not save her from.

"And Señora, perhaps when all is settled, you and I could share dinner here at my *hacienda*?"

She let her breath go in relief. "I would be honored, Señor."

Questions swirled in her mind on the ride home. She wanted the day after tomorrow to hurry. She felt an excitement in her chest she hadn't felt for a long time.

Chapter 32

Darlene

After one night at the hotel, I checked out. Darlene would stay put for a few days. I intended to drive my rental car to the Albuquerque airport and take a plane to Phoenix.

"Be careful, Jack. I'm scared for you."

"Scared for me? You're the one with a close call. Spend however long you can tolerate inside the hotel. If you go out, go with someone, preferably Will or Tommy. Call and let them know what's up. Sheila's should be safe, so if you feel like waiting tables, go ahead." I smiled and rubbed her arm.

"Can't wait to relive my youth. Maybe I'll call Tommy and see if he could use an extra hand. It is tourist season."

I appreciated Darlene. No whining or crying. Pragmatic and caring.

"And Jack?"

Whoops.

"This thing with Pendleton's mistress. Tell me if she's beautiful, and don't do anything foolish." Almost an off-hand remark.

"No matter what she is, she isn't you."

"I love you." She put her hand on my face and kissed me.

"Me too." I squeezed her and rubbed my nose in her hair.

I made the trip to the Albuquerque airport in fifty-eight minutes, a new record. Must be a symptom of my savant behavior to keep track of such things. A short hop to Phoenix, a cab to the resort, and a call to Carlos.

"Have you made the arrangements?" I hungered for action and answers. I'd be a poor detective because I lacked the patience to sift through evidence and testimony.

"Monroe, glad to hear from you. It's on for tomorrow tonight. Meet Frank and me in the hotel lobby, and we'll go through the interrogation plan we've laid out."

"Do I waterboard her?"

"Only if she won't talk."

I went to my room and called Darlene to check on her and let her know I'd arrived. I decided not to tell her about my planned trip tomorrow night. No reason to stress her further. We could talk about it later. My cell buzzed to let me know my friends were downstairs.

We gathered around a patio table. The sun had disappeared behind high clouds and a rain-scented breeze cooled the air. Frank and Carlos ordered beers and I asked for an iced tea.

Rage boiled in me, and I couldn't hold it back.

"That sick fuck attacked Darlene in Santa Fe."

I almost choked on the words.

Both men sat up straight.

"Monroe," Frank grabbed my forearm, "what happened? Where, when?"

I gave a synopsis of what I knew.

"Now it's time to wrap this thing, or I'm getting out. I can't risk Darlene."

"Monroe, we all want to close the door on this guy, but we can't do it without you. Stay strong," Carlos said.

I knew he was right. I'd needed to vent, but now it was time to get down to business.

"Tell me what to do," I said.

"The mistress's name is Rosa Lara. Here's her address and phone number." Carlos handed me a slip of paper. "El Jefe asked that we not spook her. I suspect she's on his payroll."

"What do we need to know about Pendleton?"

Frank took over. "Verify that he came to see her the night of the abduction. What did she see? The kidnapper—Mexican or *gringo*? How about a license plate on the RV? Did she hear from him after they took him? Does she have any idea who might have wanted to hurt him?" He handed me another piece of paper with the questions.

"Any background on her?"

"Very little," Carlos said. "She has a five-year-old son, and they live in a good *barrio*. Former lap dancer. We suspect Pendleton supported her, and I think El Jefe has stepped into his shoes. According to my sources, she's a very beautiful woman with a good head on her shoulders. Remember, Juarez is a tough town, more so for a single woman, and it's not unusual to use her looks to care for herself and the child. Better than the way most people there live."

"Is she involved in drugs?" It would make my trip more dangerous.

"Not that we know of. She has a reputation for being a straight shooter, and according to the girls where she used to dance, she stayed clean and sober. But you never know. Times and people change like the weather down there."

"Should I carry a weapon?"

"No." Frank again. "If a situation came up where you might need it, you'd be so out-gunned it wouldn't matter. Play it cool, and don't aggravate anyone. Plus, you're under El Jefe's protection, for whatever it's worth. He has plenty of enemies, but I think you'll be safe."

"What are the logistics? How do I get there, and, more importantly, how do I get back?"

"We fly to El Paso tomorrow morning and get a hotel. When it comes time, I'll drop you in Juarez at the same café where we met Tito. He, or a *maton* who works for El Jefe, will meet us there and take you to see the woman, and he'll bring you back. I'll wait for you in El Paso. It shouldn't run more than two hours. You have my cell number and vice-versa, so we can maintain contact. If you get into trouble, you could call, but since I won't know where you've gone, it wouldn't help much." Frank shrugged.

"Makes me feel a whole lot safer knowing I can call you to say goodbye."

"Don't worry, Monroe. You'll be okay. I can't envision anything going wrong."

"I'd feel better with my Glock stuck in my waistband, but you're right, Frank. I might be tempted to use it and end up getting my ass shot off."

"Speaking of that, we published a new bulletin at the Bureau today. I'd be remiss if I didn't pass it on."

Carlos and I both looked at Frank.

"It describes escalating violence. Drug gangs roaming the streets of residential neighborhoods, and the Mexican Army unable to control them. These guys are strapped with heavy ordinance and well-organized. Be very careful."

"I hope El Jefe's militia rules. What a fucking mess." I shook my head.

"Okay, Boys. Let's hit it." Carlos stood and grabbed my hand. "This could be the key, Monroe. Suck up those *cajones* and give 'em hell, and give my best to Darlene. She's a tough woman." He clapped me on the shoulder.

128

Chapter 33

Juarez

Come on Tito, or whoever you are. Don't make me stand here. Streets that had appeared innocuous on my last trip took on a sinister hue, and I saw danger in every person who passed. I had dressed down for the trip in old blue jeans and a tee shirt. My hair hung close to my shoulders, and I hadn't shaved in a few days. *Maybe I should have invested in a few tattoos.*

The honk startled me. I looked to my right and saw a man in a black Suburban motion with his hand. It appeared to be the same car I'd traveled in before, so I jogged to it and climbed into the passenger seat.

"*Por favor, Señor.* It would be better if you go in back and laid on the floor. Juarez is, how you say, buzzing tonight. Like a bee. *Si?*"

I didn't know what he meant, but getting on the floor sounded like a good idea. I got in the rear door, locked it, and laid down. The Suburban took off with a jolt, and I made myself passably comfortable. We drove for twenty minutes. I swear I heard gunshots, but with no way to verify, I chalked it off to nerves. Tito skidded to a halt and leaned over the seat.

"We have arrived. Señorita Lara expects you. Ring 3-D and wait until she admits you. I'll meet you here in forty-five minutes. *Comprende?*"

"*Si.*" I sat up to open the door, surprised to see a quiet, pretty neighborhood of condos and apartments. Not what I expected.

I didn't notice the tail, and Tito must have missed it too.

I rang the bell, heard the sound of a buzzer, and the door to the lobby popped open. There were two elevators, and when I pushed 'Up', the door on the right opened. It carried me to three and another surprise. It opened into an apartment entrance. Maybe 3-D occupied the entire floor. I raised my hand to knock when the door opened and a scent of gardenia floated into the entryway. Señorita Lara smiled and motioned for me to come in.

The reason Pendleton visited Juarez so often stared me in the face. The word 'beautiful' sounded inadequate to describe his former mistress. Little or no makeup, hair pulled back in a severe bun, and a facial bone structure that would make any super-model envious. She led me into a lavish sitting area that looked out onto the Juarez Mountains. I lagged behind, admiring her dancer's body in her tight designer jeans, and when she turned to sit, her silk blouse pulled against her breasts. I thought about Darlene and looked out the window at the view.

"Señor Sloan." A velvet voice with little accent. "*Mi patron* instructed me to provide you with whatever you need. I heard about the deaths of the *policia* and the attack on your friends. Please accept my condolences."

Almost staggering. Unassuming sexuality permeated every corner of the room.

"Thank you, Señorita. It's a pleasure to meet you, and I appreciate the opportunity. I also offer my condolences. Not to embarrass you, but I know of your relationship with Señor Pendleton." I kept my eyes fixed on her forehead.

She shrugged. "I considered Robert a kind man, and he treated me with respect. I miss him, but for the sake of my son, I carry on." She nodded toward what I took for her boy's bedroom. "May I offer you refreshment? A cocktail or an iced tea?"

"Tea sounds great. Sugar please." *Maybe I want to watch her walk to the kitchen.*

She returned in a few minutes and sat back on the couch, kicked off her shoes, and tucked her bare feet underneath her fabulous butt. "Now, please, what do you want to know?"

"I understand the kidnappers took Mr. Pendleton outside your building, and you saw him being forced into what you described as a recreational vehicle. True?"

"Not at all. That's what Robert told me to tell the police."

Huh? "I don't get it. Did you talk to him after the abduction? How could he tell you?"

"Let me explain. About a month ago, Robert told me we were leaving Juarez and moving across the ocean. He didn't—wouldn't say where. He intended to leave his wife and be with me and my son. His heart went out to my little boy. When I asked Robert why or how, he told me not to worry. He would handle the details. He said not to tell anyone, and I didn't."

"Makes sense. We know he moved a lot of cash offshore, but we didn't know he intended to follow it. But what about the R.V.?"

"R.V.? I don't understand. What is R.V.?"

"The recreational vehicle he entered. You said he instructed you to tell the police they forced him?"

"He didn't tell me who the people in the R.V. were." She pronounced the initials with apparent satisfaction. "He said to watch out the window and say what I said. I don't know if they were bad or good people. I don't know why he went with them." She began to cry.

"Did he call you later—after he left? Did you see anyone's face?"

"No, Señor. I never heard from him again. The people he went with—they stayed inside the R.V., so I didn't see them."

"Have you ever met his wife?"

"No, of course not." Her head jerked, and she trained her eyes straight into mine.

I knew she lied.

"What will you do now?" I asked the question even though I already knew the answer.

"Robert left my son and me well-provided for, and perhaps I'll strike up a new friendship." She paused. "Are you married?" A smile flickered on her lips.

The question jolted me.

"*Si, Señorita*. Not available. But I'm sure every man you've ever met is clay in your hands."

"Clay? I don't understand."

"*Arcilla*. You mold it to whatever shape you desire."

"You have kind eyes. Too bad you're, how do you say, spoken for?"

She smiled, and revealed the whitest, most perfect teeth I'd ever seen.

"My loss, Señorita." I felt disoriented. "Thank you for talking to me. I may ask to return. Would you be agreeable?"

"Unfortunately, I don't control things. You would have to ask my *patron*," she said.

"I understand." I stood and stretched my leg muscles. "I need to leave. My ride will be waiting." I extended my hand and she rose from the divan to take it. She pulled me close and kissed my cheek. It would take a man of stone to not feel desire.

Chapter 34

Firefight

A glint of light on metal told me Tito had pulled into the apartment driveway. The black Suburban slid to a halt in front of the door, and I crouched and ran outside and jumped into the back seat.

"Let's go home, Tito."

"Home for you, Señor, not for me. Please stay low. *Es mucho* trouble in the city tonight, and we cross through hostile territory."

"No problem, *Amigo*. Not my war."

I squirmed and made myself half-comfortable on the van floor. Thoughts of Rosa Lara swam in my head. Beautiful, alluring, but dangerous. Women like her mean trouble, and men are such fools that most would risk anything to be with them. I'm a fool, but not that kind. Once I met Darlene, the rest of the world faded into the background.

G-forces pressed me against the door when we turned hard right. Lights of a main roadway reflected from above, and I felt us pick up speed. The soft blurred haloes of street lamps provided eerie luminescence when Tito put the pedal to the metal. The causeway to the bridge that represented sanctuary from the drug wars couldn't be far.

Tito slammed the brakes and the sound of a car smashing into us, high-right, chilled my body. I knew what it meant. We thudded to a stop, pushed at an angle. The whisper of suppressed automatic weapon fire floated through the window I had cracked for fresh air. Bullets thudded against the side of the car, and the windows crystallized into scattered pieces. Tito swore in Spanish and yanked open his door. I saw the gun in his hand. Another pistol, a .44 Magnum, rested on the passenger seat. I stretched my arm around the tilt-back and pulled it to me.

Tito's Glock barked four or five times and went silent. I peeked above the window ledge and saw three *hombres* bearing down on the Suburban carrying Mac-10's, and they were aimed my way. *Fuck.* Tito had told me the doors were armor-plated so they would need to open them to get at me. I might be able to get off a shot or two before they killed me. I held no illusions about the competitiveness of a six-shot revolver against the 1000-round per minute firing rate of the Ingrams, no matter how unskilled the shooters.

I thought of the old saw about no atheists in foxholes when the *matons* opened up again, the weapons aimed at a target behind the Suburban. The sound of a different caliber penetrated the melee, the reports like thunder over the almost silent Mac-10's. I jerked my head up and saw the three *banditos* hurtle backwards, blood covering the area where their hearts—if they had any to begin with—were supposed to beat. *Christ, what now? A rival gang? El Jefe's men?*

I heard the shout, "American." I pushed open the door and poked the Magnum's barrel outside so whoever had yelled knew I packed iron. A man stood there holding a pistol. He leaned down and placed it on the ground, then moved his hands above his head, palms facing me.

I exited the car and threw Tito's gun back inside. If it was a trap, I wouldn't escape anyway. My rescuer talked to me, and I answered, but I didn't hear the words. I stumbled to his car and got in, shell-shocked. When you're shaken like I was, the rest of the world fades.

I don't know what we talked about on the ride back to El Paso. The border crossing proved easy at this time of night. After he dropped me in front of the Doubletree, I realized I hadn't asked for his name or phone number. I'd think about it in the morning. At that moment, I wanted sleep.

Chapter 35

Manuel Hoppe

Hoppe sat outside the apartment complex. Lights and flashes across the city told him the drug war burned hot tonight. He checked his watch every five minutes or so. Patience came easily to him, but he wanted to know the exact time Sloan exited. The road to the border might prove more difficult than when he had followed him in.

A black Suburban pulled up to the main entrance. Sloan moved to the car and went into the back seat. When the door shut, it took off, tires squealing. Hoppe kept his lights off until they reached a main drag, then switched on the parking beams. He pulled in close behind the Suburban.

They hung a right on Lopez Mateos. He could see the lights of the Rio Grande Mall not far ahead. They were headed for the Cordova Bridge to El Paso.

Sudden movement from an alleyway a hundred yards ahead made him turn his eyes. An old Chevie hurtled from the side street, turned so hard to its left it teetered on two wheels, and slammed into the Suburban. Three men with automatic weapons jumped from the car and began spraying it with bullets.

He saw the driver roll from his seat and return fire, only to be cut down. The three ambushers ran toward the vehicle, guns silent, but leveled. He knew they were searching for passengers.

Hoppe had stopped less than fifty feet from the firefight and blew the car horn, but the attackers paid him no mind. He slid his favorite heavy weapon, a Sig Sauer P220 Elite .45 ACP, from his shoulder holster and clambered out on the side farthest from them. The unmistakable sound of a round chambering in his pistol sent a chill up his arm. What did Duvall say in *Apocalypse Now*? "I love the smell of napalm in the morning." Hoppe loved the smell of cordite and blood.

Sloan might be the only person who knew the money's location. He couldn't afford to let him die.

He raced around to the front of the car where he could get a view of the three men. Now they saw him, wheeled in his direction like they were joined at the hip, and fired with wild abandon. Bullets smacked into the pavement at his feet, and he heard glass shatter behind him. He leveled the Sig, gripping with both hands, and put a round into each of them. The last to die raised surprised eyes at his assailant, but never had a chance to ask the question that might have played on his lips. "*¿Quien es quien?*"

He used care when he approached the Suburban. Sloan might be armed, and he didn't want to get shot. "Friend," he called out. "American. It's safe."

The back door pushed open a few inches and a long magnum barrel pushed through the slot. "Who are you?"

"American security. These guys are dead. Look." He laid his pistol on the ground and held up his hands. "Come to my car, and we'll get the hell out of here."

The door swung open and Sloan emerged, still holding him in his gun sights. It looked like he made his decision because he tossed the revolver back into the car.

"Tito's. I can't carry it across the border," he said.

"Come on. Let's go before we have more visitors." *Tito—the dead driver?*

"Thanks, friend. You saved my ass." Sloan ran to the passenger door and let himself in.

Hoppe looked with regret at the Sig on the pavement. He wouldn't have a chance to stash it with Sloan in the car, and he couldn't carry it through customs. Ah well, with two and a half million, he could buy several new ones. He slid behind the wheel, dropped the car into drive, and sped toward the bridge.

Chapter 36

Frank and Carlos

Frank, Carlos and I sat around our usual table in our favorite El Paso joint. Carlos liked it because management didn't object to cigarette smoke. After the Juarez fiasco, we wanted to regroup and see where we stood. Rosa Lara had ignited a bombshell in the middle of the Pendleton investigation, and Frank and Carlos felt the aftershock. Carlos' once-solid perception of no Mexican connection turned to jelly, and Frank smelled trouble he didn't want.

"I apologize for putting you in harm's way," Frank said. "We forget the intensity of the street violence in Juarez unless we're there to see it. Hell of a lucky break that the Good Samaritan came your way."

"Or an incredible coincidence. I've thought about it, and it's too far-fetched."

"What do you mean?" Carlos looked perplexed.

"The chances of an able, efficient, armed man being on the scene of a confrontation between two rival gangs and putting down those three thugs are a thousand—no—a million, to one. He followed me."

"What?" Frank sputtered beer down his chin. "If that's true, maybe it's the guy we're looking for. The man who killed Pendleton and maybe the two people at your place."

"I don't know who we're looking for, but whoever this was, he knew me and my destination. Maybe El Jefe put him on me like a watchdog, but I don't believe it."

"What did he look like?" Carlos said.

"I don't remember much. Tall and lean. A nondescript face—hard, but no scars or prominent features. I didn't think I'd have to ID him, or I would have looked closer. Sorry."

I rubbed my hands on my face. Talking about last night brought it all back. I'm no coward, but I believed I was about to die. That has an effect. In soldiers they call it PTSD, post-traumatic stress disorder, the same thing that had afflicted me after the shootout at the *rancho* three years ago.

The waitress stopped by, and we ordered two more beers and an ice tea for me. Frank leaned into the table and began to speak.

"The way I see it, there are three possible scenarios for Pendleton's murder. One, his wife hired an assassin and contracted his murder for the offshore money. Two, a dissatisfied client hired a killer because Pendleton stole his money. Or three, it's how it appeared at first blush— snatched and killed by a Mexican drug gang. Shot because he could identify them or for kicks." Frank paused and looked at Carlos and me for confirmation.

"Don't forget," I said, "if what Rosa Lara told me is true, he may have known the people in the RV."

Frank nodded. "Or they could have tricked him, or he might have seen the futility of a struggle. If Rosa wasn't lying, he knew in advance, so the third option doesn't work. No matter. If it is three—murdered by cartel abductors—we're chasing our tails. Chances of catching them are nil. If it's either of the other two, I have an idea."

"Spill it," Carlos said.

"If you walked up to one thousand people on the street and asked them where you could hire a professional assassin, how many would have an answer?"

"None," Carlos said with certainty.

"That means if Mrs. Pendleton or a client hired a hit man to waste him, they needed a reliable contact. We try to keep tabs on independent contract killers around the world. My guess is there are a dozen on the low end, and no more than one hundred on the high. That's not many, and you don't do business with them unless you know somebody."

Could Frank be on to the key to the riddle? I never thought of it in those terms. You read books or see movies, and professional killers seem to hang out on every street corner. I searched my mind to see if I could come up with any way to contact one, and drew a blank.

"How about the cartels? Do they have shooters?" I asked the obvious question.

"They have plenty of homicidal freaks working for them," Carlos said, "but think about Pendleton's death scene. No evidence to connect it with anybody or anything. A couple of meaningless footprints. No shell casings, fingerprints, nada. And, according to the negotiator, a single shot from a distance brought him down. An amateur doesn't fit the profile, and, like you discovered, the drug boys nail their victims with thousands of rounds from automatic weapons. Nothing subtle about it."

137

"You guys know a lot more about this than I, but I don't see how this helps."

"I can go interdepartmental and make inquiries," Frank said. "Find out how much we know about who operated where at the time of Pendleton's death. We could try to establish a geographic link with Mrs. Pendleton or one of the five clients we know about. We may have mug shots you could look over."

"A name from the files looks like a person who might have connections that would enable him to contract out the hit. International arms merchant." Carlos made a note on his napkin and handed it to Frank. "Can you pull it?"

"Sure. The way things are going, the Bureau needs us, so we'll get what we ask for. Amanda tells me they've scoped all possible forensic leads and come up with nothing new."

"Any trace of the five hundred million? Hard to pass that amount under the radar." My sense told me that if we found the money, we'd find the motive, contractor, and killer.

"It sounds like a lot of dough, but in international financial circles, it's peanuts." Frank used a table napkin to wipe the sweat from his forehead.

The A/C cranked overhead, but the sun's heat penetrated the tile roof and pushed up the temperature. He wadded the paper and tossed it at Carlos before continuing.

"There are thousands of banks, a few of which cooperate and many that don't, and boatloads of daily transactions. If it went down over a two-year period, the numbers wouldn't grab anyone's attention. Pendleton seemed like a smart guy. Go back to Señorita Lara for a moment. She thinks he intended to take her with him. He must have had confidence in his scheme, to tell her that much."

"What if Mrs. Pendleton knew about the offshore accounts, and unearthed her husband's plan to ditch her?" Carlos took a deep drag on his cigarette and washed it down with a swig from his beer. "That still makes her the prime suspect. You guys agree?"

"She'd have to know an awful lot. If we could tie her to the Ponzi scheme, I'd feel more certain. Maybe she knows more about the hedge fund business than she let on to us." I said.

"In order to find that out, we need to find her, and the Bureau's drawing a blank. She hasn't used a credit card, an ATM, or her passport. I'll buy a grieving widow wanting to spend time alone after the death of her spouse, but how alone can you get?"

"Can you locate her, Frank?" I wanted to push him.

"I'll get a priority tag on the search. She has to show up on the radar unless she's dead."

"We've ignored the possibility," I said. "But that amount of money could get a lot of people killed."

"Including us." Carlos stated the obvious. "Don't forget, she could also be traveling under a bogus identity."

"Speaking of that," I cleared my throat, "my name isn't Monroe DeLong. It's Jack Sloan. I got into a little fracas with the Sheriff up Santa Fe way, but walked away clean." I fidgeted with the pack of matches Carlos left on the table.

Frank gave a genuine laugh. "Yeah, we already knew that, Jack. I ran you a while ago. By the way, you're clean with the Bureau, so don't sweat it anymore. In fact, I couldn't find your name anywhere in our files. DOD has your veteran's records, but that's about it."

An enormous wave of relief passed through me. The best news in years.

"Thanks, you guys, and thanks for pretending." I smiled at both.

"Think nothing of it," Frank assured me. "We knew you were a stand-up guy despite the weird name. Where in the fuck did you come up with Monroe DeLong?"

I gave them a brief version of my story. The morning dragged on, and we had lots to do. I suggested we reconvene in Phoenix later that night. I wanted to get the itch of Juarez and El Paso off my skin, and an evening at the spa sounded like the perfect tonic. Maybe I should head for Santa Fe tomorrow to see Darlene.

Part 5

Mrs. Pendleton

Chapter 37

Virgin Gorda

"This is your pilot speaking." He cupped his hand around his mouth and spoke in a grave voice. He looked around the jam-packed cockpit. Nobody sat farther than five feet away. He laughed to let his six passengers in on the joke.

"Seriously," he spoke over his shoulder, "I want to warn you that crosswinds on this landing strip average forty knots. It might get bouncy on the way in, but not to worry. I've landed here without incident nine out of ten times." Nobody laughed, and he turned to look at them and grin.

"Turn your fucking head around and watch what you're doing."

The pilot started. It would be hard to miss the vicious look in the woman's eyes. He turned his to the front so fast he thought he heard his vertebrae snap.

The landing strip was no more than a thousand feet long. The plane bucked and rolled on the short approach and seemed to hang in the air before it touched down within spitting distance of the near end of the runway. The pilot jammed on the brakes and reversed the props with a roar, and they landed.

"Never lost a passenger yet," the pilot boasted and laughed. He took a peek at a pair of contemptuous eyes and abandoned his routine.

Mrs. Pendleton, Elizabeth, rented a villa about twenty minutes from the airfield in Virgin Gorda, an eight-square-mile piece of rock in the British Virgin Islands, near Tortola. Not among her usual haunts, but she wanted isolation. She could be extradited, but the chances of anyone finding her living under an assumed name with a fake passport in this part of the world were remote.

Her guidebook had said she could find restaurants and bars within easy driving distance in an area dubbed "The Valley." She pulled the rental jeep into the villa driveway and looked around. At least she enjoyed a great view and a private swimming pool. She lifted her eyes to the porch and saw the staff that awaited her. She had requested a maid and a pool boy, and had hoped against hope that one of them would look attractive. *Ugh.* Maybe she'd have better luck in the bars.

She knew people considered her a beautiful woman. The kind who made men and women stop and gape when she entered the room. She knew Pendleton thought so those first few months. But after she revealed her savage nature, his interest had waned. Not that he didn't appreciate her advice on his Ponzi scheme. He told her once that he'd never met anyone who knew so much about scamming people.

Tall and graceful, her chiseled face bespoke potential sexual delights, and she didn't like to disappoint. Her breasts were man-made, but such a perfect job, you wouldn't know unless you squeezed or sucked them and felt the implants. *Not bad for fifty-two.* She pirouetted and admired her new blond hair in the mirror.

"Piña Colada." Elizabeth sat in a Valley bar that smelled of spilled drinks and old cigarettes. The side windows and curtains stood open to the tropical breeze—otherwise, it might have been uninhabitable.

"What time does this place close?" She directed her question at the bartender, an oily-looking native.

"Ten, maybe ten-thirty—on weekends," he said. "Tonight? Depends on business." He eyed Elizabeth up and down and leered.

She glanced at the other patrons. American families on vacation. Boring. She felt like spitting.

"But there's a place down the road with music on Saturdays. Reggae." The bartender smiled at her with encouragement. "They all know me. I'll take you there Saturday night, eh?"

"Fuck off, José. Stay home with the wife and kids." Elizabeth threw a ten on the bar and left. *Jesus Christ, what a hell-hole.*

Within a week she grew tired of drinking in order to sleep. She managed to get laid a couple of times by nervous tourists who slipped away from their families for a short hour, but she hadn't slept with a woman in months, and felt horny. In other words, time to get out of Virgin Fucking Gorda—or VFG, as she called it.

Where to put down roots? She considered Caracas, Tangiers, Havana, even the Middle East, but her problem wasn't how to hide. She

142

possessed more money than anyone could spend in a hundred lifetimes and connections who could assure her safe passage, but she craved action. Scams pumped her life blood, and now that this one—her biggest, by far—looked finished except for the detail of the missing ransom money. She tried to imagine what came next. Perhaps instead of going into hiding, she'd tread the fine line between discovery and safety. Go back to the States and live under her alias and see what happened. Taunt fate. At least she wouldn't be bored.

"Reservations, please." Elizabeth called her favorite South Beach hotel. "I want your best suite for a week. I arrive day after tomorrow in the morning, and I want it ready for occupancy."

Elizabeth listened for a moment. "This is Elizabeth Mason," she said. "Talk to the manager, get my suite, and call me back in ten minutes on this number. And try until you reach me. Please," she added.

Two of her six cell phones worked in VFG, but you couldn't count on either network in this remote part of the Caribbean. Cell phones were to Elizabeth what saws and drills were to a carpenter—tools of her trade. Once in Miami, she might call a few contacts and put a new crew and a new scam together.

Chapter 38

Miami Beach

Was it safe? She didn't know, and it gave her goose bumps. She wanted to see him. The best sex ever. Why not? He wasn't about to tell the Feds she'd returned to the States. Elizabeth Mason checked into a suite at the Setai, her favorite South Beach hotel. Technically, she wasn't a fugitive, although she suspected the authorities would like to talk to her. She toyed with her cell phone and scrolled to his private number. He told her fewer than a dozen people in the world knew it.

"Please leave a name and number."

She didn't expect a live response.

"Liz," she said and fed her new cell information into his voice mail.

Later that day, she sat at the downstairs bar and sipped a martini. Her phone began to vibrate. She opened her purse and checked caller ID. 'Private Party' displayed. Him.

"Hello?"

"It's me, Liz. How are you doing? I've missed you."

The rich voice sent tremors through her stomach.

"Fine—I'm doing fine. Where are you?"

"That's unimportant. How about you? You left rather suddenly."

"Miami Beach. Sorry I didn't call. The cops made me nervous, and I wanted to get away for a while."

"I need to see you."

"Come here. I'm at the Setai. I want to see you too."

"Give me a couple of days. I have business to finish up."

When she clicked off a wave of desire swept through her body. Her hand shook when she lifted the martini glass to her lips. Maybe his 'business' included another story he could tell her. The thought of it aroused her.

Complicated. He didn't hunger for the five hundred million dollars he supposed she stole, but principles were involved. Did he have an interest in pursuing her and the money? He needed to think about it. He liked the idea of earning his own keep, and he enjoyed his work. The two and a half million that belonged to him was a different story. Jack Sloan stole it, and retrieving it would be a pleasure. Grabbing the big money might be like winning the lottery—a story that sounds good in the telling, but results in disaster. A person with that kind of financial clout could spend all their time trying to think of ways to amuse themselves.

They intended to offer him a new assignment. Not the usual hit and run, this one involved detective work. He wasn't sure he would take it, but it meant an opportunity to get close to Sloan without arousing suspicion, and he enjoyed the irony—the insurance company wanted to pay him to investigate his own crimes.

After the Juarez encounter, he knew Sloan might recognize him. Unless dense beyond belief, he might figure out that his savior's presence during the attack could not have been an accident. On the other hand, Sloan had appeared disoriented; the conversation on the ride back to El Paso, desultory. Over the years, he had taught himself to blend in and look like everyone else in the crowd. It might have worked with Sloan. No matter, he intended to plan his next move with greater care than the foray that had cost four people their lives. Heat was to be avoided, if possible. The authorities always looked harder at murder cases.

Meanwhile, he needed to consider a trip to Miami. It might be amusing. He thought about strangling her while they made love. He concluded he didn't care about her money, but she had tricked him, and he didn't like that. The logistics were challenging. Body disposal in an unfamiliar city presented a tricky problem. Same with DNA. She might be suspicious if he used a condom, which meant he couldn't climax, but he could take care of that detail later. Maybe the safest thing would be to fly there, forget about fucking her, kill her, and get back to Phoenix and prepare his move on Sloan. So many options. So little time.

Wayne Deckert played with paper clips and watched the clock. His superiors didn't like the potential outcome of the Pendleton insurance claim. They said it stunk of fraud and directed him to do something about it. He had called Manuel Hoppe and asked him to come to the office at three. The hands of the clock showed quarter past. Always punctual, Hoppe's tardiness worried Deckert. When his secretary buzzed, he almost dropped the phone in his haste to respond.

145

"Mr. Hoppe to see you, sir."

"Send him in. Please," he added.

When Hoppe entered, Deckert walked around his desk, clasped his hand, and patted him on the shoulder. Not his usual routine.

"Manuel. Good to see you. How are you recovering from your experience?"

"Fine, Wayne. I try not to think about it."

"Please. Sit." He waved toward the side of the office reserved for big shots. It included a small divan, an easy chair, and a coffee table. Deckert ordered tea and biscuits for them.

"Your favorite tea, I believe?" More a question than a statement.

"Thanks, Wayne. I'm not used to the VIP treatment. You must want something."

Hoppe disconcerted Deckert. He felt like he was laughing at him underneath the polite veneer.

"We have an assignment. Are you interested?"

"Another kidnapping? I haven't seen anything on the news."

"No. The same old crime. We want to hire you to investigate possible fraud with respect to the Pendleton death benefit claim. Our people are working on it, but we're a large company, and the bureaucracy can be overwhelming. I have less than a week before we're required by law to settle."

"My usual rate?"

"Five thousand a day, plus expenses. Plus a bonus if you come up with the answers we're looking for."

"How much of a bonus?"

"Five percent of the policy value. Two hundred fifty thousand."

"Too rich to pass up. If I don't have the solution within ten days, I'll bill you for expenses—not time. If it turns out there's conclusive evidence that the claim is valid, you still pay. Agreed?"

"You sound confident. Very generous of you, Manuel. Agreed. I'll have a contract ready this afternoon." Deckert stood and walked to his desk. He pressed the intercom buzzer.

"Please come in when Mr. Hoppe leaves. I've a chore I need you to do."

Over the speaker, they heard the clatter of her chair. Hoppe caught Deckert's attention with a rare smile.

"Email it to me, Wayne. Good seeing you. I'll have the tea next time." He rose, shook Deckert's hand, and pushed through the office door.

The fool has no idea. Hoppe laughed to himself when he strode past the security guard and entered the elevators to the parking garage. He smelled the leather of the Rolls Phantom Drophead Coupe from several feet away. He had left the top down, and admired his possession. When he was a boy, his dad had taken him on a once-in-a-lifetime trip to the city and he saw a rich man driving a Rolls. When he'd commented on it, his father had called the owner a faggot, but he knew the old man well enough not to trust the words and had decided then to have one of his own when he grew up.

He began to run his new assignment through a mental checklist. Deckert envisioned difficulties, but didn't know what Manuel knew. This would be easy. The sole question that remained was how to do it without alerting anyone. He would commence planning when he arrived back at his apartment, one of three luxury condominiums he owned around the world, all in different names.

The Rolls engine throbbed, and he edged out of the parking space, careful not to scrape against anything. He handed his stamped ticket to the attendant and pulled out into the bright sunshine. It had been cooler when he drove down—it was heating up fast. Perhaps it would be wise to raise the top.

Chapter 39

Cruisin'

Hoppe phoned a Miami associate and arranged to charter a small yacht. An accomplished mariner, he enjoyed the open sea. Another call resulted in delivery of two spare anchors and heavy fishing net cable wire to the marina in the name of the alias he used to secure the boat. Under a different passport, he booked a first class flight departing Phoenix that evening and returning the next day.

Manuel Hoppe owned several accounts with different banks, all with attached credit cards and under various identities. Cards were automatically paid in full each month, and he took care to keep the minimum required balance at each institution. When he burned an alias—like he would soon do to the one he used to charter the yacht—he stopped putting money into the related account, and John Doe, or whatever moniker he used, disappeared.

He reached voice mail when he called Mrs. Pendleton.

"Tonight at ten—meet me at the marina south of your hotel." He told her the name. "I can't risk being seen around South Beach."

Her heart pulsed under the bikini top. Elizabeth Mason sat outside a private cabana taking in sun and reading a Dean Koontz novel. She closed her phone and her eyes, and let her mind wander to the night ahead. A small droplet of fear pushed up from her stomach, but it only served to heighten the sexual tension. He reeked of masculinity and danger, and she loved it. She punched his number into her phone and called his voice mail to let him know she'd received the message and would be there.

He looked up at the almost-full moon and frowned, then shrugged. He preferred darkness, but didn't expect any witnesses to view what he planned. The warmth of the day lingered, and he breathed in the familiar sea smell mixed with the scent of flowers carried by a light breeze that blew from land. Water lapped against the dock and the starboard side of the boat. The sound soothed his soul. A perfect night for cruising.

He went to the flying bridge and checked out the instruments, fuel levels, and radar equipment. He turned the key and the deep throb of the engines erupted almost instantly. The anticipated rush of power and adventure blew through his veins. He had shown his Master's license to the marina captain and reviewed the characteristics of the boat. He should do this more often.

The below-decks accommodations were luxurious. A king-size bed occupied one room, and a dining room, living room and bar extended to the rear deck where one could sit and gaze at the heavens. The gate at the end opened two feet above the water line, a necessity for pulling in swimmers or disposing of trash over the stern. He selected Mozart's Piano Concerto Number Twenty-One on the sound system, poured himself a cold martini, and settled into the deck captain's chair to await his beloved.

"It's called erotic asphyxiation."

"What does it do?"

"You'll see. We'll do it together."

The tiny knot of fear that lingered in her gut exploded, and her hands began to shake. "Don't hurt me."

"Never, Darling. I love you."

He lay naked between her legs, supported on one muscular arm, caressing her nipples and lips with the other. He bent to kiss her and slid his penis inside. She gasped and squeezed him between legs that she lifted near his shoulders, held by hands cupped underneath her thighs. It tightened the vaginal muscles till he could sense every pulsation and movement.

"Tell me about Santa Fe." She tongued his ear and groaned.

He told her about maiming Franco and Consuela and killing the two deputies. He drew out the story and felt her passion grow with each detail. He perceived her close to the chasm and withdrew.

"Fuck me more," she begged and pushed her pelvis against him.

"You're about to come like you never have." He spoke in her ear and reached under the pillow.

"Put this over your head and breathe in." He handed her a plastic bag.

"What about you?" she said.

"One of us needs to stay conscious."

She pulled the bag over her head and took a deep breath. Elizabeth jerked when she inhaled the plastic.

"Stay calm. Enjoy the sensations and let yourself go." He spoke in her ear and blew wisps of soft air.

He inserted himself again and began to probe with serious thrusts. Her hips jerked wildly and her body shook. She labored now, and he saw her eyes dilate. She started to come, and he let himself go with her—to hell with the DNA. Her frantic gasps drew the plastic inside. Her entire being vibrated. She arched her back and passed out.

Now would be the time to save her, to bring her back from a brief visit with death, back to her passion. It wasn't a close call.

Manuel wrapped the sheet around her and tied it at both ends. He lifted her limp body with ease. He sensed a faint pulse and knew life still lingered, yearning for one final taste of honey. She hung over his shoulder like a sack of grain. He carried her to the stern deck where he'd stowed the spare anchors and fishing cable wire. He wrapped her with the wire and secured the heavy weights. She might float when the body had deteriorated enough to loosen the chains, but not before the creatures on the sea floor sated themselves, and even then, he thought it doubtful.

"Goodbye, My Sweet." He nudged her over the back and watched her disappear beneath the glassy water. He raised his face to the moon. *I did what I needed to do. She knew my identity. And the five hundred million? Fuck it.*

Sheriff Elias Hernandez' cell phone rang when he stepped out the Department's back entrance the next day.

The call snapped him out of a deep reverie, all of which revolved around that asshole, Jack Sloan. Not thirty seconds before the phone rang, he had leaned over his desk and stuck a rolled-up dollar bill in his right nostril. The pencil-thick line of cocaine disappeared like magic, and he coughed violently.

The coke lent a new briskness to his attitude. "Sheriff Hernandez," he barked.

"You don't know me, Sheriff, and I'm calling on a throw-away phone, so don't waste your time trying to trace it."

"Who is this?" Hernandez' voice turned rough.

"*This*, mother-fucker, is the guy who wasted the Pueblo deputies and hurt Sloan's beaner friends."

"Jesus Christ. Why are you calling? Who in the hell are you? What do you want?" The words poured out.

"The same things you want. I understand Jack Sloan kicked your ass good. Maybe you want to return the favor?"

Hernandez backed against the building's adobe wall.

"How do you know about me and Sloan? Where are you? I'm a goddamn Sheriff. You can't talk to me like that. Nobody kicks my ass." Elias's stomach contracted, and he thought he might vomit.

"Calm down. Suck it up. No one will ever know about this conversation."

"You're a killer? Those two cops?"

"Don't pretend you give a shit. You need money and cocaine—and a whore once in a while."

"You don't know jack-shit. I don't do no drugs or run with hookers."

"Here's the deal, Sheriff. I want your help, and in return, I'll keep a lid on your vices. Wouldn't want to spoil that re-election campaign. I'll also give you a hundred thousand dollars in cash."

"What kind of help?" Hernandez was trapped. He pulled at his necktie and loosened it. His shirt stuck to his armpits, and sweat rolled down his chest.

"Sloan's been gone a while, but eventually, he'll return. When he does—you let me know."

"How in the hell am I supposed to do that? You already said your phone's temporary."

"Are you on Facebook?" The man chuckled like it might be an inside joke.

"Fuck no. That's for teenagers."

"Get on it. Create a profile. When Sloan comes home, post a message on your page. 'I'm planting green chilies.' Understand?"

"Fuck you. Keep away from me. I don't want nothin' to do with you." The cell phone shook in Hernandez' hand.

"In that case, I'll drop an envelope at the local newspaper in the next couple of days."

"Whadda you mean? You stay the fuck away."

"I go where I please. The editor will be very interested in my pictures of you. That's one nasty coke habit, and your foul language is abominable."

"If I tell you when Sloan comes home, what's gonna happen?"

"That's not your concern, Elias. Follow instructions, and you'll be fine."

Hernandez chewed on his lip. If he weren't standing outside, he'd do a line.

"All right, goddamn it. But you gotta promise to give me them pictures when it's over."

"You have my word, Elias."

"When do I get the dough?"

"Afterwards. I'll deliver it personally."

"No. That's okay. I...."

The phone clicked off, and Hernandez was left talking to air.

Chapter 40

Making Port

Hoppe moved to the rear of the main cabin. Liz's purse, clothes, and shoes lay in a heap on the floor. *Careless.* He scooped them up and walked toward the rear platform. The boat's auxiliary anchor would work to weigh them down. He glanced at the purse and felt an irresistible pull. He sat on a bench and opened it.

The contents were unremarkable except for two items. The key to her suite at the Setai and another—one that looked like it might fit a safety deposit box. A rush of adrenaline hit his brain. *I know what this is. Why not use it? No sense leaving the contents of the box for the hotel manager or the Feds.*

He unfolded a slip of paper and saw a copy of the registration form she had used when she checked in. Not Pendleton. Further examination of the items in the purse revealed a passport in the name of Elizabeth Mason, the same one used on the hotel document. His mind raced. He pulled out his cell phone and speed-dialed the number of the highest-class madam in Miami Beach.

"Grace," he said. "This is Manuel. I need an escort. Long hair, a little older, well-dressed and sophisticated. Can you do it?"

"Yes, but it may take time. It's too late to schedule anyone like that tonight, but I just recruited a new, young Cuban you'll love. I could have her at your hotel in two hours."

"No. I want what I said. Your girls don't get up early, but I want this one to meet me at nine in the morning. A special assignment that shouldn't take more than a few hours."

"It'll cost you extra."

"Five grand if she's what I asked for. Sound okay to you?"

"Perfect. Love doing business with you, Manuel. Where are you staying?"

He gave her the hotel name and his room number.

The escort buzzed his suite at nine the next morning. He told the concierge to send her up. When he opened the door, he knew he'd bought a winning lottery ticket.

"My name's Annie." She extended a manicured hand.

"Pleased to meet you, Annie. Come in and I'll explain what I want you to do."

"May I please use my phone to check in with Grace first?" She smiled and displayed a perfect set of teeth.

Annie called, and they settled on the sofa with coffee while Hoppe briefed her. Not on the motive for the mission, but there were details to take care of. A trip to a salon for a hair color and comb. A stop at a makeup counter for the right shade of lipstick. He showed her Elizabeth's passport photo.

"How close can you come to this?"

"Pretty damn close. Gorgeous woman. Who is she?"

"A close friend who needs a stand-in to impersonate her. We're going to open a safe deposit box here at the hotel, retrieve what's in there, and I'll take it to her." Hoppe stood. "Come over here to the desk and practice the signature. I'll call and make an appointment at the hair salon."

"Why don't I do both? I have a fab hairdresser who'll see me on short notice. He'll do the makeup too."

She walked across the room and Hoppe felt a tinge of desire. She knew how to carry herself and possessed a body that didn't take prisoners. Maybe after they were finished.

Hoppe realized that he could have brought an eighty-year-old African-American woman with him, and the clerk wouldn't have hesitated to give them access to the safe deposit box. Still, he considered himself a cautious man and felt pride when he looked over at Annie. Close to Elizabeth and better than one could expect with an hour's preparation. He thought again about sex with her when they finished.

The room behind the front desk felt cramped, and Hoppe pressed against Annie's thigh when she inserted the key. She looked about to open the box, but Hoppe held her by the arm and moved her away.

"Best you don't see what's in here. I don't want to put you in danger."

He noticed the alarm in her eyes. Her breathing became more pronounced.

A woman who likes to take risks.

Of course, he should have known that. He always wondered about the moxie it took to knock on a stranger's door knowing the person inside intended to fuck you. And you couldn't refuse if he happened to be old and ugly—only if you felt yourself in danger. He enjoyed his conversations with Grace about the nuances of the business. Fascinating stuff that reminded him of his own profession. Once he took an assignment, his employer expected results, no matter the extenuating circumstances.

Hoppe removed the oilskin-wrapped parcel from the box. There was also jewelry, but nothing else. He turned to Annie and handed her a necklace that was worth at least twenty-five grand.

"A bonus," he said.

She smiled and kissed him on the cheek, almost like she knew in advance he'd give her a gift that day. Very smooth, but he noticed her face flushed with excitement.

"Thank you, Manuel. Grace told me you were a gentleman."

"Let's go back to the suite. You do have more time, don't you?" He stuffed the package into his inside jacket pocket and the remaining baubles into his pants. He shut and locked the box, then pressed the buzzer. The clerk popped into the room.

"We're finished here, and thanks for your help." Hoppe extended the box to him. The clerk held the door for them when they exited.

He looked at the bedside clock and knew the time to leave had arrived. Why stick around, even with his confidence that Elizabeth wouldn't rise from the bottom of Miami bay? Annie lay asleep on his arm.

He moved it from under her and felt the tingle of circulation returning.

"Wake up, Sweetheart." He nudged her and kissed her forehead.

The sex had met his expectations. Annie looked like a possible keeper.

"Will you call me again?" She sat up in bed, her perfect breasts and more-perfect nipples pointing to the sky, and reached for her purse. She took out a small card and pen and wrote a note before handing it to Hoppe.

"My real name and cell number. You can reach me directly, and I'll let Grace know so neither of us gets in trouble with her."

Hoppe read the neat scrawl. *Megan Donahue.*

"Pleased to meet you, Megan." He smiled at her and climbed from the bed. "We'll talk again."

155

After she left, he removed the packet from his coat pocket and opened it, letting its contents fall to the bed. Two hundred million in bearer bonds landed on the sheets. *What did she do with the rest of it?* Idle curiosity. The sight of so much money didn't do anything for him. He expected to find her trove stashed in the safe deposit box. He drew satisfaction from knowing his reasoning had been sound. Other than that, the wealth held no allure. Maybe he should walk to the nearest homeless shelter and hand it over to one of the denizens. Then again, maybe not. They might use it to start a fire.

It presented a complication he'd rather be without. He needed to decide how and when to dispose of it without attracting attention. With his connections in North Africa, it shouldn't pose a problem, but he needed to go there in person. He yawned and ambled toward the shower. The money Jack Sloan stole from him was of a different color. He thought about the various punishments he could mete out to a thief and smiled. That part would be fun.

Part 6

Jack and Darlene

Chapter 41

Break Time

The intensity of the past two weeks had enervated me. We talked it over and decided a day off sounded good. Carlos would call Maria and have her fly to Phoenix, I'd ask Darlene to come, and Frank would introduce us to Amanda. Lie around the resort for a day. Swimming, hot tub, massages, margaritas, and a good dinner at a nice restaurant. When I called the hotel in Santa Fe, Darlene sounded excited.

"Exactly what we need. I'm going out of my gourd waiting for something to happen, and I jump whenever I hear a strange noise. From now on, I think I should travel with you."

"Stick a bag of John's good weed in your pocket. It'll be fun to see Frank stoned."

She laughed, and it soothed my soul.

"Get the first plane out. Come tonight and take a cab to the resort."

"10-4, Big Daddy. See you soon."

I called Will and asked him to drive Darlene to the Albuquerque airport, then checked the clock beside the bed. Five p.m. I had only slept four hours the night before, and a nap would feel great. I pulled down the bedspread, put the 'Do Not Disturb' sign on the door, threw my clothes in a pile next to the desk, and crawled under the sheets.

Half-awake, I dreamed of gunshots and tequila. I lay stretched out on a slab in the morgue, covered with hundred dollar bills while a naked woman danced at my feet. I tried to look at her, but a toe-tag blocked my vision.

Two thoughts always give me the heebie-jeebies. The worst—trapped in a cave head-first with no way to wiggle out. The second, the imaginary feel of a wire wrapped around 'this little piggy goes to market' with my name on it.

The sound of a key in my door, and my heart leapt to my mouth. I had taken my Glock from my suitcase and stuck it under the pillow. I whipped it out, sat up with the sheet over my lap, and leveled it at the door. My finger tightened on the trigger when the door swung open.

"Maid service," a sing-song voice called. She stepped into the room, saw the weapon, and looked like she might faint.

"Aieeee," she managed and held her hands in front of her face.

I put the gun under the sheets and held up my hands.

"Perdon, Señorita. Policia. I thought you were breaking in."

"The ... sign ... Maid Service Requested ... Señor," she stammered. I'd turned it wrong-side out.

"I'm so sorry. Terrible mistake. Please, accept my apologies, and, no, I don't need service."

She backed out of the room, never taking her eyes from mine.

Darlene showed up an hour later, and we spent a quiet night—the perfect antidote for raw nerves.

About noon the next day, the phone beside the bed rang.

"*Amigo.* Maria is here and we're having lunch by the pool. Why don't you join us?" Carlos sounded excited.

"How about Frank and Amanda? Have they arrived yet?"

"He called, and they're on their way. Should be a blast."

"Give us twenty minutes. Darlene's in the shower."

"*Hasta luego, Amigo.*" He hung up.

When I told Darlene, she reminded me of our massage appointments at 4:00. Plenty of time.

Whichever of us came up with the idea of a day off was a genius. We ate a fabulous lunch washed down with Silver Coin margaritas. Amanda and Marie proved delightful—like their partners—and good conversation dominated. The first serious note sounded around 3:30.

"We may have a lead on Elizabeth Pendleton." Amanda's eyes sparkled.

"Where, what?" I dripped guacamole on my swim suit.

"We dug deep, and found a maiden name. Pendleton turned out to be her fourth husband, which explains the difficulty in tracing her. People watch television and get the idea we can plug in a fingerprint and ID a criminal anywhere in the country. That's a crock, of course. Very few law enforcement agencies are connected, and almost no civilian ones."

She must have saved this news because Frank let out a low whistle.

"What's the name?" He leaned forward.

"Mason. The best news is that there's a live passport in that name, and it's been used—recently." Amanda beamed at Frank. "A round-trip from Mexico City to the Caymans. We don't know where she went after that, but she came and went on the same day."

"My God, she picked up the money." Carlos looked visibly excited.

"That's one possibility," Amanda said.

"So what's next?" Darlene interjected.

"We'll see where she turns up and look for signs of a money transfer. If she did go to the Caymans to retrieve Pendleton's dough, she must have changed it into paper. Otherwise, she would have done it on the Internet. That makes tracing it a lot more difficult."

"I have two concerns—the cash I found and finding the dude who wasted the cops at our place, but I'm ninety-nine percent sure those things are tied to your investigation. If you can locate Elizabeth Pendleton-Oliveras-Mason, it could be the key." I felt excitement tickle my stomach.

Carlos, Frank, and Amanda nodded.

"Give us a little time, Jack. We'll find her." Amanda sounded sure of herself.

"I'm encouraged. If you've come this far, you should be able to go all the way," I said. "By the way, we made spa appointments at four, so we're heading there now. What time do you want to reconvene?"

"We're doing the same at five," Carlos said. "We can meet you guys here by the pool at seven?"

Frank and Amanda exchanged a look that told me they intended to spend the next couple of hours in their room.

Doubt washed over me when I saw my massage therapist. An older Asian woman who stood no more than four feet six inches and weighed about seventy-five pounds, wearing a kimono and soft fabric slippers. I'm a solid two thirty-five and felt about twice her height. I looked around for a treatment table, but a thick blanket on the floor with a small pillow comprised her equipment.

"You lay on stomach."

A no-nonsense voice. I obeyed.

"Make sure you comfortable."

Not an easy command to obey, seeing that I was face down and pressed into a hard wooden floor with little padding.

It started near my ankles. A firm muscle penetration. It took a minute or two to realize she'd gained a solid purchase on my legs. She walked up toward my butt, her toes working my muscles. Up and down, never losing her balance. She did the glutes, then moved to the lower back. Spine, shoulders, the backs of my arms. When she hopped down and told me to roll over, my body felt completely relaxed. She repeated the process on my thighs, stomach, and chest, then worked my hands and the soles of my feet. The greatest massage of my life.

We spent the rest of the evening eating, drinking, and laughing. We imbibed enough so that the corny mariachi band that played for the tourists sounded in tune. A fabulous and much-needed respite. The hard stuff would come with the morning.

The next day, Darlene and I decided it was time for both of us to go home. We couldn't put if off forever, and we didn't want to sell the *rancho*. Anger ate at me every time I thought of my wounded friends and the dead Pueblo police, but that wouldn't go away no matter where we lived, and under no circumstances would I agree to Darlene going alone.

"Let's pack up the day after tomorrow and go back to Santa Fe." I touched Darlene under the chin and lifted her eyes to mine.

She nodded, and I saw tears.

"It'll be tough, Sweetheart, but we don't have a choice. The animals have survived alone way too long, and it's where we live. I'm not going to let what some psychopath did keep me away, and if he comes back, I'll kill him."

My cell phone rang, and I scrambled to pull it from my jean's pocket. I didn't recognize the number on caller ID.

"Jack Sloan."

"Jack." It came across like more of a scream than a statement. "It's me, Rosa Lara. You told me to call if I needed you." She cried and talked at the same time.

"Calm down, Rosa. What's the matter?"

"El Jefe's missing. The Mexican army came in and started shooting everybody. The gangs shot back, and many were killed. I'm in El Paso. I crossed the border with my child, but I need a place to go."

"Do you have money?" The most important question.

"*Si*. Not a lot, but Robert insisted I keep a small sum in the apartment for emergencies."

"Passport or driver's license?"

"No. I paid a coyote to smuggle us over. I don't have identification that will allow me to get on a plane. I'm afraid, Jack. El Jefe fought many enemies, and they'll try to find me."

"Can I call you back on this number?"

"*Si*, but soon, *por favor, Señor Jack*." Her voice shook.

"Half an hour, at most." I clicked off the phone.

Twenty minutes later, I conferred with Frank and Carlos. Frank said her witness status in the Pendleton crime could gain her immunity from deportation. Carlos said he'd work things on his side of the border. They told me that getting her on a plane would be impossible given her lack of credentials, and Frank didn't think he could swing a chopper. They agreed that I should drive to El Paso in the 'vette and transport her back to Phoenix.

"One of you guys drive to El Paso. You think I'm the FBI's fucking private taxi service?" I felt a flush rise to my cheeks. "I'm goddamn tired of running your errands. You're both grown boys with access to cars."

"Jack, you know this is off the grid. If either of us gets involved, it could blow the whole case. You have to help us out one more time. I swear this is it." Frank pleaded with his eyes.

I'm not sure Darlene loved the idea, but she didn't object. She would catch a plane to Albuquerque and take the shuttle to the hotel in Santa Fe and wait for me there. She promised to let Will know her plans. I called Rosa back.

"Where are you?"

"I'm at the bus station. It's creepy. Everyone is watching me."

"That's your imagination working overtime, Rosa. You're scared and on the run. Do you know anyone in El Paso you could spend six hours with?"

"My cousin lives here. I could phone her and ask."

"Do it. If she agrees, take a cab and call me with the address. I'm coming to get you."

"*Gracias*, Señor Jack."

We hung up and I called for the car.

162

Chapter 42

Rosa

I drove to the El Paso address Rosa gave me and waited outside while she and her cousin stuffed things in the 'vette's rear seat and trunk. She made it clear that she didn't want me inside the house. After they loaded her worldly possessions, I put the top up. The sun shone with a fierce intensity, and we faced a six-hour drive.

"Your son will stay with your cousin?" I looked at her across the car top.

"*Si*. I don't know what's happening, and I'm frightened to take him to Phoenix." Rosa opened the door and slid into the passenger seat.

I moved behind the wheel and couldn't resist. I turned sideways to view her startling beauty. Perfect, even features, no makeup, and an earthy aura. Mixed Indian and Hispanic, I guessed. Her dark copper hair hung across her shoulders, gleaming from a recent shampoo. Her fresh scent held a hint of perfume that I couldn't identify. She looked down at her fingers, either unaware of my scrutiny, or so used to men's reaction to her that she wasn't fazed.

"*Vamos*." I smiled at her and started the car.

I looked at the house and saw a woman holding a small child.

Rosa waved and the little boy started to cry. Her shoulders shook. "*Vamos*," she said, choking. "*Pronto*. Before I change my mind."

I slammed the 'vette into first, and we left the curb with a screech. It might be a long trip.

Rosa leaned back against the head rest and fell asleep. She didn't stir until east of Deming, New Mexico.

"Señor Jack. Could we please stop? I need to use *los baños*."

"Me too, Rosa. There's a convenience store at the next interchange. Maybe a restaurant where we could get coffee, and I could use gas." I was drowsy after hours on the long, boring Interstate.

163

We parked in front of a run-down building that advertised the best Bar-B-Q in the Southwest. It didn't look that bad, and they boasted indoor plumbing. I opened the door for Rosa and admired her slender grace when she moved past the counter toward the ladies' room. I headed for the men's.

The waitress showed me to a booth remarkable for its cracked linoleum table top festooned with paper place mats depicting a pig roasting over an open fire. I ordered coffee for two and asked for menus. The young girl popped her gum and nodded at a blackboard hung behind the bar.

Rosa slid onto the bench across from me.

"You order for us, Jack. I'm not very hungry."

"Coffee?" I looked at her, and she nodded.

"Two coffees and two pulled pork sandwiches. Extra sauce." I love barbeque.

The girl laboriously wrote our order down on her pad, biting her lower lip in apparent concentration.

"Raht back." She ambled to the open window of the kitchen and shouted an order to the cook. She returned with cups of steaming coffee and several mini-moos.

"Thanks." I emptied a couple of the creamers in mine and stirred in sugar from one of the packets on the table. Rosa did likewise.

"What happens when we get to Phoenix? I have relatives there, but I haven't spoken to them in years, and I don't know much about them."

I felt like I'd agreed to adopt a homeless person. Why my responsibility?

"I think the Feds will put you up in a hotel. You're a key witness to a crime they're investigating."

I didn't know if I told the truth or not. Small pangs of guilt nibbled at my conscience, but I brushed them aside. All for the greater good, I reasoned. My perfidy would visit me later when the devil came to collect his due.

"If they don't, can I stay with you and your wife? I want my son to come and live with me, not with a second cousin in El Paso, and a hotel wouldn't be a good place."

I saw the strain in her eyes. It's easy to forget how difficult things can be for the other person. None of this could have sounded easy to her, and a sudden rush of sympathy made me say something I shouldn't have.

"I'll ask Darlene. There's nobody in our *casita* right now. I don't know, Rosa. You might not like it. Two policemen died there."

"I'm sorry for them, Señor Jack. Terrible." She reached across the table and put her hand on mine.

I don't know if electricity flowed both ways, but it shot through my arm and straight to my groin.

"We'll talk to Frank Hunter and Carlos when we get to Phoenix. If there's a problem, I'll call Darlene." I moved my hand from under hers to my coffee. She didn't seem to notice that it was a giant step back.

It turned out to be the best Bar-B-Q in the Southwest.

Pulled into Nazareth, I was feelin' 'bout half-past dead. The Weight played on the oldies station. The Phoenix skyline came into view, and my muscles relaxed for the first time since I had picked her up. I wanted a hot shower and a soft bed. I opened my cell phone and hit Frank's speed dial number.

"You've reached Agent Frank Hunter. Please leave a message."

"It's after seven. I'm fifteen minutes from the hotel. I'll check our friend into a room. Call me."

I repeated the process with Carlos and achieved the same results.

Rosa drifted in semi-sleep beside me in the car. I shook her arm with care.

"Rosa. Time to wake up. I couldn't reach Frank or Carlos, but I told them we were headed for the hotel. I'll check you into your own room."

"*Gracias*, Señor Jack." She stretched and yawned, the fabric in her loose blouse pulling tight across her breasts.

A half-hour later, we stood in the hotel lobby. I handed Rosa a room card.

"I'm whipped. Order whatever you need from room service, and call me when you wake up. We'll sort this out in the morning. And don't use your cell phone to contact anybody. Call on the hotel's land line. I doubt if anyone's looking for you, but why take the chance?" I leaned over and gave her a peck on the cheek.

"Thank you again. I don't know what I would have done if you didn't come for me." She pulled my hand to her lips and kissed it, turned, and walked toward the elevators.

I felt the tingle move up my fingers. The scent of her perfume lingered after she left, but I shook my head and moved to the bar. One drink while I called Darlene. Both would help clear my brain of the visual images playing there.

Two Johnny Blacks and an hour later, I popped an Ambien and crawled into bed.

The light tap on my door woke me from a half-sleep. I stumbled over and opened it. Rosa pushed by me, her scent caressing my nostrils. She walked to the side of my bed, removed her robe, and crawled under the covers. Stretched out on her back, she smiled. I caught a glimpse of her body and didn't hesitate.

"What?"

She pressed a finger to my lips then rolled on top of me and kissed me. I felt her breasts push into my chest and shuddered when they moved to my stomach, then my thighs. I've enjoyed a few great blowjobs, but nothing like this. I thought of the study that must go into such a common act to render it special. Rosa proved a great scholar.

I stopped her before I came and moved atop her. I spread those gorgeous legs that wrapped around my waist like smooth, soft silk. My nose went behind her ear and I inhaled her. I kissed the fine hairs on her jaw line. I wouldn't call it making love; I would call it exceptional fucking. So often, the first time is a bust, but not with her. I like it when a woman can climax at will, and Rosa came whenever she felt like it.

She teased me with her tight pussy until I thought I would have a stroke, then pulled me full inside her and did tricks with her muscles I still don't believe.

The phone jarred me. My seven a.m. wakeup call. I sat up in bed and looked around. No Rosa. My boner pushed against the covers, and waves of relief and regret passed through me. A great dream, but that's all it was.

Chapter 43

Connections

The identity of the stranger who had saved my ass in Juarez plagued me. Who and why? Too much of a coincidence to be one. I called Frank to talk about Rosa and decided to press him for answers.

"I need to get the hell out of here and back to Santa Fe. Rosa's your witness and the Fed's problem."

Frank agreed to meet me in the hotel coffee shop. We sat in a corner for privacy.

"Jack. *Amigo.* I couldn't get money approved to put her in a hotel. My bosses think she's told us everything she knows. We're not chasing El Jefe, we're investigating Pendleton's murder/kidnapping." He shrugged and held his hands out, palms upward.

"So what am I supposed to do with her? She has no place to go, and you and Carlos told me to bring her here." My irritation boiled to the surface.

"You did a good thing. I don't think she would have survived in El Paso, given her connection to El Jefe. Our intelligence says he's still alive, so that means he'll plan a counterstrike. The war's going to heat up, My Boy, and it's no place for a young woman with a child."

"So I did my good deed for the day. You haven't answered my question. She can't live in this hotel for the rest of her life. Will you try again? Invent a story. Tell your boss she knows who killed Pendleton. Anything."

"Why don't you take her home? She could stay in your *casita* until we sort things out."

"Darlene would love that. Frank, for Christ's sake, look at the pickle you've put me in. Rosa thinks I'm her savior, and you ..." I couldn't finish.

I picked up my cup and took a long pull of coffee. A tequila shooter would taste fine right now.

"What else is bothering you?" Frank looked at me and raised an eyebrow.

"The guy who rescued me in Juarez. Have you found out anything about him?"

"We checked customs logs. There are a couple of possibilities." Frank stared at an object across the room.

"Like what? Or who?"

"You remember the name of the *hombre* the insurance company hired to manage the Pendleton hostage situation?"

"Hoppe? Something like that." A tingle ran down my spine.

"Yeah, Manuel Hoppe. Turns out he visited Juarez that night. You have to ask yourself if it's a coincidence, or is there a connection? If it's the latter, it opens up all kinds of investigative avenues. Why Juarez? And what are the odds of him crossing your path?"

"The man who killed those thugs moved like a pro. Three shots. Three dead. No fucking around. Does Hoppe fit the profile?"

"We don't know yet. We're running a deep background. I shouldn't be telling you this, Jack, but you've stuck your neck out for me. If we get anything, I'll pass it on, but don't do anything rash. Don't contact him. Understand?"

"I wouldn't have any idea how to do that. Don't worry, Frank. My desire is to get far away from this bullshit. I want to ditch the money I found and pretend it never happened." Thoughts of Franco and Consuela in hospital beds flashed across my mind, reminding me that I would never be able to do that.

"The money's our bait. After we wrap this up, I'll take it off your hands, but in the meantime, keep your head low and wait to hear from me or Carlos. Anything else?"

"You said one of Pendleton's clients might have the wherewithal to hire a hit man. Did you check him out?"

"Dead end. The guy's cleaner than Carlos," Frank said.

The air in the restaurant was thick and humid. I wanted to get outside and on the road.

"I'm going to call Darlene. If she agrees, I'll take Rosa north. Keep trying to get her a witness relocation package. Promise?"

"I promise, Jack. Stay safe."

"This doesn't mean I'm not totally pissed off at you and Carlos."

He nodded, which made me infer he understood. Not that it did me any good.

We rose at the same time and I threw a ten on the table. I didn't want to wait for a check.

"Later." I shook his hand and watched him shuffle toward the exit. A good man, and I trusted him. I needed to get over my anger.

"I'm coming home, Sweetheart. I'll leave Phoenix in about an hour. How are the patients?"

"Good. They'll be released in a couple of days. I've contacted a nursing service to care for them, but we need you here. Be careful on the road. It'll be late when you hit Santa Fe."

"Uh, there's one more thing." I hesitated.

"I know the sound of trouble. What's going on?" Her voice sharpened.

"The Feds won't put Rosa Lara up in a hotel, and she has no place to go. Frank asked if we could take in her and her child for a short time."

I heard Darlene hold, then release her breath in a whoosh.

"What's a 'short time?' A day, a week, a month?"

"I don't know. Until she can go back to Juarez, I guess."

"My God, Jack. We need time alone, and we have Franco and Consuela to consider. I don't mean to be uncharitable, but you're stretching it."

"I swear, it's not my idea. I don't know what else to do. I don't feel like paying for a month of hotels. Frank promised to try again, but its decision time. I don't think I can abandon her."

"Is the child with her?"

"We left him with a relative in El Paso. We can send for him."

The mention of the little boy must have pushed her over the edge.

"Do what you have to do. I think your heart is bigger than your brain, but it's one of the reasons I love you."

Darlene and I sipped tea on our back deck. The half-moon backlit the cottonwoods, and the Milky Way clustered over our heads. A light breeze carried away the heat of the day. Rosa and her boy were ensconced in the cleaned-up *casita*, safe for now. Two days of travel, phone calls, a new ID card, missed flights for the boy and his aunt, and myriad other issues had taken their toll. I felt bone-tired.

An ambulance had brought Franco and Consuela home, and they were settled in the west section of the main house with the night shift nurse.

"You're pensive tonight. What's on your mind?" she said.

"Death. How little regard we give it because of what we see on TV and in the movies—and what we read. How many people are murdered each week on *Law and Order* reruns? Dozens, at least. We've inured ourselves to what it means."

"Morbid thoughts. What triggered them?"

"The usual. Franco and Consuela's near-miss, the deputies shot down in our driveway, and others. A person dies by violence and the shock waves travel like a small tsunami through families and friends. It happens too often, and I've seen too many."

"You blame yourself, but you don't have to. There are people capable of terrible things. You didn't invent them, and you can't control them. I'm proud of you."

It took a moment for me to answer.

"I'll think about it. You know that's how I deal with things. I try to do the right thing, but most of the time, I feel like the proverbial bull in the china shop."

"Come to bed. You've had a tough couple of weeks, and I think you need lots of affection." She rose and offered me her hand.

"One last tour of the property," I said.

Since our return, I'd become obsessive about patrolling the perimeter and checking things out. Also, I wanted to stop by the *casita* and make sure Rosa and Raoul were tucked in. I pulled my Glock from the gun cabinet, stuck it in my waistband, and went out into the dark.

Chapter 44

Manuel Hoppe

"*Issallamu alaykum.*" Hoppe greeted the Moroccan banker. "*Kayfak?*"

"*Kullish zane, shukran, winta?*" The banker's Iraqi accent carved through the polite response. He lifted his coal-black eyes to Hoppe's.

"*Ana ham zane,*" he replied in perfect Arabic, then switched to English. "I need to make a deposit." He opened his briefcase and placed the bearer bonds on the banker's desk. "Convert these to cash, and put what's left after your commission into my numbered account." He saw envy flash across the other's face, covered by a slight bow of the head.

"As you wish, Monsieur Hoppe." The banker used the mixed argot common to Tangier. French cultural influence remained strong. "Are you staying in the usual place?"

"Yes, The Villas. Please forward confirmation to me there."

The canned Middle Eastern music that played in the background jangled in his ears.

The banker wrote out a receipt and handed it across the desk.

"A pleasure doing business with you, sir. *Fi amin Allah.*"

"*Ashkurak. Allah wyak.*"

He had flown in from London the night before and called one of his favorite consorts, an exotic, dark-skinned beauty he'd met the year before at a party at the Four Seasons in New York hosted by the Sultan of Brunei who was rumored to own the hotel. The evening in Tangier had surpassed his expectations, now he pondered staying an extra day. He had settled into the back seat of the limo when his cell phone rang.

"Manuel, this is Wayne Deckert." The connection faded for a moment.

"I'm not in the country, Wayne. I can't hear you very well, but go ahead."

"An FBI agent came in here asking questions about you. Why would they do that, Manuel? It made me very nervous."

"What kind of questions?" For the first time since his arrival, he noticed the searing Moroccan sun that beat on the window glass. He rubbed his finger across the surface and felt the heat.

"They asked if you were working for us in Juarez two weeks ago. He wouldn't tell me why he wanted to know, but it brought the Pendleton matter to mind. That's the last thing we worked together on down there."

"What did you tell him?"

"The truth, of course. You weren't on assignment for us. Were you there?"

"That's my affair, Wayne. You did fine. Did he say he intended to come back?"

"He said there might be more questions. Apparently, your name has surfaced in one of their investigations, and they're doing a background check."

The phone connection sputtered.

"Thanks for the heads up, Wayne. Nothing to worry about. I'll call you when I'm back in the States." Hoppe pressed disconnect and leaned back in the leather seat. Plans were being made for him, and he didn't like it.

He phoned British Airways and booked an evening flight to London and an early morning flight to Phoenix. There were things he needed to take care of.

Two days later, Wayne Deckert chewed the end of the eraser-tipped pencil and considered his position. He and Hoppe had worked a scam for years. He overpaid for Hoppe's services, and half the excess came back to him.

What if the FBI knows about or suspects my relationship with Manuel? I could preempt them and turn on my partner, or hold my tongue and hope for the best. Which way to go?

He glanced up at the clock on his wall and saw it registered almost five—time to call it a day. He could head home to his boring wife and a tasteless dinner, or he could call her and say he was working late. The money stashed in his wall safe beckoned. Drive to the casino, play a few hands of blackjack, then call a hooker to meet him at the hotel. He laughed to himself. It was a no-brainer. He moved to the wall, dialed in

172

three numbers, and slipped a five thousand dollar pack into his coat pocket.

The dealer knew him and tried to cheer him up.

"Come on, Wayne. Call it a bad night. You'll get it back."

Deckert gazed with malice at the ten and six that lay on the table in front of him, then shifted his eyes to the dealer's up face card. He'd won three hands in a row and parlayed his bet. The two thousand sitting in the betting circle represented the last of the five pulled from his safe. If he lost, he wouldn't be able to afford a hooker.

"Surrender," he said and smiled at his own weakness. "I'm done for the night. Show me the next card."

The dealer shoved half his money back and flipped over the five of spades.

Deckert groaned, picked up his remaining chips, and headed for the cashier. He punched his speed dial and reached the woman with whom he had scheduled a date.

"Can you come now? I'm going to my room." He tried to make his voice upbeat.

"You either won a lot or got killed," she said.

"Please meet me there soon." He closed the phone.

He pocketed the thousand dollars and began the long walk to his hotel room. The buildings weren't connected, so he walked outside. He knew a path across the courtyard to a side door his key would open. Five minutes shorter, and he would avoid the risk of seeing anybody he knew.

Chapter 45

Rosa

I finished slicing the peaches onto the granola Darlene had concocted using her secret recipe, and we settled in at the table on the porch. I heard the front door open. I stood and yanked the Glock from the back of my Levi's. Darlene ducked and reached for the shotgun propped in the corner. My coffee cup tipped on the edge of the table. I reached and snatched it before it toppled.

"Señor Jack?" Rosa's voice drifted through the screen.

I felt the adrenaline work its way back to my heart and I returned the gun to my waistband. Darlene and I had talked it over and decided to keep ordinance nearby at all times.

"Rosa, for Christ's sake. You scared the hell out of us." I wanted her to know I felt irritated, and she had intruded.

Rosa came out on the porch. She wore a yellow string bikini covered by a lacy, see-through jacket. Her son, Raoul held her hand.

"Is it okay if we go for a swim?"

"Me too," said Raoul, a nice kid who looked a lot like his mother.

"Rosa, I've told you many times. Go whenever you want, but please use the downstairs entrance." I tried looking other than her direction while remaining polite. My peripheral vision showed Darlene glaring at me.

"Okay, Señor Jack. You like my swimsuit?" She removed the jacket and pirouetted in front of us.

"Lovely," Darlene cut in, ice in her voice. "Can we please have a little privacy?"

Rosa's eyes showed alarm. Her face reddened, and she covered herself and slipped back towards the door.

"Of course, Señora. *Gracias.*" She turned and pulled Raoul toward the stairs.

"Now, Sweetheart…"

"Don't 'Sweetheart' me, you bastard. Did you sleep with her?"

I felt pain in the question.

"No. I didn't—and I won't. I'll get her back to Juarez soon."

"What's soon? Whenever you get tired of ogling her?"

This wasn't going to go away.

"Frank and Carlos promised to look into a witness protection program. I'll call them today."

Darlene stood. I saw anger in her eyes and knew this was no drill. She turned, and had taken one step towards the sliding doors into the living area when a staggering explosion from the direction of the front gate rocked the house.

"Get under cover! Grab a weapon!" I shouted and ran for the corner of the house. The southerly wind blew great plumes of smoke towards the rear of the property and I caught the unmistakable scent of dynamite.

I rounded the giant cottonwood in the front yard and stopped and stared. The gate had disappeared. Total silence except for the sound of my breathing and the dogs going nuts. I whistled for them and they ran to me.

"Stay." Hopeful, but it would be damn near impossible to keep them at bay. I didn't want them hurt.

An engine started and, like an apparition, the black SUV from Juarez burst through the opening. I knew it couldn't be the same vehicle, but a shiver ran down my spine.

"Call the dogs to you," I said in Darlene's direction. "Lock the doors and take the shotgun to the front bedroom window."

I heard her whistle and summon our boys. They jerked towards the SUV, but Jem, the leader of the pack, led them into the house. I heard the door slam and lock at the same time I saw the car doors spring open.

Four men jumped out holding sub-machine guns at their hips. I didn't shout a warning. I took aim at the one closest to me and put three in his chest before he knew what hit him. The others swung in my direction, looks of amazement on their faces. The twelve-gauge boomed from the bedroom window. One of them flew backwards and slumped against the car, blood pumping from a large hole in his stomach. The remaining two jumped for the open seats. It looked like a slo-mo shot in an action movie. Darlene took out the rider's side door with a fusillade of double-ought pellets, and I emptied my clip into the windshield.

Gun smoke and cordite drifted on the breeze. The SUV wheeled and tore out the ruined gate.

175

"Call 911!" I yelled in Darlene's direction and shoved in a fresh clip. I sprinted toward the downed men.

The *maton* with the holes in his chest still lived. Darlene's target looked finished.

"*Habla ingles?*" I pulled his shirttail from his pants and pressed it onto the wounds.

He looked at me with blank eyes and uttered one word. I leaned closer. What I heard sounded like El Jefe's real name, Villenueva, but I couldn't be sure.

"*Repetir de nuevo,*" I said.

His head flopped to the side and his eyes glazed. Nothing else to tell.

I squatted next to the corpse, sweat running down my face, until I heard sirens. I used my own tee-shirt to wipe away the perspiration, rose, and walked through the wreckage of the gate to make sure ambulances and police cars could see a clear path. I pulled my cell phone from my pocket and pressed Frank's speed dial number. He answered after three rings.

"Frank, this is Jack. Find Carlos and get your asses up to my house with a chopper. Rosa leaves today. If you can't get the Feds to pay, figure it out yourself."

When I said her name, it struck me that I didn't know where she and Raoul were. I hoped they had stayed in the pool area.

The afternoon sun burned into my eyes, and a light breeze rustled the cottonwoods. What had gone down didn't seem possible.

"Calm down, Jack. What's up?"

"There are two stiffs in my driveway, a blown-up front gate, and an abiding suspicion that it's connected to El Jefe." I told him the dying man's words.

"I'm not sure we can do anything. It's complicated."

"Either you do it, or I talk to a friend of mine at the Santa Fean. They haven't grabbed a scoop for decades, and this one would pump circulation through the roof."

"Now, Jack. I thought we were partners." I heard chagrin in his voice.

"I'm tired of getting fucked over, Frank. If we're partners, hold up your end of the bargain."

"Okay. I'll call Carlos and get back to you."

"You have one hour, then I make a call." I pressed disconnect.

I looked toward the west side of the house and saw Franco standing in the open porch door. He weakly raised his hand, I presumed to let me know he, Consuela, and the nurse were okay.

Hernandez rode in the lead car with Will driving. Two ambulances followed. Will pulled up beyond the bodies, which gave the EMTs a clear path. He and Elias jumped from the vehicle and trotted toward me. Elias drew his service revolver while he ran.

"Drop the gun and put your hands on your head." He sounded hysterical.

I looked down and noticed I still clutched my Glock. I moved with care and placed it on the ground, then raised my arms. I heard Elias cock his pistol.

"Take it easy, Elias," I said.

Will stepped back and aimed his gun at Hernandez' back.

"Sheriff," Will said, "he did what you asked. Let's holster our weapons."

Hernandez glanced over his shoulder and lowered his revolver.

"Your ass is mine, Cowdry." Flecks of spittle flew from his mouth.

"We'll see." Will kept his voice under control. He looked away when another two cop cars wheeled into the driveway.

Pueblo police. They would claim jurisdiction even though we weren't technically on Tribal land. My shoulders relaxed when I recognized Vernon, the head sergeant.

"What happened here, Jack?" Vernon planted his sizeable body between Elias and me.

I told him what I knew and tossed out my suspicions. Elias stood in the background, snorting.

"Shut the fuck up, Hernandez."

I knew Vernon didn't like him any better than I did. He turned back to me. "So they came from a Mexican drug cartel?" Vernon sounded dubious. "You wanna tell me what's going on here? Consuela, Franco, two cops, and now this? What the fuck, Jack?"

"I can't tell you everything. The FBI will be here soon, and the lead agent will explain. Things have become complicated." I sounded like Frank.

I heard footsteps on the gravel and turned when Darlene approached our group. She still toted the shotgun.

"You take out one of these guys?" Vernon couldn't hide his admiration.

Darlene nodded, her eyes fixed on what remained of her target's stomach. She turned her head and threw up, then swung back toward us like nothing had happened.

"They invaded my home, Vernon." She wiped her mouth with the back of her hand. "Nobody gets away with that."

My cell phone rang. I looked at the caller ID and Frank's name glowed.

"Excuse me. FBI."

I walked four paces away, and turned my back.

"What's the verdict, Frank?" Not a civil way to answer a phone.

"We'll be there in two and a half hours. We're sitting in the chopper as we speak."

"There may be lots of questions. The cops here are mighty curious about the carnage on my *rancho*."

"I'll tell them what I can. Hang in there, Buddy." He clicked off.

When I turned back to the group, Vernon was speaking with his phone pressed to his ear, walking in a circle in what I presumed was hope of clearer reception. After a moment, he closed his phone.

"My guys have a black SUV in a ditch about a mile south of here. One wounded in the driver's seat, one dead in the passenger's." From the tone of his voice, he loved this cops and robbers stuff.

"The Feds will want to question him, Vernon, so I'd make sure he's safe if I were you."

"Don't sweat it, Jack. I'll put half a dozen of my troopers on him." He glanced at Elias, who glowered in the background. "Keep your dipshits away, Hernandez. Don't fuck with Tribal affairs."

Elias stomped to the Sheriff's cruiser and opened the passenger door. "Let's go, Cowdry. Back to the office."

"Drive yourself, Asshole. I'm not going anywhere alone with you." Will shot a dismissive look at Hernandez.

"I'll fucking crucify you," Elias snarled and walked around the front of the cruiser to the driver's side.

I gave Will a questioning look.

"He's up to his ass in something," Will said, "and I think it pertains to you. He babbles when he does coke—which is every day—and I listen."

They bagged the bodies, set up little yellow flags on the terrain, and were packing up to leave when the thump of helicopter rotors came from the southwest.

178

"The cavalry. Vernon, you want to stick around and talk to the Feds?"

"Sure. I have four guys sitting on the wounded dude at St. Vincent's, and these two," he nodded toward the other troopers, "can handle the intake on the stiffs. We'll need your statement, but it can wait until later."

The chopper hovered and started to sink toward an opening in the trees. I'd once again forgotten about Rosa, but recovered my senses when she made a sudden appearance by the pool gate.

"They came for me," she wailed, clutching her son who stood mute at her side, his eyes huge. She still wore the yellow bikini, but the cover-up was missing.

"Rosa. Are you okay? Is Raoul okay? Everything's under control. Go to the *casita* and get dressed. We need to talk." I tried to keep my voice composed.

She nodded. I don't know if in answer to my questions or to indicate she understood, but she and Raoul staggered toward the *casita*, Rosa's arm tight around her son's shoulder.

"Jesus Christ, Jack. Who's that? You hidin' something from me?"

"Down, boy. She's a guest, courtesy of the FBI." Despite the circumstances, I laughed at Vernon's reaction.

After everyone had said goodbye, I walked up the rise to the side of the house where Consuela and Franco were staying. I knocked, and the nurse answered.

"I hope you weren't too frightened." What I really meant was that I hoped she wouldn't quit.

"I spent three years as a nurse in Iraq," she said and grinned. "I've seen worse."

"How are the patients?"

"Believe it or not, I don't think Consuela woke up. I gave her some pain meds about an hour ago, and they knocked her out. Franco was a different story. It was all I could do to keep him from running out there with you."

"Please tell him I'll stop by later and fill him in. And thanks for your patience and bravery." I reached out and took her hand. A cool customer.

Chapter 46

Explanations

I managed to get everyone to the back porch, including Carlos and Frank. Darlene had gone to the *casita* to help Rosa. The two of them joined us a few minutes later, Raoul in tow. Since Franco had a personal interest, I'd invited him, and he rested with his feet up on an ottoman. He'd lost maybe thirty pounds, and his hair had turned gray.

Darlene retrieved a soda for Raoul and propped him in front of the TV with a *Bad Santa* DVD. He still looked stunned, but therapy would have to wait a little longer.

"Tell us what happened, Jack." Frank leaned forward, concern on his face.

I told them what I knew.

"I guess it's the same gang from Juarez that came after me. How they found me here is anybody's guess—same with what they wanted." I meant to continue, but Rosa interrupted.

"No, Señor Jack. They came for me. Those men work for El Jefe. I've seen them around his *casa*." Her voice shook.

"You know something you haven't told us." A flat statement from Carlos.

Rosa hung her head and looked up at him under her eyelashes.

"Nobody asked me." Her voice so quiet I strained to hear.

"Godammit, Frank. If you'd taken her like you promised, you could have debriefed her, and none of this would have happened." Anger consumed me, and I jumped up and began to pace.

"Sorry, Jack. We dropped the ball." He held his hands out, palms upward in what had become a familiar gesture.

Carlos threw a pack of cigarettes on the table. We all reached at the same time, and within seconds, a small cloud drifted up from the deck.

Frank turned back to Rosa. "Tell us what we don't know."

"It's confusing," she began. "I heard these things at El Jefe's. He found out what I knew. That's when I ran." Her nervousness showed.

"I don't understand," Carlos interjected.

"Him. He did the thing with Roberto. He wanted his money."ow iHo

Frank, Carlos, and I all shouted "What?" at the same time.

Rosa pulled away, perhaps frightened by our vehemence.

"Easy, Rosa." I placed my hand on her arm. "Relax and give us the story."

She spent the next fifteen minutes in a rambling discourse about El Jefe's mansion and what she had seen and heard. It seemed obvious that she was telling the truth. El Jefe conspired first with Robert Pendleton to launder money, then with Mrs. Pendleton to have her husband kidnapped and to split the bearer bonds after his death. Early on we had discussed the difficulty the average person would have in locating and hiring a hit man, but with El Jefe's connections, it wouldn't have presented a problem. It answered a lot of questions.

"Robert wanted out, and El Jefe said he would help, but after he met Mrs. Pendleton, he—how you say—double-crossed Robert."

"You told me you never met Mrs. Pendleton." I shot an accusing look Rosa's way.

"I'm sorry, Señor Jack. El Jefe told me to say that."

"Rosa," Frank said.

She stopped talking and he turned to her. "We're taking you to a safe house. You and your son. We'll want to know everything. Details matter, and you may not even understand how much you overheard or who you saw at El Jefe's."

"Am I arrested?" Fear flashed in her eyes.

"No. You're a material witness. From what you've described, a crime took place on U.S. soil, and we intend to get to the bottom of it. You can help."

"And you can help the Mexican authorities too," Carlos said. "El Jefe's involvement makes this Mexico's problem to an extent. You and your son will be cared for. Trust me."

Darlene and I sat alone in the darkened living room. Everyone had left, including Rosa and Raoul. Frank and Carlos had helped Franco back to the guest area. I tried to lift the glass of cold vodka to my lips, but my arm refused to obey. I felt drained and ineffective.

"It's an unending nightmare, Jack," Darlene held her hands over her face. "They won't stop until they have what they want."

"We don't know what that is." I shook my head. "Rosa? I doubt it. Her silence? Perhaps. The money in the bag? Peanuts. Maybe now that she's in Federal custody, they won't bother us."

"Can we count on that? Get rid of the money, Jack. That's what ties us to them. This isn't our battle."

I heard the fear in her voice and it reminded me of what she did today. Most people wouldn't have the guts.

"You may be right, sweetheart, but I stuck my nose in the middle of it when I went to Juarez. How do I convince El Jefe, or whoever else is involved, that we don't have a dog in this fight?" I lit one of her Marlboros.

"Have Will announce the discovery of the ransom money. It'll take the pressure off."

"And what about Consuela and Franco? I want the bastard that attacked them, and the money's our link." I crushed the half-smoked cigarette out in the ashtray.

I saw her stop and consider.

"Sorry. For a moment, I forgot. You're right. We'll keep fighting until we find him or her. Don't count out Mrs. Pendleton."

"I wonder what happened to her. Frank said she's dropped from sight. But we can worry about that tomorrow. Let's hit the hay."

I stood, took her hand, and pulled her from the chair. We hugged, and she headed for the bedroom while I went to engage the alarm—not that it protected the front gate any longer. The dogs heard me moving and yawned and stretched. They had suffered a long day too.

Within fifteen minutes, most of the household slept. I went to sit on the porch and gaze at the night sky. The innocence of the stars belied events. Would life ever be as uncomplicated as the enduring heavens? I didn't know, but I'd guess not. Franco and Consuela's ordeal would haunt me forever, along with thoughts of the two cops who had died to protect them. Pride is a dangerous thing to cling to, and mine had contributed to their fate. I promised to never let it happen again. It wasn't enough, but I had little else to comfort me.

Chapter 47

The Long Walk

Wayne Deckert walked with hunched shoulders through a light drizzle, wishing he had taken one of the umbrellas stacked by the casino door. His depression over losing at blackjack faded when he contemplated the delights that lay ahead. A slight noise to his right made him jerk his head up.

"Who's there?" The words echoed in the emptiness of the courtyard.

Lots of critters and stray cats out here at night. He dismissed his anxiety and plowed on, but the glow had disappeared. Thoughts of Manuel Hoppe and his predicament flooded his mind.

What if I'm arrested? My God, everything will be ruined. I should never have listened to Hoppe.

For the past five years, the extra money he'd earned through hiring Hoppe at inflated rates had changed his life. He'd discovered hookers and blackjack. It made him feel like a Player, not a drudge who worked for an insurance company. He wished his friends knew about his secret life.

Another two hundred yards, and he'd be in the hotel lobby. He heard the noise again, but didn't bother to look this time.

A strong hand clamped over his mouth and yanked him backwards into the darkness of an alcove. He felt a stinging in his back, and a sharp blinding pain roared from his liver to his brain. His knees began to collapse, and he felt the knife enter his chest to the left side of his breast bone. He actually felt his heart falter and bright lights flashed before eyes that were already rolling back in their sockets. He died before he hit the pavement.

Manuel Hoppe braced the body under the armpits and lowered it to the ground. He removed the plastic slicker that covered him from neck to ankles and threw it over the corpse. Something about killing with a knife offered more satisfaction than a long-range gunshot. He loved feeling the victim's spasms and the surprise that always suffused their faces. Of course, it didn't compare with the plastic bag he'd used on Liz—a once in a lifetime opportunity.

With hands sheathed in latex gloves, he reached inside Deckert's jacket and removed his wallet and the thousand dollars. He lifted the limp wrist and removed the wristwatch and gold wedding ring. A robbery without a doubt. He picked up the slicker and shoved it and the rest of the detritus into a plastic trash bag. The cash went in his pocket. He looked around to make sure no one was watching, then grabbed the trash bag and moved cat-like through the side gate of the courtyard to the rental car parked in the lot. He had disabled the surveillance cameras when he arrived, and it pleased him that apparently, no one had bothered to check on them. The little red lights on top that signified they were operational were not blinking.

He stowed the trash in the trunk and moved behind the steering wheel to start the car. He still wore the gloves. He wouldn't leave prints anywhere. The radio was playing classical music. He switched to a twenty-four-hour news channel, then rolled down the window to breathe in the moist night air. One more problem disposed of.

The desert sucks up moisture, and by the time Hoppe arrived back at his hotel, he couldn't tell that it had rained for the past hour. He felt discombobulated. Why did the money Jack Sloan stole obsess him so? He possessed all he would ever need in the Tangier bank account. Liz and Deckert, the two people who could connect him to anything illegal, were both dead. But, Godammit, Sloan had affronted him. He needed to be dealt with.

He tossed the plastic bag with the remains of Deckert's day into the dumpster behind the hotel. The surgical gloves and knife disappeared down a rain sewer. He doubted if there would be a police search thirty miles from the crime scene.

He inserted the key card into his hotel door while dialing Elias Hernandez' number. The radio news reports he'd listened to in the car describing a shootout on the Sloan ranch north of Santa Fe alarmed him.

"Sheriff, remember me?"

"You said not to call," a strangled voice croaked.

"I told you to post on Facebook when Sloan returned to town. It looks like he's back, but I didn't receive a message from you."

"I wasn't sure. I'll do it now."

"Listen carefully, Sheriff. I need two days. If he's still there day after tomorrow, send the message. Now, tell me what happened."

Hernandez spun the story, his voice rising when he described Will's insubordination.

Hoppe pulled the phone away from his ear in annoyance.

"I don't give a shit about your deputy. Take care of business, or you'll find yourself in a world of hurt. Understand?"

Hernandez sputtered obscenities, but indicated he understood the message.

When he finished, Hoppe pressed the off button and pondered. *So, Villanueva came to New Mexico. That explains the rest of the bearer bonds.* He'd been played, and it didn't sit well. Many things to consider.

He opened his room door, threw his keys and the contents of his pockets onto the desk, took off his shoes, and laid down on the bed's dust cover. Within five minutes, he was sleeping the sleep of the righteous.

Chapter 48

Unfinished Business

The man Jack Sloan called 'El Jefe', Eduardo Villanueva, shot a withering look at his second in command.

"*Cuatro matons*," he shouted in Spanish. "Big tough guys get wiped out by a *gringo* farmer and his wife. My mistake—three were waxed—the other one is in jail. I'm in the middle of a political campaign. What if he talks and gives them my name?"

"Jefe, I take responsibility, and I'll resolve the problem."

The man who spoke, Ignacio Valdez, looked like he could deliver. Tall and thin with black eyes and hair, he sported a week's growth of stubble. A thin cigar hung in the corner of his mouth. Born and raised in a rural village in central Mexico, he was fluent in five languages: Spanish, English, Italian, Portuguese, and Tepehuan, a rare Aztecan dialect. His darker-than-usual skin pegged his ancestry, and the citizens of Juarez averted their heads when he approached. Many knew his connection to Villanueva and were aware of his own ruthless reputation.

"I want our man released from jail or killed. I want Rosa back here. Sloan and his wife? I don't care. He can't hurt us any more—not without Rosa."

"She's in FBI protective custody. It may be difficult...."

"Find a way. Bribe an official if you have to, but get her out."

"And if we can't?" Valdez pressed for the answer he wanted.

"Then eliminate her." Villanueva hung his head in apparent regret.

"*Sí*, Jefe. It will be done."

Valdez used a valid U.S. passport when he purchased his first-class ticket and didn't receive unusual scrutiny by airport security when they swept the plane. His destination was a safe house on a secluded lot just outside Phoenix where the cartel maintained a stash of weapons, cell phones, and other things he might need to complete his mission.

Valdez unlocked the front door, stowed his luggage, and telephoned a number in Juarez.

"Come to Phoenix today. I need your help."

"Are you insane? I can't help you with anything in the U.S. I don't even like talking to you. Leave me the fuck alone."

"If you love your family, you'll come. We have a unique problem that you may be able to solve."

A vast silence boomed from the other end of the line. Valdez heard heavy breathing and a sigh. It sounded like acquiescence to him.

"Does that mean I can expect you?"

"What choice do I have?"

"None. Call me when you arrive. I'll pick you up at the airport."

He hung up the phone and went to the refrigerator. He hoped it had been stocked in anticipation of his arrival. It would be a long afternoon and night.

On his way to the airport to pick up the visitor from Juarez, Valdez decided the first order of business would be to spring their man. The cartel's contact in the Phoenix Police Department told him the prisoner was locked up in the Santa Fe County Jail, pending charges. Should be a piece of cake. He double-checked the driving route on his laptop. It looked like a six- or seven-hour road trip. He thought about flying and renting a car, but it would leave a trail. Better to drive and remain anonymous.

After picking up his passenger and returning to the safe house, he assembled a small overnight bag and walked to the living room. His contact from Juarez sat on the sofa. The man had told Valdez he possessed no information yet on Rosa's whereabouts except that the Feds had placed her in a Phoenix hotel under an alias. He promised the information by the time Valdez returned from Santa Fe.

"Sit tight and wait for me. I'll be back tomorrow. Unless you want dead children, don't call anyone. Understand?" Valdez pressed a finger into the other's chest.

Carlos nodded, a look of despair on his face.

"The television has cable. Enjoy your movies." Valdez sneered.

He carried a briefcase that contained his credentials naming him the detained man's attorney, along with business cards and a forged writ of habeas corpus. A syringe filled with potassium chloride nestled in a side pocket. Almost a cliché with the mob, but Valdez wasn't concerned about originality.

The prisoner, Hector Marichal, current resident of the Santa Fe County Correctional Facility Sick Bay, located on Highway 14, the route to Madrid, New Mexico, would be very happy to see him. He checked into a second-tier motel on Cerrillos Road, north of the jail. Dinner at one of his favorite New Mexican restaurants, two excellent margaritas, and he headed back to his lodgings. The hooker from Albuquerque should arrive a little after ten.

Chapter 49

Carlos

Carlos looked at the façade of the Federal Building where the Phoenix FBI Field Office was housed. It depressed him, and he didn't want to take the next step. He forced himself through the front door and security, entered an elevator, and pressed the button for the third floor.

"You look like hell." Frank jerked up from his desk when he saw Carlos approaching.

"Not much sleep last night. We're working on a big bust, and I need to talk to Rosa," Carlos said.

"What for? Is she involved?"

"Don't know, but she might have information. We think El Jefe's tied to part of it, and she might remember critical details."

He stood by Frank's desk shuffling his feet. He had failed to anticipate how difficult this would be.

"You came in from Juarez? Could have called your old pal and given him notice." Frank stood and hugged Carlos, then stepped back and held him at arm's length. "It can't be that bad."

"Sorry, *Amigo*. My mind is in a thousand places. I want to get this over with and go home."

"What do you need?"

"A half hour with Rosa. If you could take me to her, I need to ask her what she knows about an El Jefe rival who came to visit him when she was there."

Frank frowned. "One problem, my friend. I don't have access to her and don't know her whereabouts."

"She's not in FBI custody? I thought you guys wanted her for a material witness to the shootings at Jack's."

Thoughts of Maria and their children flashed through his mind. *If I can't do this, my God...*

"Sorry, she's in Witness Protection. They're tight with information. Not a chance they'd agree to an interview."

189

"Who can I talk to over there?" Carlos tried to keep desperation from his voice.

Frank opened his desk drawer, rummaged through it, and came up with a business card. "Call her. She might be able to help."

Carlos studied the card for a moment, then shoved it in his suit coat pocket. "*Gracias, Amigo.*"

"How about going downstairs for a cup of coffee?" Frank reached for his jacket.

"Can't do it, Old Man. I'm on a short leash. Thanks for this." Carlos squeezed Frank's arm and almost ran out the office door.

The agent handling Rosa's case looked disinterested in Carlos' request.

"First of all, I can't even acknowledge I know who you're talking about. Once a witness moves into our program, their old identity disappears. It would take an order from the President of Mexico, countersigned by our President, to put you anyplace near one of our clients. Sorry, I want to help you, but it ain't gonna happen."

The answer Carlos expected. How to explain this to Valdez? He needed time to think this through.

Back at the safe house, he poured himself a couple fingers of Silver Coin tequila and slumped back on the sofa. Valdez had threatened his family. But had he made a fail-safe arrangement to have them harmed if Carlos didn't deliver? Had it come from El Jefe, or Valdez? If not El Jefe, then it might be empty talk. A way to make him cooperate. If Valdez never returned to Juarez, Maria and the kids might be safe.

What are my options here? Very few. The Rosa contact isn't going to happen. He realized what he needed to do, then felt a strange sense of relief and calm. Valdez would return from Santa Fe tomorrow. Carlos would be waiting.

He hit the speed dial for home. Maria answered on the second ring.

"Take the kids and go to LA to visit their godfather. I'll call him and make the arrangements."

"Are you in trouble?" Calm and measured.

"Maybe. But I'm not in danger. We've talked about this before. The situation at home might get serious for police and their families. I'll call you tomorrow to fill you in. Please, *Corazon*, do it for me."

"*Si*. Call tomorrow. I won't sleep tonight. *Te amo.*"

"*Te quiero, Carina.*"

190

Chapter 50

Valdez is Coming

The ease of springing Marichal surprised even Valdez. The clerk examined the writ, and within a half-hour, three bulls escorted the limping prisoner to the release holding area. Valdez signed for him, and they walked out the door. *Mierda, these Yankees are stupid.* The syringe of potassium chloride rested in his suit pocket.

"*Gracias, Amigo.* I thought you forgot me."

"No problem. We don't forget those loyal to us."

"What now? How do I get out of this accursed country?"

"We go to the safe house in Phoenix. A new passport and documents should arrive tomorrow. In the meantime, we have a small job to take care of."

"*Qué?*"

"Remember the woman, Rosa Lara? The boss wants her back."

"I don't blame him. What a beauty."

"She's in FBI custody, so it's no cakewalk. When we get to the safe house, you'll meet one of the boss's contacts, who will lead us to her. Keep your mouth shut about who he is. *Comprende?* Do you feel up to it?"

"*Si*, Valdez. I'll say nothing—and my wound? It's a scratch."

Must be getting old. The five-hundred-mile drive tired Valdez, and he was looking forward to a hot shower and a quick nap before they laid out their plans for Rosa. Carlos would have tracked down her location by now.

What have I done? Betrayed my friends, my country. What choice did I have? I must make it right. I'll take care of things when Valdez returns. Carlos' mind ran at a frightening pace.

He checked the action on his Beretta 90two F. He had chosen the .40 S&W caliber because he believed in its increased stopping power over the 9 mm. Eleven in the clip and one in the magazine. Should be enough to kill Valdez.

He heard one car door slam, then another. *Caramba.* Valdez must have sprung the prisoner. *Ay Dios mio.* Would he have to kill both? A key in the door and it swung open.

"*Alto!*" Carlos menaced with the pistol and motioned them inside.

"Are you out of your mind, Carlos? You dare threaten me?" Valdez reached into his jacket pocket and palmed the syringe.

"The prisoner must be returned. You threatened my family."

Valdez moved behind Marichal and held him with a strong arm around the chest.

"You want to arrest the prisoner? Go ahead, but first you have to shoot him, then me. Get control of yourself, Carlos. If you do this, your family is dead."

Valdez slipped the tip off the syringe and plunged it into Marichal's neck. Marichal twitched in the cradle of his arm for a few seconds, then jerked hard and fell to the floor.

"What have you done?" Carlos held the gun steady. He crab-walked closer and knelt to check Marichal's pulse. "He's dead. *Jode culos.*"

"So what? Now hand me the pistol and tell me about Rosa. I'm willing to forget this nonsense." Valdez walked to the nearest chair and plopped down. "I'm tired, Carlos. It's a long drive from Santa Fe, and I need a shower."

"There's a problem, Valdez. I can't tell you about Rosa, because the information is not available, so you see, I have no choice but to kill you. You've made it clear that if I fail this mission, my family will be harmed. I believe you would do it, but I don't think you've made arrangements."

"If I don't return tomorrow, Villanueva will know something's wrong. He'll take care of business. Shooting me solves nothing."

He's one tough hombre. *Not a hitch in his voice. I know what I must do.*

Carlos felt the weight of the Beretta begin to cramp his arm. He'd never shot anyone at close range, and it made him sweat. *Now or never.* His finger tightened on the trigger.

Valdez helped. He exploded from the chair and threw himself at Carlos. The pistol's thunder deafened Carlos, so he didn't hear Valdez' scream. He didn't stop firing until he expended the full magazine.

The stink of cordite and blood rushed to his nostrils, but he forced himself to look at the ragged heap scrunched in front of him. Twelve shots, and it looked like none had missed the target. Out of habit, he took a new clip from his belt and shoved it into the Beretta's receiver, chambering a round.

Carlos studied the carnage. He knew the only people who used the house were cartel members. One of Valdez' compadres could come tomorrow, or a month from now. When Valdez turned up missing, Villanueva might send someone looking. He noticed the syringe still protruding from Marichal's neck.

He searched Valdez' bloody corpse and found his gun in a shoulder holster under the left armpit. *Fuck.* A .45 caliber. Not that the cartel would perform a forensic check, but it must look plausible. He went to the kitchen and found plastic sandwich bags. He filled one with his expended shell casings. He took Valdez' weapon, stood a few feet from Marichal's body, and aimed at Valdez' corpse. Once again the house reverberated with large caliber explosions. Ten shots, and the slide popped open, signifying an empty gun. He didn't think whoever found Valdez would stop to count the holes. He placed the gun next to Marichal's hand and turned him so he faced Valdez. Let them figure out how a guy with a needle in his neck had enough juice left to ice his killer.

He gathered his things and went outside. Valdez' rental sat in the driveway. If he took the car, it would announce his presence. He needed to walk, then take a cab. Good thing the late afternoon sun had lost much of its sting. He set off in the direction of the Phoenix skyline.

Chapter 51

Jack and Darlene

Adrenaline can become addictive. I read an article about people who take life-threatening risks on a regular basis. It's not that they're more courageous than the average person, but they don't recognize the peril, and the rush they get from doing what they do is how they cope. The more the Pendleton case sucked us in, the easier it became to sympathize with daredevils. We had been living with the consequences of this situation for so long now, it was beginning to feel normal.

"We need to wrap this up, Darling," I said.

Darlene looked at me, and I knew she understood.

"What comes next? Don't forget, Jack, we lived through more intense times three years ago. None of this latest conundrum would have snared us if you hadn't picked up that bag. I'm not blaming you or the event. It's the way you live that brings us to the edge." She played with her fingers which meant an uncomfortable conversation.

You hear, then you can't; smell, and it stops; see, and the page goes blank. Few days pass in the arroyo *when ravens and turkey buzzards don't circle over a critter's carcass. The cycle of life. We draw it out until an event happens to stop it. Maybe it's our fault or someone else's. It doesn't matter in the end.*

"I hold myself to account for what happened to Franco and Consuela and the Pueblo police. Nothing can change that." I felt the catch in my voice.

That's the rub with living the way I did. You endanger those around you. So you skate, but they don't always glide down the ice with you. Did I have a way to atone? I didn't think so.

"I need a drink. How about you?" I rose and headed towards the bar.

"Absolut on the rocks. A couple of those anchovy olives." She hesitated, then began to speak again.

"If you want to go back to normalcy, then you know what we have to do. That satchel stuck in the Corvette trunk needs to go. Your chum in Juarez—the cartel boss—has to know we're out of the action. Jesus Christ, Jack, we gunned down three people in our front driveway. That's not a usual family activity."

"I called Frank earlier today. Amanda's putting together a wrap-up, and they'll come here to show us. My gut says we're close to the end, but let's hear the FBI's opinion."

"Who's coming?" We switched to idle conversation.

Women are much better than men at turning on a dime. Darlene didn't waste time rehashing. Say it, and move on. It often disconcerted me, but I always appreciated it.

"The usual suspects. Carlos, Frank, and Amanda. I think she has new things to tell us." I took a huge gulp of vodka and savored the heat that raced to my head.

Later, I walked outside. A cold front moving in from the eastern mountains caused the temperature to drip forty degrees from the warm high of the afternoon. Not unusual in the mountains. I sucked in deep breaths and blew out to watch the fog dissipate between me and the stars. *Maybe tomorrow will bring answers. I hope so.*

Chapter 52

Manuel Hoppe

The text came in the afternoon. "Ransom 2 B returned – original hiding place, 2morrow." No caller ID or signature on the message. Must be Villanueva, or, more likely, one of his henchmen.

The timing suited his plans. He knew he needed to return to Santa Fe, if for no other reason than to take care of the big-mouthed Sheriff. Hoppe harbored few doubts about Hernandez' inability to keep a secret. Drive to Santa Fe, take care of both business matters, and be out of the country before anyone knew what happened. Time to retire. He had plenty of money and a blown cover. No sense pushing the envelope. He could always kill for pleasure whenever the urge became too strong.

"I have the money I promised you. Be ready to move when I call again. We'll meet in Santa Fe." Hoppe's voice on the phone carried a notch above a whisper.

"When? Where?" Elias Hernandez sounded nervous.

"A time and place of my choosing. I'm not going to let you set a trap for me."

Hoppe counted on greed to make the Sheriff do what he wished, and he harbored no illusions about the danger he might be walking into. If he were Hernandez, he'd figure out a way to get the money and kill his opponent. He pressed the electric window button on his rental car and let the cool air flow across his face. He'd miss driving trips like this. Nothing like New Mexico to revitalize your spirits.

A few bars and restaurants around the Plaza and on Guadalupe stayed open late, but by and large, Santa Fe was saddled with a rep as an early-to-bed town. Hoppe checked into his favorite hotel, ate dinner at the in-house restaurant, and contemplated where to meet Hernandez.

He knew where the Sheriff lived. He intended to make sure Hernandez arrived home from work before he called. Two important factors—no police cruiser, and the execution site had to be within ten minutes of Hernandez' house. He didn't want to give him time to make preparations. Hoppe needed to consider that the Sheriff might use his cell phone on the way to the encounter, but he doubted it. They were committing a felony by meeting to pay off a bribe. How would Hernandez explain that to another party?

Disposing of the body wouldn't pose a problem. He meant to light up Hernandez' car. Hoppe knew from experience that the most difficult crime to solve is a random one. Sure, his cell phone number would be on Hernandez', but it was a throw-away. He checked his weapon, the same silenced .22 caliber Colt Woodsman he had used on Franco and Consuela, and called a valet to bring up his car. He stuck a backup Beretta .40 caliber semi-automatic in his belt. Time to scout out an ambush site and case Hernandez' house.

Hoppe sat in his car in front of the motel office off Cerrillos Road, south of the Plaza. The note on the door listed a phone number to call if he needed information on rooms or rates. The few cars scattered across the parking area told him there were numerous vacancies. He checked for security cameras and found none. Management might have hired a private patrol company to check the premises, but, judging from the appearance of the place, he doubted it. He worked the slide on the Woodsman and chambered a round, then picked up his cell phone to call Hernandez.

"Drive to this location. Leave right away. It's twelve minutes from your house. Don't be late. When you arrive, roll down your window and pull next to my car, facing the opposite direction. I'll pass you a bag. I'm driving a white sedan. I'll give you three minutes to go outside and start your car. If you're not here in fifteen, I'm gone. Don't call anybody, and don't get cute. We'll take care of our business, and that will be it. *Comprende?* The clock starts now." He clicked off.

Hoppe savored the wait. Others might get nervous or fidgety. He breathed in the fresh night air and fantasized about the moment of the kill. Nothing could compare.

After eleven minutes, an enormous SUV he recognized as Hernandez' pulled into the parking lot. He silently congratulated himself for taking the time to check out Hernandez' home. The SUV had been parked in the driveway. The almost indistinct blur of movement in the rear seat behind the passenger compartment didn't escape his notice. He took his backup weapon from his belt, chambered a round, and placed it on the seat beside him.

Hernandez turned and smiled when he pulled his car next to Hoppe's. "*Buenas noches, Señor.*"

Hoppe shot him three times in the front teeth. The surprised look on Hernandez' face made Hoppe laugh. He emptied the pistol into the rear compartment behind the passenger seat and was rewarded by several anguished cries. He ejected the spent clip and jammed in a fresh one. He had to make sure. The latex gloves he wore would conceal any prints.

A twisted body lay in a pool of blood on the back seat floor. Hoppe shot the person once in the back of the head, then did the same to Hernandez. He returned to his own car, reached in the open window, and pulled out a plastic zipper bag.

He removed a small bottle of gasoline and a kerchief from the bag, then opened the gas cap on Hernandez' vehicle. He stuffed the rag into the opening, poured on the gasoline, and put the empty bottle on the roof. After stripping off the gloves and placing them beside the bottle, he took a book of matches from his pocket, struck one, and lit the cloth.

Hoppe walked to his rental, no hurry in his steps, started the engine, and left the motel parking lot. He could see a small glow in the rearview mirror. He'd almost made it back to his hotel when a bright flash lit the southern sky.

Part 7

And So the Story Ends, We're Told

The poets tell how Pancho fell, now Lefty's in a cheap hotel,
Death is quiet and Cleveland's cold, so the story ends, we're told.
Pancho needs your prayers, it's true, but save a few for Lefty too,
*He only did what he had to do, now he's growin' old.**
*Pancho and Lefty by Townes Van Zandt (1972)

Chapter 53

Answers

Frank, Carlos, Amanda, Darlene, Franco, and I sat in our living room.

"Here's how it played out." Amanda looked at Darlene and me.

"Pendleton and his wife staged the kidnapping. They had worked together on the Ponzi scheme. When it began to unravel, Pendleton figured he couldn't avoid prison, so he decided that the best escape would be to disappear. He didn't count on his wife's resourcefulness."

Amanda had set up a flip chart and drew on it while she talked.

"What do you mean?" Darlene said.

"She had promised to leave the country with him when the smoke cleared. He intended the ransom money to finance his abduction and pay for living expenses until they tapped into the mother lode."

"So what screwed it up?" I said.

"Mrs. Pendleton found out about his affair with Rosa. She went to visit, and Rosa told her Pendleton didn't love her—the missus—and he intended to divorce her and take Rosa and her kid to a new home in another country. Apparently, Rosa didn't know anything in advance about the swindle or the planned abduction. She thought she'd found true love."

"So both women kept their mouths shut. Mrs. Pendleton, because she didn't want to tip him off, and Rosa, who didn't want to jeopardize her passport to freedom." Frank's first contribution.

"And in stepped El Jefe—Villenueva," Amanda said. She drew another box labeled "El Jefe."

"Why? What tipped him to Pendleton? How did he know about the offshore accounts?"

"Again, Rosa represented the key. Pendleton aroused El Jefe's curiosity when he started making regular visits to Juarez. El Jefe checked him out and deduced the Ponzi scheme. Rosa told us he brought her to his house for a sit-down. Said he wanted to talk to Pendleton about laundering money."

"How did you come up with this?" My curiosity itched.

"A lot of it from talking to Rosa, but finding out that the hostage negotiator doubled as a hired assassin didn't hurt. Thanks to you, Jack, we had access to Rosa, and once the shit went down in Juarez, and you rescued her, she wanted to help." Amanda took a sip of water.

"When El Jefe sprung the prisoner in Santa Fe, we feared he might be after Rosa too," Frank said. "We took precautions that went beyond normal witness protection." He avoided eye contact with Carlos.

"Go on." I motioned to Amanda. I wanted to hear the rest.

"El Jefe's men identified Mrs. Pendleton when she visited Rosa. Villenueva came to Phoenix and invited her to dinner. They must have struck up a sexual relationship. I'm speculating, but I think he saw in her the path to her husband's money."

"So you think she came up with the premise, and El Jefe helped her execute it? Or the other way around?" What I heard made my head swim. So many players, so few answers.

"These are the facts: Pendleton paid the men to kidnap him in front of Rosa's apartment so he'd have a witness. He used Hoppe to line them up. To refresh everyone's memory, that's Manuel Hoppe, the hostage negotiator and, we now believe, the person who shot Pendleton. They drove across the border and headed North towards Los Alamos. Hoppe's idea. He knew the territory, and wanted to work in familiar surroundings.

"Mrs. Pendleton had also located Hoppe through El Jefe. She hired him and made a separate deal. He whacks the husband and takes the ransom money for payment. Of course, the insurance company also engaged Hoppe's services as a negotiator—his legitimate profession. Pendleton thought he'd get in the RV in Juarez and disappear in the Caribbean."

"So he didn't know where they were taking him?" Now, it made sense. He wouldn't have gone along with his own murder.

"Right. Like I said, Hoppe arranged the snatch and paid the kidnappers to take him to Los Alamos. I guess Pendleton ended up more surprised than anybody when he discovered they hadn't transported him to a Mexican port." Amanda ran her fingers through her hair and brushed a couple of stray strands away from her eyes.

Carlos scratched a match on his fingernail and lit a cigarette. He blew the smoke away from us. Darlene pushed her chair next to his and joined him.

"But the coincidence of Hoppe being both the killer and the negotiator...?"

"Maybe good fortune for the missus, but no coincidence. Hostage negotiations provided the perfect cover for his professional hit-man career. Freedom to travel, inside information about the kidnapping trade in Juarez, and recognition from law enforcement as one of the 'good guys.' He didn't work exclusively in Mexico, but almost. When we looked at his dossier, it stood out that no one ever connected him to multiple assassinations. The indications were in plain sight, but the rationale? Too long a stretch."

"And the famous secret message that almost got Carlos killed?"

"Che. 214466-A. An encoded password—a code within a code. If you use the period and the dash, it comes up invalid. Put it in backwards, with no special characters, and it unlocks the keys." Amanda looked proud of her deduction.

"What keys?" Darlene asked.

"Fourteen separate offshore accounts. The passwords and account numbers were accessible in sequence by following the program the password opened. The most sophisticated lock our guys have ever seen."

"And what happened when you could view the accounts?" I said.

"*Nada.* Mrs. Pendleton and El Jefe, we presume, had cleaned them out."

"You can't walk into an offshore bank and withdraw cash. You must have a computer trail to where it transferred."

"Whoever grabbed it converted it to bearer bonds. We think they disappeared into Mexico or the Caribbean. Maybe Venezuela. Or North Africa—Morocco. I doubt we'll ever locate the paper or the owners."

"No matter where the dough ended up, it solved my problem. The Mexican government issued a statement this morning. *Turistas* are now safe in Juarez." Carlos shrugged and smiled.

"*Salud.*" I raised my drink. I noticed the sadness in his eyes.

"Who did the money belong to?" Darlene looked at Frank.

"Pendleton's investors—another presumption. We'll never know for sure, but it explains a lot. Our forensic people estimate that the accounts at one time held more than five hundred million dollars. Plenty of motive to wax Pendleton and anyone else who was in the way." Out of habit, Frank reached for one of Darlene's cigarettes, but didn't light it.

"You said the password let you in. On what computer?" When I had asked Carlos earlier if they found a laptop at Pendleton's house or office, he responded in the negative.

"You're talking the real beauty of it. Any computer that could access Facebook. He stored the program nowhere and everywhere."

"My God. Anything else on the Facebook page?" Carlos asked.

"Yeah. A message to you."

"What did it say?"

"*Chinga su madre.*"

"Where's Mrs. Pendleton?" Darlene asked the question in all our minds.

"No trace of her," Frank replied. "After we discovered her maiden name—Mason—we tracked her to a hotel in South Beach, but after that, gone. We'll find her one day. These types always turn up because they can't resist flaunting the money. Only a matter of time." Frank sounded like he didn't believe his own words. "If we'd had a chance to question the *maton* we captured here, we might have discovered the information we needed. We should never have allowed him to be held in a county lockup."

Loose ends—Manual Hoppe and the two and a half million stuck in the Corvette's trunk. The others left Carlos and me alone on the deck.

"We're returning it to the insurance company." I hoped my resolve showed.

"Of course you are, *Amigo*, but first, let's use it to find Hoppe." Carlos looked intent.

"Why do you care? You said your boss liked the outcome."

"This guy works for the cartels or anyone else who wants to run a pick in Mexico. And you must admit, he's smart. Who else could kidnap a person, negotiate their release, kill him, and collect the ransom? I want to take him down."

"You and the Feds work on that. I want out."

"I need you to take me to the place you found it. Afterwards, hand the money over to Frank and let him deal with the insurance people. I understand there's a good reward."

"I don't want a reward. Maybe you can use it in Juarez."

"Hey, there are plenty of people there who could. I don't want it for myself, but I won't turn it down. You take it and gift it to me. We need to clean up the open spaces in my neighborhood."

"I still don't see how the money gets us any closer to Hoppe."

"The guy worked for the insurance company. If the money goes back to them, chances are he'll know it. He couldn't have done it alone, and whoever brought him inside will tip him off. And, he's the only person who knows its hiding place except you. He must be pissed since his employer pulled the plug and left him without a payoff. I'll get word to El Jefe that you're tired of being a target, and you intend to put the money back where you found it."

"It might take a long time for him to inform Hoppe—if he ever does. What's in it for him?"

"Hoppe's a liability. His cover's blown, and he won't be working the Mexican kidnapping trade any more. It might please El Jefe if we take him down. We know Hoppe visited Phoenix yesterday, and it's a long haul back to your place. I bet he'll be on the prowl in a couple of days. What do you say?"

"Provided Frank takes the cash today. I want it off my hands."

"I'll talk to him. I don't think it'll be a problem."

I grilled great rib-eyes served with buttered edamame and Jack Daniels. We ate on the deck, the fire pit glowing behind us, the smell of burnt *piñon* in the air. Although I'd seen my view of the sky hundreds of times, my mind still boggled at the immensity of the universe and how one glance upward could blast our insignificance in my face. A voice interrupted my thoughts.

"We'll set up HQ here, at your house—if it's okay with you." Amanda turned all business.

"No sweat, Amanda. Carlos and I will be ready to move early." I felt the adrenaline start to pump.

Carlos sat on the edge of his chair.

"I hope the *mierda* takes the bait," he said and pounded a fist into his palm.

"I hope he does it soon," I added.

Chapter 54

The Arroyo

Hoppe parked in the same place he had used for the attack on Sloan's *rancho*. He took the rifle case, a small duffel, and a canteen from the back seat of the Hummer, then shut and locked the door. The sun still burned hot at this hour of the afternoon. He thought about when he had stood here after whacking Pendleton, and how she was waiting for him. Maybe the time to quit had come. He missed her.

The text message he presumed had come from Villanueva said that Sloan intended to put the money back in the crevasse today. He knew the route. He tugged the bush hat lower over his eyes and set out. His long, athletic strides ate up ground. He could walk the two miles in less than twenty minutes, even given the rough terrain.

He almost stumbled into them. He knelt on a small bluff that overlooked his childhood lair. Memories came back, and he thought about how many times he had run through these same outback ridges playing cowboys and Indians. A horse's whinny jerked his attention to the moment, and he saw them, heads down, toiling up the hill.

He dropped to the ground and moved behind a rock outcropping with a clear view and little danger of being seen. The two men carried bags, and he recognized the money satchel. *They must be cops, and the one in front walks like a Mexican.*

He unlocked and opened the gun case, watching for a reaction, but their position below masked the sound. He assembled the rifle and fitted the scope. Not enough time to zero in, but he could estimate his distance and reset the bullet drop. This close looked like a shooting gallery anyway.

He intended to take down the greaser first. He looked more professional than the other. If he did it right, he could drop both with one salvo. If he missed one, the steep angle would preclude return fire. There was enough water in the canteen to wait out a survivor and

205

sufficient spare clips in the duffel to lay down a siege. He looked through the scope and saw the second man raise his head. His stomach did a flip-flop. *More than he'd hoped for. Sloan.*

Four rifle shots spaced a second apart ripped the air. I heard a cry and saw Carlos go down. I crawled across the rocky shelf where his blood started to pool. I kept my shoulders hunched, anticipating a bullet. A loud thwunk about fifty yards downrange told me the shooter didn't have a clear field of fire.

I inched up beside Carlos' motionless body and reached to turn him over. I pulled, and the back of his head came loose. I started to vomit, but held it in. I withdrew my hand, wiped it on my pants, and took a few quick, deep breaths.

Whoever was hiding on the ridge could outlast me. I had no water or long-range weapon. Besides, he was good. Must be Hoppe. A matter of time till he picked me off. The heat felt intense, but maybe my predicament exacerbated the temperature. I felt underneath my armpit for reassurance that my Glock still hung there, although I didn't think I'd get a chance to use it. Still, if he came to root me out, I might get a shot off.

Come on down here, you bastard. Give me one opening, and I'll make it count. You killed a damn good man.

The strains of "Bolero" stopped, then started again. *Carlos' cell phone.* I reached for his coat pocket, and a fusillade of shots ricocheted off the nearby rocks and careened into the *arroyo.*

I found the phone at the same time it stopped ringing. I lay on my back, opened the cover, and looked at the missed call notification. Frank Hunter. I pressed the 'call' and waited for the ring. Another dozen shots caromed from rock to rock above my head.

"Carlos, what's your location?"

"It's not Carlos, Frank. It's Jack Sloan."

"Jack. Why do you have Carlos' phone?"

"We followed the plan and came to where I found the money. Somebody beat us to it."

"And?"

"Frank, Carlos is dead. I'm pinned down. Can you help?"

"Oh my fucking Christ. Are you sure he's dead?"

"Head shot. Like Pendleton. I'm sorry, Frank."

The shooter unleashed another clip, and I pulled my hands lower.

"He's shooting at you."

"Yeah, Frank, and he's going to hit home pretty soon."

"Give me directions. I have another agent with me. Hang on."

"Don't come here, or you'll be up shit creek with me. Ask Darlene. There's a road a couple of miles south of here that Hoppe must have used to come in on. You can get there in ten minutes and come in behind him. Wear boots. It's a long hike to where I'm stuck. Your ETA will be about forty-five minutes."

"Roger that. Oh my Christ—Carlos. How will I tell Maria?" He sounded broken.

I heard the phone click off.

Carlos and I had come on horseback. Sapphire and the bay gelding I boarded for my neighbor were hobbled at the bottom of the rise. I had carried the canvas satchel stuffed with newspaper, and Carlos a duffel bag of supplies—food, water, extra ammo, sleeping bags. His load tumbled back down the hill when he was hit. No way could I get to it.

Our idea was to reconnoiter the area, plant the canvas bag, and stake it out until Hoppe showed. Either bad luck or poor planning, but the shooter arrived first.

I needed to think of a way to move without Hoppe picking me off. Forty-five minutes sounded like forever, and I doubted he'd let me stay alive until help arrived. A four-foot high cut in the rocks lay ten feet to my left. *If I can make it there...?* At a minimum, I might have a field of fire so I could force his head down when Frank and the other agent arrived. *Fuck it. Have to try. Sorry about this, Carlos, Old Buddy.*

Carlos lay upslope from my position, his right arm hanging almost into my face.

I gathered his tee shirt in my fist and pulled. He slid a few inches in my direction. I worked my toes and ankles to free up circulation, took a firm grip on the fabric, and yanked with all my strength.

Carlos' corpse tumbled over me, and half a dozen shots erupted from the high ground. I jumped to my feet and flew toward the rocks. Bullets splattered Carlos' body, but none came my way. I couldn't believe it. I eased up and looked over the rock that shielded me from his view. I saw Hoppe, but he didn't see me. The rifle barrel started to move back and forth, and I knew he was using the scope to search the terrain.

I ducked down and considered my problem. I could get a clear view of him, but he lay out of pistol range. I needed to get him to come closer and do it without his spotting me. A rock tumbled over the precipice above Carlos' body and rolled on down the hill. He must be on the move.

It hit me like a sledgehammer. He'd pumped Carlos' dead body full of bullets, but we had dressed alike. He must've thought he just popped me. I pushed against the rocks and tried to make myself smaller. More rocks fell, and I knew I'd see his face soon.

He stood with his back toward me, his left toe prodding Carlos. I saw him look down the hill, then start to swivel in my direction. The sweat on my body turned cold.

"I promise to shoot you in the back, Hoppe, unless you put the rifle on the ground and turn to face me. Do it slow and no sudden movement."

He hesitated a beat, and I saw his body jerk, but at the moment I began to increase trigger pressure, he bent forward and placed the rifle in front of him.

"Put your hands out to the side where I can see them, and turn."

He held his arms like a diver, straightened up, and inched around until he faced me.

"You're the thief who stole my money." His voice showed no emotion other than anger. "It's been a while since Juarez. You remember, don't you? I saved your life."

"Fuck you, Hoppe."

I watched his eyes and saw the appraising look while he calculated his chances against a person he presumed to be an amateur. I knew in my gut he intended to make his move soon, rather than wait for any possible backup coming our way.

"What's next, Thief? You going to arrest me?"

The sneer on his face told me he had no respect. The first opening he detected, he'd come at me. Then I saw something else—Carlos' face, his wife, the photograph of Pendleton's head, Franco and Consuela. The FBI needed Hoppe to find out what had happened to Mrs. Pendleton and the five hundred million from the safe deposit boxes, but suddenly, I didn't care. I didn't care about any of it.

I think he knew I meant to pull the trigger. The Glock covered his face, and maybe he remembered the way blood sprayed when a bullet tore off the back of a man's head. I couldn't hold him like this for much longer. My arm already ached, and sweat ran into my eyes. *Fuck it. Fuck the money. Fuck the law.* I squeezed.

Epilogue

When Frank found me, he said I didn't recognize him. I have an eerie memory of riding Sapphire back to the barn. I left Frank and the other agent with the crime scene and the bodies. They asked why Hoppe's rifle lay behind him, but I didn't respond.

Later, a forensics team visited the shootout site, bagged the bodies and dusted the scene. If they found anything to implicate me, it never came up.

A month afterwards, Darlene and I pulled up to a modest ranch house in suburban El Paso. Two children played in the front yard. They laughed, but their eyes held a sadness that might never disappear.

Frank had turned the ransom money back to the insurance company, and they paid Darlene a ten percent reward. She'd sent the IRS twenty-five percent of the amount, and we kept the remainder, one hundred eighty-seven thousand dollars, in a briefcase that she was carrying now.

Maria Santiago answered the door. The government had done the decent thing and relocated her and the children to the States and provided her with a Green Card.

"Thanks for the phone call. I've been expecting you. *Por favor*, come in and sit down. It's been a while." She led us to a well-worn living room and patted the divan. I thought it was up to me to begin.

"Maria, you know how we feel. Carlos was a brave man, and in the few weeks I spent with him, I learned to like and respect him."

"Thank you. He said the same things about you. You were with him when …" She choked and her words trailed off.

I nodded, not trusting my own voice.

"I remember how much fun we had when we met you at the hotel in Phoenix. Carlos laughed and drank tequila." She wiped a tear from her cheek.

"We want you to have this, Maria. For the children." Darlene put the briefcase on the coffee table and opened it. "It doesn't make up for your loss, but it will put them through college."

"I can't. You …"

"It's the reward money. Carlos deserved it. Please. We don't need it, and your kids do. Please, Maria. Do it for Carlos."

We never heard from her again. I hope things worked out for her and the children. I think about Carlos every time I ride the *arroyo*, and once in a while, I think I hear him laughing. Maybe I do, or perhaps it's only the wind in the cottonwoods along the river. No matter. I imagine it's him, and it eases my mind.

The End